Death Below Zero

Library of Congress Control Number: 2013948958
Casebound: 978-1-937356-34-7
Trade: 978-1-937356-35-4
Ebook: 978-1-937356-36-1

Publisher's Cataloging-in-Publication Data

Anderson, Richard
Death below zero / Richard Anderson.
p. cm.
ISBN: 978-1-937356-34-7
1. Murder—Fiction. 2. Trans-Alaska Pipeline (Alaska) —History—Fiction. 3. Prudhoe Bay (Alaska) —Fiction. 4. Fairbanks (Alaska)—Fiction. 5. Labor unions—Alaska—Fiction. I. Title.
PS3601.N5449 D43 2013
813.6—dc22
        2013948958

Book Design by Frogtown Bookmaker
frogtownbookmaker.com

Cover photograph by Antony Spencer
http://www.antonyspencer.com

M K Stencil display font by Manfred Klein
manfred-klein.ina-mar.com

http://DeathBelowZero.com
Published by BearCat Press: www.BearCatPress.com

DEATH BELOW ZERO

Richard Anderson

 BearCat PRESS

I've always been a story teller. DBZ is due to my wife Gayle who figured out how to make me write some stuff down. Our friend Tashery's clever encouragement and maneuvering amplified. Their demand was write it or speak it to a camera. So, I wrote it.

Prudhoe Bay, Alaska

March 1976

Chapter One

What first gave me pause about coking up was seeing Allen get down on his hands and knees to lick the rug. He simply wouldn't concede that our cocaine stash could be absolutely gone. I watched in fascination as his tongue darted delicate little strokes, zeroing in on the exact spot where the spilled powder of an earlier hour had dusted the floor.

I was vastly surprised to catch myself wondering if I really wanted another bump. Once we had a toot session going, I had always wanted another hit, and another after that, then more later on. A few friends had turned into nose hounds, screwing themselves up, getting hopelessly paranoid about their high. One even destroyed the membrane lining of his nose and after that set about exploring how to smoke the stuff, but I felt personally immune to any danger from cocaine. It was just thrills, an exquisite rush, even if each hit was less potent and yet more wildly demanded than the one before.

That winter Prudhoe had constant cocaine with plenty more down along the pipeline. The construction camps were hard and strange places, with a lot of cash floating around and Arctic bozos going nuts in the corners. And, there was always the relentless and painful cold. A stray cocaine binge was one of those crazy ways to stay sane, but at that moment I could see myself licking the rug and I didn't like the image.

Back about three or four a.m., when it seemed that there would be toot forever, Jack had bungled an exuberant move and dumped a mirror-load on the floor. At the time the three of us had scooped up the spill, whiffed it and carried on, free-falling through acres of cocaine, enjoying the absolute hell out of the night. By about six, the supply was going invisible on us and that seventy below zero chill factor lurking outside began to infiltrate my mood.

There didn't seem much point in trying for breakfast. The crew bus would be taking off too soon and we weren't quite done with the dancing powder. We scraped the final lines together, did them, and then started getting inspired about how to come up with that one last hit before going out to deal with the daily blizzard.

We picked every single, tiny white flake out of the grungy rug in that Construction Camp Two room, chopped all of them into powder and whiffed away. Seemed quite natural to me at the time, perhaps even charming to indulge in any desperation that kept the cocaine flying. Then, Allen announced that we could dissolve what we'd missed and retrieve it with an eye dropper. In a second he'd splashed some water on the rug and had dropped down into position, licking around to locate the heart of the spill.

Jack was leaning over him, intently staring. After a few strokes Allen called for the dropper. As I handed it to him, I considered that tearing up a night with cocaine might become less than pure, radiant fun. I'd always enjoyed the powdery frenzy and the extremities it encouraged in me, but this time, I was torn between laughing at Allen's manic improvisation and a sense the earlier excitements were spoiling.

Those thoughts were new to me. I pushed them away, assumed that the next snort would be a kick and squirted up an eye-dropper shot. Kerblamo. A low-grade high, only a thin and wavering rush compared to the first thrills hours before, but I liked it.

Crappy roadflex—letting the party go on like that, jam up on time to hit the bus. The last threads of linger time were finally gone and we had to split. Jack grabbed his outdoor gear and ran for the front door. I dashed down the hall toward my room, feeling great and persuading myself that I deserved a touch of celebration, even if it did have a ruggy aftertaste. The Pipeline had come along to rescue me from Arctic poverty and I didn't see any problem with holding on to a manual labor job that paid me fifteen hundred a week. I already knew how to deal with the weather, the rednecks and the work, so I figured I could carouse one night since I didn't have to pay attention to much, except trying to get laid in a camp almost devoid of women.

I went left at the main hallway, charged another thirty yards and leaned into a hard right at A Wing. I burned twenty seconds in my room gathering down coveralls, down coat, duffel bag and boots. The front door was a no-go by then. The Randolph-Lightner crew bus had surely pulled out. I ran down to the far end of A Wing, butted the door open and stepped outside. An immensely cold, bitter wind raked snow off the ground. The chill cut through my jeans and flannel shirt like they were cheesecloth.

I didn't leave any skin behind barefooting it down the metal steps covered with nice warm ice. The bus was churning around the corner with its lights on. I waved and ran for it. The bus slowed. Cocaine flashes were surging through me and I found myself laughing at how close I was cutting it. My feet were freezing as I pounded across the parking lot, but the cold was not a concern, just thrilling, and something more to laugh at. My laughter threshold always did get perilously low behind a load of toot and I had definitely managed to forget about my passing cocaine unease.

I hurried past the path of the bus and stood there as Phil Dalira braked it down. He opened the door and I climbed aboard into a heat wave. The crew was laughing and hooting at my barefoot arrival. Not Phil. He was pissed.

"You're lucky I stopped. Barriss is ticked off at guys being late, holding up the whole crew," he lectured seriously in a deep, smooth voice, interpreting the world as did our hard case superintendent.

Phil was in his late thirties, five-ten and strong, with dark hair, a bushy moustache and excessive vanity. He was the Randolph-Lightner Teamster foreman and resident salesman. He also had a pompous side that made me feel like irritating him. I gave him my best Laborer's smile from behind my armload of Arctic gear and said, "Get it straight at least, Phil, I'm on the bus so I'm not late. Besides, I was the one who had to wait on you. I was actually standing still before you got the bus stopped."

More laughs from the crew, but Phil was not amused. He took off with a jerk as I did a sideways shuffle down the aisle. Phil tried to throw me by slamming into second and tromping on it. I kept my balance and had my way eased by a spontaneous outburst of proletarian justice.

"Smooth it out, Bussie. You're spilling my coffee."

"Fucking Zero," another sneered, "probably got his driver's license mail order."

Phil relaxed and eased off the gas. He was fairly attentive to protest. I stepped over a guy lying across the aisle asleep on adjoining seats and walked on back.

Huey caught my eye as I was shuffling past him. He gave me a very hot look. His rough, pudgy face was clenched as his dark, close-set eyes glowered at me through black horn-rimmed glasses. He wasn't bright. Reading the newspaper was an Olympic event for the guy.

I was surprised. I hadn't had any run-ins with him my first two days on the job. We'd hardly spoken. He operated the crane. I humped it on the insulation crew. As far as I could tell his anger came from nowhere. I ignored it and slid into an empty seat.

5

The uproar over my arrival died down and then flared up again in a new form, this time as disgust with the elements. I got confirmation on bad weather news. My seatmate told me that the weather board had the temperature at minus forty-one and the wind at fourteen mph, which put the chill factor down to minus seventy-one. I dragged clothes out of my duffel bag to get ready.

Lovely cocaine flashes allured me, but I subjugated my mind and threw it below decks to row my body into two sets of cotton long johns. Most people at Prudhoe wore wool, but my skin long ago declared itself in a state of permanent revolution against that substance as a result of certain medieval tortures I endured as a child. Cotton was warm enough. Besides, the idea was to get several layers between the flesh and the frost.

"This week's your last shot at the heavy money," Phil yelled back over his shoulder, out-shouting the roar of the engine to tout his primary hustle. "If you want in on the Denali Checkpool, you gotta sign on by Friday."

Phil cocked his head up toward the inside mirror and looked over the crew. He smiled his crooked smile, his left cheek climbing higher than his right.

"I'm telling ya, someone as disgusting as one of you Laborers is gonna retire Friday night."

"Get off it," Jack shouted over the engine roar. "Who wants to blow a thou on a checkpool?"

"Doyle?" Phil said, asking for confirmation.

"You don't need to get your money down," Doyle told him with imperial condescension. "I'm already going to win enough to become an entirely different person. How much are they holding for me now, Phil?"

"Seventy-two thousand as of last night, rising fast. Only it's all gonna be mine. That's why I want you worthless Laborers to sign up, because I got more luck than the Pipeline's gonna have leaks."

Checkpools were common. Every payday somebody like Phil would collect twenties. They'd get three or four thousand dollars together and whoever had the paycheck with the best poker hand would win it. But this one was different. It cost a thousand bucks to get in and they were shooting for a hundred players. With five thousand deranged workers at Prudhoe, that plan looked realistic. I was brewing a sarcastic remark about how checkpools had been fiddled before, but about then the cocaine overdrive mellowed out into a glow and I kept quiet to savor it.

The checkpool talk faded away into a whiskey deal, Phil selling at twenty-five bucks a fifth. I pulled on two pairs of socks and shoved dry felt insoles and liners into my Sorels. The year before had been my inaugural session with the Laborers, Local 942 of the International Hod Carriers, Building and Common Laborers' Union of America, with the emphasis on common. Praise the local brother. Since the entrance requirements were a strong back or a quick tongue, we got all sorts.

Union work had reversed my long-term trend of increasing debt. Reversal didn't mean I had broken through the waterline, however. When I took the dispatch from the Hall the Friday before the temperature was two above at

Prudhoe Bay and I was broke. March wasn't the complete middle of winter, even at the extreme northern edge of North America. I went with the cold weather boots I already had, Sorels. Then the temperature buried itself and I was wishing I'd hit someone up for the hundred to get bunny boots. Sorels were good, but at the far end of the thermometer, bunnies were the only boots you wanted. They were big, white, bulbous rubber things and they were ultimo warm. Everyone else on the bus wore them. Phil himself wore bunnies and he didn't need to because he was a prima donna Teamster who rode around in vehicles all day. I was going on second-best gear. That was dumb.

The rest of the way over to where we were slapping on insulation, I completed my metamorphosis into Arctic worker by getting into a down vest, down coveralls and heavy down coat. My rigorous double standard regarding wool was flexible enough to allow me wool liners inside my leather mitten shells and two wool stocking caps under my coat's down hood.

The cigarette smokers had asserted total domination over the air shed in the bus. Apparently they were trying for unconditional surrender from the few remaining oxygen molecules. When the bus stopped I was ready to get outside, no matter what the weather was. I headed down the aisle feeling foolishly happy behind my cocaine high and the fact that I was working on the highest-paid construction job in historical time.

That mood changed in an instant. Huey was in his seat fiddling with his gear as I went past. He stepped into the aisle right behind me and I felt his presence immediately. Alarms rang inside me. I knew he wanted to smash me.

Huey was about forty. He was a big man, a very big man. I heard that he'd walked on with the Colts out of army football and had stuck until the last cut. He was the sort of guy who thrived on getting the boss' permission to pound on irregular persons. My shoulders wanted to tense and rise. I relaxed them and held my air low, cocking my head back to track him as I walked down the aisle. At the door, I stepped off the bus and turned around in the same movement. Huey got off. His eyes were burning at me. His face looked set in cement, but he didn't move on me. He just glared and stalked past. From that moment on, I paid attention to where Huey was at all times. That saved my ass, but it got to my mood.

The glow evaporated and its place was taken by a very particular old sour feeling that I had a lot of experience with. This feeling accompanied a memory of the day they ripped up my private eye ticket. Together, that got me rankled about doing this damn construction work as economic penance. And then I was wondering what exactly was so much fun about tooting up white powder and watching a friend lick the rug. I went off to stash my gear in a wary and changeable frame of mind.

Two empty eight-foot by eight-foot insulation crates twenty feet long were bolted onto a steel skid, one on either end, with a generator mounted in between. The one in front was a work room. The rear crate was the warm-up shack. I tossed my duffel bag in there, then unreeled the air lines and walked them around to the front of the skid.

The other guys on the line crew were carrying the pneumatic tools out of the work shack. We went down the bank to the two oil lines coming from the wells on E Pad toward Gathering Center Two. The pipes ran on steel supports which rose two feet out of the frozen tundra. I whipped the hoses across the pipes and climbed over.

We snapped the hoses onto the air tools and started crimping down the insulation section left over from the day before. Jack went along the seam first, knocking it into place with a rubber mallet. He moved so well in the narrow space between the oil lines that you'd never suspect he'd had his left leg half blown off by incoming fire at Danang. Paddy followed him with the clamper and Doyle finished the seam with the button punch. Those two were very Irish.

Paddy was the oldest guy on the job. Late fifties. He had silvery hair. His face showed heavy mileage and the love of whiskey. He had a hinky, jerky walk, but he was out there with the younger guys. Doyle was thirty, tall and thin, with a wry sense of humor. He had a beard and long dark hair, but he didn't like it when Paddy said he was working with anarchists on all sides. Me, I was the rookie on the crew and they had me coming along behind banding the sections together and taking off the belts. The wind was ripping out of the northeast, cutting across my face from the left. I cocked my head away from it, tucked in my chin and cranked that bander.

The North Slope stretched across a flat plain from the polar icecap eighty miles south to the Brooks Range. We were getting a dozen hours of daylight, only at that latitude the sun barely got above the horizon, shining no brighter than a full moon through the thick white haze of ice fog. Cold, dense air supported the zillions of tiny ice crystals stripped off the ground by the wind. When you looked at the sun the ice crystals blowing by glinted like sparks thrown off a huge grinder into the whiteness. The ice fog thickness cut visibility down to fifty yards. Beyond that, the ice fog merged with the ground into an obscure, impenetrable white.

Up on the road two other Laborers dragged the next insulation section out of the work shack, three hundred pounds of awkward load. They horsed it onto the sawhorses between the skid and the crane, rigged it with straps to the hook, and Huey boomed the section down to us. One of the shack crew guys had the load on a tag line or the wind would have swirled it away.

I watched Huey carefully. Cranes are dangerous even when you get along with the operator. Huey swung the section in a tight arc and never put it over our heads. His control was excellent as he lowered it gently onto the pipes ahead of us. We unrigged and he returned the boom to hover over the sawhorses. He didn't have anything to do until the next section was ready. He sat there in his heated cab and watched us.

We got that section on and the next and the next and the next as we worked our way along E line twenty feet at a time. The work was as repetitive as any assembly line, but I was determined to enjoy it because after all boredom is a self-inflicted failing. Our pace hindered conversation, but we managed a constant flow of abuse directed toward Randolph-Lightner. You can never have too many bitches against the company you work for. Running down the full indictment daily helped with the cold.

The foreman, Theo, was decent and we said little about the man. We did a lot with Barriss and the timekeeper came under fire frequently, of course. Nobody knew him, but nobody needed to. Go onto any construction site and you'll find all the workers hate the timekeeper, convinced the little spider is sitting in a warm office figuring ways to short their pay.

The dominant, ever recurring complaint, however, was about the trashy insulation material we had to work with. I learned that, back in prehistory before I came on the job, there had been far lighter insulation to install. The present stuff looked exactly like it, was also manufactured by Arctic Wrap and came out of the same Arctic Wrap crates, but the foam was screwed up. It was twenty-five pounds apiece heavier and that extra hundred pounds a section made it very awkward to handle down on the line. Heavy as it was, we were putting on seven or eight hundred feet a day.

Whenever we finished off a section before the shack crew had the next one ready, we dropped the tools in the snow and copped a short break. We checked each other's face for the gray spots that mean frostbite is close, then gathered into a tight group, our backs to the wind like so many musk oxen, and talked about things.

"You think this is hittin' it," Paddy said in the slightly mocking tone of an old timer. "We were getting a thousand feet a day until last week."

"Don't even listen to that," Doyle said. "A thousand with the regular is easier than seven hundred with this crap."

"Right," Jack added. "It's worse now with the man around all the time and that Arctic Wrap fool birddogging us."

"Never before lunch, you can be sure," Doyle said and they all laughed.

"You mean that indoor hero who never gets out of the truck, always waves Theo over to him?" I asked. "I thought he was with Randolph-Lightner somehow."

"No. He just drives one of their pickups. He's some kind of phony engineer Arctic Wrap has up here to see how we put on their insulation," Jack explained.

"What's his name?"

"Wayne Tyson," Doyle answered. "He only talks to bosses. He comes on sounding like Mr. Science, but he trips over words and doesn't really make sense. A joke."

Huey boomed another section down to us and talk turned to grunts as we strained to get it in place. My high had completely evaporated into the cold, but staying awake after pulling an all-nighter was no trouble. The chill factor saw to that. That, and tracking Huey's crane work. Watching him swing the boom back slowed me a count in belting down the section. Paddy misinterpreted that as easing back on the throttle.

"You best stay right on it," he counseled gently, turning his craggy face into the wind to speak to me. "I don't tell any man his business, but Barriss is a fast one with a pink slip. He's gone through a lot of men on this show."

I snapped to and thanked him so he wouldn't feel embarrassed at advising me.

Suddenly plenty of conversational momentum appeared and we were all talking as we worked, speaking up to be heard over the wind and the kachunk, kachunk, kachunk of the air tools.

"Barriss ran off three Labes from the other crew last week," Jack said angrily. "For nothing," he added, deliberately knocking a dent in the insulation for emphasis.

"Didn't a thousand feet a day keep Barriss happy?" I asked. "I heard Green hardly gets that on their insulation show and they've got better material to work with."

"Two thousand feet a day wouldn't make Barriss happy," Jack said, whapping another dent into the metal, "because Barriss can't be happy."

"Barriss is always around you know," Paddy said slyly, "even when he isn't."

"Theo?" I asked.

"Theo's all right," Doyle said. "He wants the footage, but he never yells. It's Huey he means."

"Yeah, Huey," Paddy confirmed. "He sits in that crane all day and watches."

I could see Doyle decide the time had come to bring up a certain point concerning me. "Say, didn't you used to be a private eye?"

It felt like he'd kicked me in the stomach. I never got over how hard that "used to be" always hit me.

"One of my past lives, Doyle."

"What happened in that Arthur case? The *Tribune* said Lou Devery was a friend of yours and you deliberately

14

screwed up the cops' arrest, somehow got them to violate his rights to blow the prosecution."

"It played the other way around. Devery was no friend of mine."

Doyle had more questions, but he saw how much the subject got to me, so he let it go.

The crew fell silent. We kept putting on the insulation, with the rhythmic kachunk of the air tools counterpointing the howl of the wind. Gradually my good spirits returned and I had a nice moment when Jack made a cryptic joke about the rug.

Then Theo appeared on the road and waved me up the bank. That was odd because we were right in the middle of banding on a section.

Theo was a stocky Dutchman, about five-ten, with a quiet, dour manner. Everyone's nose ran in the cold, but Theo was the only guy on the crew who didn't wipe it off. He was old school, pre-pipeline, and didn't like anything to interrupt him on the job. He ran things effectively and got along with everyone.

"Barriss wants to talk to you," he told me.

"What's it about?"

"Didn't say. He had that pink slip look so I told him you were a good hand and I didn't want to lose you."

"Thanks."

Theo almost smiled, motioning me past the crane to Barriss' green Ford pickup with the Randolph-Lightner logo on its doors. My breath had frozen my stocking cap to my beard, like always. Walking to the pickup, I slid the cap forward over my head and then squeezed my beard with my hand to melt the ice, so I could pull it off.

Barriss had a big barrel chest, short dark hair and mean brown eyes. He was tall and walked with a swagger. Somehow he managed to sit with one too. A thin white scar ran along his jaw toward his right ear, pulling tight as he managed an icy smile when I climbed in.

He shoved it in gear and took off without a word. After two hundred yards, he pulled up beside an unopened crate sitting in the snow a few feet off the road. Barriss got a clipboard off the seat, flicked over a couple pages and ran a thick, knobby finger down a column of figures.

I was curious. Extracting company secrets was second nature. I hoped to stir something to build a rumor on, a little one maybe, for the boys to laugh at on break, but Barriss was being careful. He shot me a glance to make sure I wasn't looking over his shoulder. I faced straight forward and observed the countryside, which was done in all colors of the spectrum, from white to less white to more white. I got to thinking how unusual the situation was. A superintendent, a nonunion man, was driving a union worker around, namely me. Very defiant of the Teamsters. The labor contract called this a manhaul and Teamsters did all manhauls, the pipeline being a highly union job.

I kept my head facing forward but, being basically snoopy, I pulled my eyes down over to the left to see what was available. I could see a half page of typed memo or letter with two columns of numbers under it. Maybe a dozen numbers in each column. I couldn't make it out, except three words typed in capitals, "DO NOT INSTALL."

"Get a bar," Barriss said in a flat, rough voice, pointing his thumb at the bed. "I want to inspect that crate."

Considering the junk we were working with, that seemed a good idea. I zipped up and got out.

The three-eighths inch plywood skin was excessively nailed to the crate and had become brittle from the cold. I tried to pop a whole sheet off the end, but it tore every place I got the bar under it. Usually we'd knock a hole in an end wall, chain up the crate framework and rip the whole works off with Theo's pickup. I didn't even suggest that. I did it the hard way, piece by piece.

When I had it open, Barriss got out holding the clipboard. He was wearing a green parka over brown slacks and leather boots. He didn't look comfortable out in the wind. He jerked his head toward the truck for me to wait there. I got back in and looked around, but mostly just the usual stuff was there — Thermos, flashlight, tape measure, Buck knife, Polaroid camera and assorted boss paraphernalia. And, an AM radio. Pipeline trucks always had a CB, but an AM radio was unusual. I turned it on and ran the needle to 680. KBRW came in from Barrow a couple hundred miles across the Slope. They were playing The Stones. "Jumping Jack Flash." Those Eskimos went for solid rock. I leaned back and felt warm as the music throbbed on.

The door opened with a rush of cold air. Barriss flicked off the radio as he got in. I remembered someone saying that Prudwad Bay's a penal colony on an asteroid. Barriss turned

17

around and drove back through the ice fog to the show. He stopped the truck and finally looked over at me. Not even the icy smile. Just a frozen look and hostile eyes.

"Scanlon didn't forget about you, Rezkel. You're lucky you got this job. The one day in a week he didn't read the list of new bodies, you slipped through. He told me about you."

"Yeah? What'd he say?"

"He didn't like the way you crowded him on that Arthur case."

"That's too bad for Scanlon. What's it got to do with you?"

"I'm warning you. Don't mess with me."

"You see me doing anything other than work on this job?"

"No, but if I do, I'm not seeing it twice."

We sat there staring. My job suddenly seemed founded on quicksand. I wasn't canned yet, so I broke eye contact. I got out into a razor blade wind and slammed the door.

As I walked back toward the skid, Phil jammed the nozzle into the fuel truck pump and came storming past me. He jerked open the pickup door and shouted at Barriss, "God damn it, that's a manhaul. You trying to get me in shit with the Hall?"

Phil got in and they argued, stabbing fingers at one another. Phil had a point, being the Teamster foreman, but I was surprised that he jumped on Barriss so strong and so open, and that Barriss looked to be taking it.

Theo held up his fists and twisted them apart like he was breaking a stick. The line crew instantly threw down their tools and we all headed for the warm-up shack. Doyle fell into step with me. He pointed back at Phil and Barriss, and then shook his head with a smile.

"Barriss hates everyone. He even got mad at the R-L front office boss, guy named Scanlon. Over Phil. Shouted at him, 'If he didn't get it from you, who did he get it from? Naturally, we all figured it was the clap.'"

Theo had his green Randolph-Lightner pickup parked behind the skid. He took his breaks there so the office could reach him on the radio. The rest of us piled into the warm-up shack. First man in turned on the space heater and shut down the deafening pounding of the compressor chugging in the back. Last one in wired the door shut against the wind.

I took off my coat and sat down on the bench. I unzipped the chest and legs of my down overalls, then took off my Sorels. Nobody bothered to take off their bunny boots. My liners pulled out easily, but the insoles were frozen. Felt sucked up sweat like a magnet. I peeled the insoles out and put the whole works off to the side of the space heater to dry. A direct blast would have fried them. That monster had the size and power of a five hundred pound bomb. It was either full on or off, nothing else. The shack was already up to ninety-five degrees and stinking of diesel. Ninety-five above was better than thirty below, so we left it on and unfolded the layers of our clothing like tropical flowers.

I changed both pairs of socks and stuck my feet up on a tar bucket. I hadn't gotten my Thermos filled, much less had breakfast or made a lunch. Very slack, very cocaine. Jack gave me a cup of hot water from his Thermos. I reached a teabag out of my duffel bag. Maté Orange Spice. I leaned back against the plywood and at that moment considered break had begun.

Huey was on the opposite bench, next to Doyle and Paddy. Usually he blathered on about heavy equipment in a dim way, telling us how he remembered the sound of every rig he'd ever operated and other dreary stories. A quasidodo. But that day he was quietly lusting through a skin magazine.

"What did Barriss want with a low-caste Laborer like you?" Doyle asked me.

"Read me my rights. Told me not to make him mad."

"What's he got against you? You're doin' your job."

"Me and Barriss, we got mutual friends it turns out."

The conversation flowed on. We were only rope-pullers hauling rock for the Big Oil Pyramid, but we were getting Pharaoh's pay scale. Only job I've ever seen where the workers made more than the bosses. It was sweet to listen to the boys piss and moan about the strain of the eighty grand tax bracket.

Raps sounded on the door. Jack got up and unwired it. Phil Dalira came in with a swirl of minus-thirty air, scowling.

"Close the door, Zero," somebody yelled.

Teamsters were Zeros, a flexible term that might refer to anything—morality, intelligence or job effort. In Phil's case it wasn't the last two. He wired the door shut. When he turned around again he had three-quarters of a smile in place.

"I got a fifth for you, Paddy. Come by the room after work."

"Last chance to get in the Denali, right?" Jack asked.

"Wrong. Last chance is Friday afternoon," Phil said, relaxing.

20

Catching snickers in response to his sales pitch was familiar to him. He straightened up in the cockpit and flew on through the flak. He put his right foot up on a bucket of silver paint and tapped a clipboard on his knee.

"Here're seventy-two guys already who aren't wiseasses. They're the ones with the play for real money."

"Let me see that," Jack said and held out his hand for the clipboard.

"Hey, Phil, how do we know this Denali is straight?" Paddy asked. "What if some Carpenter has the front office wired and gets five aces on his check?"

"Listen, that's not a problem. I told you people this already," Phil assured us wearily in his soothing voice. "It's like any other checkpool, but we're going to use cards too. You get five cards dealt to you to start with. The you add the cards to the last three numbers off the serial number on your paycheck and the cents off what you actually got paid, in order like, and that's your hand. If you got a four on your check and you're dealt a nine, that's thirteen. You use the three. And so on for your five cards. Best poker hand wins like usual. See, someone else shuffles, cuts and deals for you. That way nobody pulls nothing."

I listened along, automatically interested because cards were involved and I liked playing cards. I was OK at bridge. I liked poker too much.

When Jack finished looking at the list, I took the clipboard. The top pages were a long list of names, companies and union affiliations for the workers in the Denali Checkpool. I thumbed over the page. Timesheets and stray papers. Why am I doing this, I asked myself. Snoopflex. I checked Phil. He was rattling on, not paying attention to the clipboard. I scrunched down on the bench and flicked through the sheets.

"What about face cards?" someone asked.

"Face cards don't count. You get dealt another card."

I found it toward the bottom. A letter from Arctic Wrap to Randolph-Lightner, copies to Barner Oil and its management contractor, Harkell Associates. Phil was preoccupied so I did a quick read. One page had a riff about excessive water content in an early production run and insulation crates mistakenly shipped to Prudhoe Bay. Yeah, real mistakenly, I thought. "DO NOT INSTALL" in caps. I ran down the list of crate numbers and bingo, there was Arctic Wrap crate number sixty-three, the very crate we were working out of.

I felt something so I looked over at the other bench. Huey was staring right at me. Then Phil turned toward me. He was about to catch me ransacking his papers. I had hold of the clipboard near the top. I handed it to Phil upside down so all the pages flopped down. His eyes started down toward the pages, suspicion trying to build in them. I covered by saying, "I didn't see Barriss' name."

"Fuck no," he snapped, "and we ain't letting no fucking superintendents in."

Theo blew the horn on his truck. Break was over. On that job we got fifteen minutes and that didn't mean sixteen minutes. Going from plus ninety-five back out into the minus-seventy factor was a jolt to the body. If you survived such jolts, it made you very healthy.

We slapped on insulation the rest of the day. The wind died down some toward noon and then came back worse than ever in the late afternoon. The bosses came and went. We put sections on the line and all was routine until the third time we moved the skid.

The shack crew stowed their gear and the line crew walked the air hoses ahead. It was my turn to rig. I got the tow cable out, then stood on the ice in front of the skid. I held the cable with my right hand and signaled Huey forward with my left. He brought the twenty-ton Pettibone crane up and stopped before I signaled him to, a few feet from the skid. I caught his eye and held up my left fist to keep him stopped. His left cheek was twitching in a funny way I hadn't seen before.

I stretched out the cable. It wouldn't reach the tow hook on the front of the crane. I straightened the fingers of my left hand and motioned Huey forward, rubbing my thumb and fingers together to tell him to take it slow. That was the standard signal. I made sure he saw it.

The Pettibone started moving. I signaled and watched the hook. Suddenly the crane jerked forward. A yellow wall of steel closed on me. I stepped back and began to give the fist sign for him to stop. Then it was too close for anything but jumping. I dropped the cable and leaped over the front skid step into the shack. The crane banged into the skid right after me and knocked it back a foot. No way it would

23

have killed me, only taken off a leg or so. An image of Barriss flashed into my mind.

I gave Huey the finger and screamed a dozen things at him. He was smiling as he backed up the crane. The whole crew came running up. Theo burst around the corner of the skid.

Huey opened the door of his cab and leaned out. His cheek was no longer twitching. He had the least bit of contrition on his coarse features.

"Gee Theo, I'm sorry. My foot slipped on the pedal."

Huey looked at me and shrugged.

Doyle slammed the cable onto the hook.

I caught up with Theo walking back to his pickup.

"Huey has a decent touch with that Pettibone. You ever see him do anything like that before?"

"No. First bad mistake I ever saw him make."

Chapter Two

Phil Dalira braked down to a crisp stop thirty yards from the orange and white modules of CC2, as they called Construction Camp Two. He could have gotten closer, but he made it easy for himself to pull out afterwards. I didn't bother with zipping up. Seventy below was no factor at all on the way in after work. Anyway, I was still hot from Huey's crane move. What I felt like doing was unloading on him right then, right there, only I knew that whatever went on in his pea brain, it wasn't dreaming up the idea of trampling me with his Pettibone. That had to come from Barriss.

Throwing a couple at Huey wouldn't settle anything. It'd feel good for a moment, but the only positive thing that could come out of it would be to get him fired too, which would surely happen, since whenever a fight broke out in the camps, both parties were automatically down the road, no matter who started it. I managed to let go of revenge fancies, still being innocent enough to imagine that I could hold onto my job, and hustled across the ice with the crew, into camp.

Inside the double doors, everyone surged left into a small, windowless room with a mail rack on the wall. I reached through the horde to the R box and discovered that, through some incomprehensible postal miracle, my mail was actually being forwarded. The thrill faded as it was only a bank statement disdaining my $14 balance and announcing an obscure service charge, likely for wear and tear on the vault.

A Laborer on the other insulation crew elbowed past, claiming he'd heard a rumor we were going to twelve-hour days. I liked it. Another $300 plus a week for two more hours a day on the job.

When the crowd thinned I cut across the flow and went into the front office to check on the newspaper situation. I didn't want to lose contact with basketball right when the NCAA playoffs were happening because maybe the UCLA candle was being snuffed out at long last. It turned out, on the authority of the desk clerk, that since it was a Monday, there would be no newspaper.

In the lobby, I bumped into Wayne Tyson, the Arctic Wrap field rep. He was a tall, thin and snooty guy in a blue sport coat and tie, actually wearing slacks. Unusual clothes for Prudhoe Bay, but they went well with sleeping in until ten, never consorting with the troops and maintaining an attitude that being an engineer conferred some sort of intellectual distinction. Doyle had told me the guy could fuck up a wet dream. I didn't hold it against him. I'll talk to anyone when I get curious.

Tyson made a distant, mumbly sound and turned away when I said hello. I didn't take the hint and persisted with a couple friendly little questions.

"How about this crappy foam we're putting on out on E line? What kind of insulating job do they imagine it'll do?"

"What do you mean, it's all the same," he said, hesitating as he realized he was talking to one of the barbarian Laborers.

"No way. That stuff is much heavier than the other material, like fifty percent heavier. Isn't that just what you don't want in foam?"

"It's a new, advanced foam with an exponential thermal index."

"You wouldn't kid me, would you?" I asked, leaning toward him slightly and slapping him on the chest with a playful backhand. He was getting angry despite my maximum smile. I was getting amused.

"Are they trying to slip it in so they won't have to junk it?"

"It's all within spec," he bit off and walked away.

I considered that a conversation with him was not likely to shore up the shaky foundation beneath my job. Wasn't worth dwelling on.

CC2 was done in Barner Oil's rendition of institutional beige, with green plastic carpets and framed objects on the walls that a blind man might mistake for art. Along with the mail room and front office, the camp had a theater offering a different lousy movie each night, a couple recreation rooms heavy on pool tables, a dining room appropriately called a mess hall, and a commissary that mostly sold toothpaste and *Hustler* magazine. A barber chair in a side room was attended nightly by a man called Fearless Bill. For ten bucks, he'd take a flyer on any head of hair.

Long hallways led off in either direction to double-story wings of living quarters. Five hundred men lived there and about twenty women, an incendiary ratio. I took a right and padded off to my room.

My cellmate was back from work, though he was barely present. Days, he welded. Nights, he was catatonic, doing his best trances over a bottle of bourbon. He had stayed on the Slope too long and zombied out. As usual, he sat in his chair and didn't respond to my greeting as I stepped back to my half of the room, shrugging myself out of the space suit.

The room was about eight by fifteen with a bed, a desk and a locker along each wall, leaving a narrow passage in the middle. I had the wall locker doors pulled partly out of their tracks so that, when swung full open, they met and divided the room in two. My roommate had been there first and could have taken the secluded back half. It didn't seem to have occurred to him. In fact, he hadn't even looked up or spoken a word when I'd moved in three nights before. Maybe he didn't need privacy anymore.

I always liked to stay sharp physically. That meant karate and Frisbee. I pulled on a jockstrap and sweatpants, then headed down to the theater to get in a workout before show time. I pushed back the front row of chairs and had plenty of room, but it wasn't a very good session. My kicks and combinations were alright and I did my kata, Sochin, a dozen times. My mind got in the way, though.

28

There's little point to flailing away at the air. For training to be of much use, you must imagine an opponent. Often my best karate self turned up before me, or, sometimes, my teacher. That night the round face, small nose and crooked teeth of Huey dominated my imagination. I went flat out at him, but I couldn't stay calm. I kept getting angry and toward the end pulled a neck muscle. I took it as a message from the gods of karate, got hold of myself and finished off properly.

On the way back, I saw Phil strolling down the long hallway beside a new lady in camp. She might have been good looking, though a quarter inch of makeup made that uncertain. She definitely had a great figure, but on balance, she didn't appeal to my aesthetics. Even worse, she was a Teamster, judging by the button on her clingy orange top.

Phil wanted to walk past with a nod. Perhaps he was still ticked off about me nearly missing the bus. More likely he didn't want yet another man prowling after his companion. I didn't give him the chance. I stopped and launched right off into conversation.

Phil's strained, disinterested manner was more than I got from her. She wasn't putting anything out in my direction. At least, Phil relented as far as providing the minimum introduction.

"Lori, this is Nick. He insulates."

Maybe she didn't like the way I was dripping wet from training. She looked at me as though I were yet another peasant who had broken into a sweat at the mere sight of her. For my part, I felt myself trying to attract her by habit, then wondered if I really wanted to. Reminded me of that surprising feeling I'd had watching Allen load up the dropper from the rug.

I'd always loved the stray all-night coke binge, but then I was done with it for weeks or months. Suddenly, I was unsure exactly what I felt about cocaine. That made me want to find out what I felt about it, to clear away any ambiguity right off.

Phil was the man to score toot from. I didn't figure he'd mind me bringing up the subject in front of a sexy third party, since he always liked to talk it up around the ladies, so I asked him if the store was open.

"No have got, pal. See me in a day or so."

Lori was looking into the middle distance, ready to move on.

"See you, Nick. We gotta go."

I forgot about it, took a shower and went over to C Wing to Downer Dave's. Well before his room I could hear rock flooding the hallway. A *High Times* marijuana centerfold was taped to the door next to a "Daysleeper" sign. The start-stop switch from a generator was fastened to the doorframe. I pushed start and in a few seconds the door was opened. Music engulfed me.

The front half of the room was conventional down to the photo of three kids on the desk. This was the roommate's turf. He was most unlike Downer, but he made a superior roommate anyway since he worked a nightshift and was never around.

The back half was a black-light environment, with Indian bedspreads hanging from the ceiling and vibrant posters pulsating on the walls. Late hippie, which was common on the pipeline. A mass of stereo equipment poured forth Led Zeppelin. Amid the sound, incense and candles, three longhairs passed around a joint

"Hawaiian Senseless, man. Two toke weed," proclaimed the guy who handed it to me and he was right. That's all it took. Of course, I had a lot more.

Downer sat on the floor rolling another. He was in his late twenties, slight and sharp featured. The acute angles of his face made him look alert and active, which he wasn't at all. He was dissipated and slow about everything, from his work to his entertainments, but he was a pleasant person to be around and he liked sarcasm.

A fire truck light came alive on the desk, pulsing out bright red flashes. I was closest, so I opened the door and another Randolph-Lightner Teamo came in, a natural-born skeptic by the name of Luke.

We all sat around and smoked some more of the finest weed there ever was. Luke razzed Downer for putting down a grand to get in the Denali Checkpool and then carried on about checkpools in general, dismissing them all down as hustle, but always returning to harassing Downer in an amusing way.

Luke had a resonant voice, which he needed over the volume of rock and roll. His thin fringe of hair fended off total baldness. He had a wrinkled brow and a large nose that had been pushed aside more than once. This slightly battered look somehow lent an odd credence to his insults.

Downer took it all in good humor, immediately confessing to the essential justice of any charge laid against him and attributing it to the permanent mental damage he must have suffered when he first beat off at the age of thirteen.

Eventually, I wandered down to the mess hall for dinner. The best part was the formerly fresh fruit. The worst part was this young plumber in line ahead of me. He was enthused, somehow, over broccoli cooked gray and mushy. He turned around and beamed at me.

"Ain't this the best chow you ever ate?"

"Right, the best chow ever. As chow, definitely great."

After dinner I wasn't ready to crash, even to get my sleep quotient caught up. Took off my shoes and rounded up Jack for a few Frisbee throws to keep the hand in. We looked at his rug, shook our heads and laughed. Then we went and tossed a few.

The long hallway was fifteen feet wide and made a nice court. The walls were playable and the putting green carpet was good for skips. Behind-the-back catches on the jump were tricky as the soundproofing panels in the ceiling were rather low, so I had to bend my head forward on leaps to keep from wiping out.

We played between the C and D Wing cross hallways so that no one would have a 119 gram surprise flicking past the face while coming around a corner. And we held it up whenever traffic came by. That pretty much kept the locals on the side of the Frisbee game. Nobody bitched to the management even though it wasn't a natural Frisbee crowd.

Jack had an ulterior motive for wanting to play just there. The women lived in D Wing, including this certain bull cook who inflamed his imagination. To keep the creatures at bay, most women on the pipeline spoke not a single unneeded word to a male or paired off fast with just one. Some women exploited the ratio and figured promiscuity didn't start short of one new lover a day. Do the math and you'll see that after a month, thirty turned down ex-lovers were all living and working together. That got too interesting at times.

Jack's fantasy lover had taken the first line. She tossed up a completely impenetrable, invisible shield to shut out the high volume sexual pressure from all those horny construction workers who figured their best chance was to come on louder and stronger than anyone else. Myself, I wasn't interested in her, but I was pleased to go along with Jack's hope that the flight of the friz would create an opening for him. I told him he had no chance with her, but of course that made absolutely no difference whatsoever to his imagination. For all that, she didn't even walk past.

The game went pretty well anyway. Jack had a hot night and I was on sometimes, especially with two-finger snap throws. Then he threw a high one and everything got different.

I skipped back, tracking its course, waiting for it to come down to a catchable height. Behind me, I heard footsteps come out of D Wing behind me. There was just enough room to go up for a behind-the-back and get down without crash landing on whoever was coming along. I looked over my shoulder to indicate that I knew someone was there and that I had it timed. All I took in was that she was a strawberry blonde and incredible. I leaped and put on my flashiest catch.

"Showing off again," she said in a throaty voice, devastating me with a smile and all the light streaming out of her gray-green eyes.

"Only at the last second."

"Can anyone play?"

"Definitely not. The board of directors is making an unheard of exception for you."

I handed her the Wham-O Frisbee and stood aside to watch, stare, leer, drool or whatever I was doing. She tossed her grayish Air Force issue parka onto the floor and squared up to throw. She was beautiful, willowy in flowing green cords and a tight canary top with green trim. Her skin was pale, reddish, freckly, somehow just exactly right to fascinate me.

She rolled her head to the side and long, silky hair washed across her shoulders. A wheat field at sunset. She wore bunny boots with figures painted on them, a juggler on one and a dancer, maybe an elf, on the other. Even wearing those awkward boots, she whipped a hard skip shot that came up off the carpet right to Jack. Then she made a deft catch of the return.

"I'm Nick Rezkel and you're..." I said, hanging on her name.

She paused a heartbeat and I started to fear there would be nothing more. Her mood had shifted and she stood there, measuring and distant, unfocused. Then, I could feel her energy again as she said, "Jeanne Dalira."

"I bet you've come to visit your brother," I guessed.

She tossed another to Jack, then turned and looked at me. A gold speck in her left eye glinted curiously. Her face briefly tightened, then relaxed.

"You know him?"

"Sure, I work with him," I said, thinking that I hadn't realized how fortunate that was until I saw his surpassingly beautiful sister. "You don't live in this camp, I know that."

"No. I'm an expeditor for Livingston at CC1. Well, thanks for the throws. I have to go meet Phil."

She picked up her parka and I felt a quiet desperation.

"Can I entice you by my room later for some of the best dope in town?"

She paused, considering, then shook her head no and said, "Sorry, I can't make it." Disappointment must have hijacked my face. She seemed to read me most quickly, no doubt having lots of practice with this particular situation. Then she added, "Not tonight."

I proceeded to make another try.

"Tomorrow night I'm making a run over to Parsons. Want to come and indulge in illicit nasal pleasures?"

Full smile, eyes locked. Suddenly she was right there, saying yes intensely with her smile, though teasing me on with suspenseful silence. Her high cheekbones and delicate features accentuated the flow of rapidly changing expressions across her face as she played my feelings adroitly and enjoyed the effect it had. I liked it also, and wanted her to keep playing.

After an agonizingly long interval, she answered, "Sure. Do you have a truck?"

I had a quick flare of the old cocaine anticipation. The doubts I'd been having flew straight out of my head.

"I'll get one," I told her. "Pick you up at seven. What's your room number?"

"C219. At seven." She flashed me a last smile and walked off.

I let Frisbee slide and gave myself over to the pleasure of watching her walk down the long hallway. I dismissed my misgivings over Allen's tongue job on the rug and reaffirmed that cocaine must be a most wonderful substance, since Jeanne Dalira wanted to do some with me the very next night.

Phil and Lori came out of C Wing and they stopped to talk. I couldn't hear anything they said, but sparks clearly flew between Jeanne and Lori. Then Jeanne and Phil walked away from Lori. Phil looked back over his shoulder, shrugging to Lori that he couldn't help it.

Jack had watched it all with a bemused look. We threw a few more and then hung up reality for the night.

Chapter Three

Tuesday the job went well. The factor warmed up to minus sixty. I watched every movement of the crane, but Huey kept it clean and nothing happened. Barriss gave me a couple hard looks. Maybe he was hoping I'd get offended and drag up. Maybe he was still building his pretext to fire me. I didn't get distressed over it. I just put up with the work and the weather and got on with my immediate business, which was to get hold of a truck. I hit on Theo to borrow his after work, but he said he already had it promised. When Phil came by, with Lori sitting aloof as the crew stared at her through the ice fog, I gave him a try, but he said he was using his truck that night. So, I was essentially blameless. I was forced into grand theft truco by the press of circumstance.

After work I showered straightaway and put on my ceremonial clothing—tan jeans and blue shirt embroidered with Rousseau's *Sleeping Gypsy*, the image of a lion standing guard in the desert over a gypsy sleeping in a cloak of many colors. That was a way to handle Pruderude Bay. Put your gypsy to sleep and ride it out on your lion. That night I wanted to give my gypsy some air and a lady to be with, so I skipped training for an early dinner. The lettuce had certainly been fresh just the month before.

I went outside in my down coat and Sorels, with down coveralls slung over my shoulder just in case. A line of pickups and busses was parked out front, plugged into electrical outlets mounted on a wooden fence. You could always tell an Alaska vehicle by the head bolt heater plug dangling through the grill. Winter on the Slope, you plugged it in or let it run all night.

None of the trucks had a key hidden in any of the obvious places. If I hadn't managed a lifetime of evading contact with the internal combustion engine, I might have hot-wired one of the damn things and been off. As it was, my truck theft career developed under such laboratory conditions that I never bothered with anything I couldn't find a key for.

As I was trying to find my personal vehicle, I saw Theo's pickup roll by. I ducked behind a bus because I didn't want to be noticed casing the company rigs or else I might have seen who was driving. Could have been Theo, but I didn't think so.

Then I came across the Randolph-Lightner timekeeper's green Ford pickup. It had the same R-L script logo on the doors as all the other Randolph-Lightner equipment. The truck was locked.

The timekeeper spent every night in camp watching the movie and shooting pool. He clearly wouldn't lend his truck to a peon such as myself. On the other hand, he wouldn't notice if it was borrowed. I noted the number and circled back behind camp to the Randolph-Lightner office. Wind was ripping out of the west. It had blown constantly as long as I'd been at Prudhoe, but after work and with Jeanne on my mind it didn't seem so very cold.

Randolph-Lightner operated out of a corrugated metal building behind the kitchen complex. The side and back doors were padlocked, but the large sliding doors in front were not completely secured. That sort of door can be fastened from the inside, but mechanics will often leave it open to the proper touch so they can get in after hours for free time on the company phone or private enterprise like torching Alaska maps out of the big pipe. I patted the "Authorized Personnel Only" sign for luck, wiggled the lower right hand corner and was able to ease the door away from the frame enough to slip inside.

No one was there, but the lights were on. Typical pipeline economy. Racks of tools and parts stood against the walls, along with an overhead hoist and a horde of defunct space heaters. Barriss' pickup was parked in the middle of the gravel floor. Its engine had been pulled and sat half-assembled on a metal table.

A small office was tucked away in the left rear corner. My first day on the job, Luke had brought me there to check in and fill out a W-4. I noticed then the usual board hanging on the wall next to the office with a lot keys. On one hook were two spare keys for the timekeeper's pickup. I took them both and headed off for my wheels.

The truck was almost warm by the time I'd done the seven miles along the spine road over to Construction Camp One. I parked in front of the red modular buildings and went inside. Jeanne was waiting in the lobby. She looked tense, perhaps angry, but brightened instantly when she saw me. I marveled at how quickly she changed gears. She was wearing a lavender top and jeans and looked so fine walking toward me in smooth gliding steps, her pale, rose gold hair shining. She touched my arm and all was delicious from the first moment. We spoke easily with an eagerness in the air. I could hardly keep my eyes off her long enough to back the truck around.

"Let's pass on the usual route," I suggested.

"Sure. You know a shortcut?"

"Better. There's a longcut by the romantic Prudhoe docks."

"Show me."

We went through the Gathering Center Three site and out along a thirty-eight inch pipeline toward the compression plant where they pumped the natural gas back underground to maintain pressure below. No other trucks were on the road. Nothing but snowfields and a rusty pipe that hadn't been insulated yet.

"Are you from Fairbanks?" I asked.

"For a month. I just moved up from Anchorage."

"Who do you live with?"

"A friend."

"What's she do?"

"She works at a travel agency in the Northward Building. How did you know it was a she and not a he?"

"I'm lucky who I meet."

"And you? Who do you live with?"

"I live alone, now."

Snow had drifted across the road. I kept it rolling at thirty and blasted on through. It would have been a cold and lonely place to get stuck, miles from anywhere with a CB radio made problematical by ice fog conditions. A large drift appeared, with a second immediately behind it. They both went across the road three feet deep. I glanced over at Jeanne and could see that she liked the chancy ones. I changed down to second and stayed on the gas. We hit the first drift and hung a moment before we went through. Little speed remained for the second. The truck plowed into it, slowing way down and straining against the snow, tires slipping. She looked at me and said, "This is close." Then the tires bit and we were through and laughing at it together.

Past the gas plant we went left and drove the five miles out to West Dock. The ice fog thinned out and our headlights lit the road for several hundred yards. I kept looking at her. In the faint glow of the dash lights she looked calm and contained. I tried to figure her age. With the play of so many expressions across her face, one easily after another, I couldn't be certain. I was guessing late twenties.

Jeanne turned and moved slightly closer to me. Then she tapped a foot against the floorboard and hummed quietly. I liked it.

"What did you do in your previous incarnation, the one before the Big Pipedream?" I asked her.

She hesitated, became serious and then lightened up again.

41

"Different things. Newspaper stuff. Hey, look at that," she said with a sudden soft wonder in her voice, "in the middle of nowhere."

It took a moment to get past a sense that I'd been pushed away from a sensitive subject. Then I looked where she was pointing and saw a tugboat that appeared frozen into the snow. It seemed a good moment to stop the truck, the better to view this odd sight.

The previous summer's sealift to Prudhoe had skinnied in through the least sliver of open water. It took gutty seamanship to try it at all, but they got the barges in. Then the winds shifted, blew the ice back against the shore and slammed the passage shut, catching the barges and tugs. When Prudhoe Bay had frozen solid as steel, they unloaded the equipment, material and even completely assembled modular buildings from the barges, dragged them across the ice and carried on with the season's construction. After that, the fleet sat there, frozen into the ice, waiting for the next year's open water.

The earth and the ice were both drifted over with snow and they were indistinguishable. The ice in the bay was only ten or fifteen feet thick, but the earth was frozen more than a thousand feet down, permanently. I stopped the truck when the road brought us three hundred yards from the lonesome tug Jeanne had pointed out. There were more tugs and barges looming further ahead through the ice fog.

I made the classic opening move, man's arm to back of seat. I trailed my fingers down onto her shoulder. She leaned back slightly and turned her head to me. My heart started pounding.

Then she pulled away and sat up, reaching into her coat pocket. Before she had her hand halfway out I knew she was bringing out cocaine. I felt a tiny, minute pause, the least hesitation, but then I stopped all questioning and only felt how much I wanted her.

She flourished a mostly empty little bottle in the dim light from the dashboard, unscrewed it and put a small straw into the white power. "There's hardly any, but, maybe, you'll like it," she said, leaning in close to me, offering me the straw.

I snorted up about half of it in two quick bursts and fantastic rushes surged through me, an energy mingled with a burning want for her.

In a flash she finished the cocaine and leaned back savoring the rush. I started to reach out for her, but she pulled away and motioned at the tug boat across the snow. She sat up and with a sexy smile said, "Let's check it out."

That isn't quite what I wanted to do, but I liked the way she said it. We pulled on our coveralls and zipped up. I turned the truck toward the tug so we'd have lights to return by. I stuck a flashlight in my coat pocket and we got out, leaving the truck running, with the defroster on high.

We stepped off North America onto the ice. Jeanne took off running. I chased after her. The wind had blown the snow into little waves and troughs. It was much firmer along the top where the snow had a stronger crust. We raced along the ridges. I caught up and tackled her. We crashed to the snow and rolled. The flashlight lumped under me, but there was nothing in her pockets and I could feel her against me even through all the clothing. For a second her hand traced a curve up my thigh. We wrestled to our feet and ran hand-in-hand the rest of the way. The wind was blowing, but it didn't feel cold.

We kicked around the tugboat deck and then went into the wheelhouse. Once we were out of the wind, the mood got much warmer. Jeanne definitely made up for the twenty below, though a surprisingly coy and shy sense had come over us.

Out the windshield, looking up above the ice fog we watched the beautiful intensity of the Northern Lights. No bright colors, like south around the Arctic Circle. Rather brightly glowing white, rolling in long wands. The streamers flowed, faded and then jumped to a new place across the sky, getting much brighter in an instant. White balls of light washed across the horizon and merged into a glowing cloud.

Cocaine rushes and desire surged up. We looked at one another, standing close. I cranked the steering wheel around and asked, "You ever see me put one of these through a one-eighty? They handle like a big snowmobile."

"Well, full speed ahead, Cap'n."

That's just what was on my mind. I caught her eye and looked her over to the stairwell. I snapped on the flashlight, grabbed the rail and swung down the steps three at a time. Jeanne came after me. At the bottom I put my arms around her. She squeezed against me. We were poised, hesitating an instant, then we kissed, exquisitely moist, sharing and exploring. I opened my eyes a bit and up through the stairwell saw a glimpse of the Lights shining on.

44

I got a terrific hard-on and wondered if she could feel me through the layers of down. She could. She slipped a leg between mine and rubbed against me. We took our coats off and by flashlight managed a more or less direct course to a narrow bunk.

"I'm glad you're so hot, lover," she whispered in my ear, "cause this is the coldest place I've ever done it."

"I'm getting all the heat from you," I answered through a kiss.

I unzipped her down coveralls. I slid up her canary top. She was glorious. All undressing stopped as I sucked her breasts and ran my tongue over her nipples standing up so firm.

We went through the layers getting me uncovered and then Jeanne did some funny, sexy gyrations to slip her coveralls over her shoulders. I ran my hand along her stomach and stroked her pussy while I undid her pants with my other hand. She scrunched her pants and coveralls down and they clunked oddly against the bulkhead. Then she got my pants down. I turned around and she was under me, taking my cock into her mouth. I licked her pussy, sucked on her and played around with my tongue until she was slick with juice and moaning. She slipped my cock out of her mouth wet into the air. I felt a jerk of cold. She blew on me, first amazing cold and then hot and wonderful as she sucked again. I felt a flash of the cocaine energy, but that scattered and I felt only how much I wanted her.

Jeanne made a lingering cry, then turned under me, licking up my body until we were face to face. I moved

45

between her legs, slid a hand up her flank and cupped her left breast. "It's very dangerous here. The ice can crush a ship's hull like an eggshell," I said squeezing her and making a crunching, squishing sound.

She squirmed and purred, saying, "Oh, show me the danger."

We held each other tightly against the cold and I slipped into her. Waves of heat from her mingled with ripples of cold air. I wanted to come from the first instant I was in her and I wanted it to go on forever.

She moaned and shifted. I went more deeply into her. We thrust together, slowly for a long time despite the freezing air washing over us. Then the intensity built and we moved together quicker and deeper. We fell out of sync once, for a moment, but then our energy pulled us together and we found our rhythm again. She kept getting more excited, not quite coming but wanting to, trying to. I marveled at her incredible surging energy. Then she came, crying out "Yes, yes, yes," and just then we were surging exactly together, in a wonderful frenzy. And then coming became inevitable. It rushed through me, carried me off and I was ecstatic.

Afterward we lay still in the darkness.

The cold cut short our lounging. We zipped up and went back across the snow to the truck. I turned it around and we took off for Parsons Camp with a burst of talk about how fine a few more snorts of cocaine would feel.

"Let's get some toot and do it again, someplace warm this time," she purred.

And that's exactly what I wanted to do. Only, soon, something went out of the mood. Jeanne became distracted. Maybe it had happened too quickly for her taste, though I doubted that. I wasn't sure any more if the cocaine had made the pleasure greater or not.

She seemed in a hurry to get somewhere and that put a strain in the conversation. She sat on the far side of the seat. I wondered whether her light gaiety on the way to the tugboat had been forced or if she actually changed that quick and strong.

We fell silent and drove miles through the gathering ice fog. I was considered whether getting stoned was likely to restore the mood or if it would be just another vain, hopeless chase after the initial high. And I thought about how often I got it wrong with women, even when it worked out, as it just had, sort of.

Chapter Four

We pulled into Parsons Camp and rolled past two or three hundred trucks and busses in the parking lot, looking for a place to plug in. All the outlets were taken, so I stopped in front of trailer wing eleven, which was fairly close to the center of camp. We sat there and chatted some about the toot awaiting inside, covering the tension with a lot of forced anticipation. A raven was waddling around the hood of the pickup next to us. The bird walked as awkwardly as we were talking. Then the raven took off and curved away over the roof, becoming beautiful in flight. I hoped it was a good omen and looked over at Jeanne.

She was smiling again in the half-amber light of the mercury vapor lamps shining over the camp. Her expression had an oddly practiced quality. I wondered if there wasn't another way to take that omen.

"I have to see a friend," she said, not quite meeting my eye. "Let's arrange a place to meet."

"For long?"

"Uhhh, no."

"OK. I'll score and meet you in the Rec Room," I said, going through the motions with declining hope. But she turned toward me and her face lit up. She wanted to toot some more dust. I got a sense of that which was palpable and sharp. It gave me hope that our passion would as quickly surge again.

"Alright." she agreed, with her spirits quickly damped down again. "I'll see you there."

Somehow, I didn't think she would. She flashed me an almost smile from another time zone and got out. I watched her go inside and my heart sagged. Then I shrugged my way out of my coveralls, getting down to indoor clothes. I had two keys to the truck, so I left it locked and idling, defroster on full.

As I went through the Arctic doorway, an older guy in a bathrobe tiptoed out of his room, eased along the ragged out carpet and opened the black door of the furnace room two doors down. He did it slow and quiet. When he got the door open, he reached in and fiddled the thermostat. He tried to close the door carefully, but it squeaked. He left it ajar and scurried back to his place. The door between his room and the furnace room had a crude felt tip slogan scrawled on it, reading, "Fueled by Speed, Powered by Greed." It snapped open and another old guy stormed out, barefoot and in pajamas. He was a lot bigger than the first guy. He jerked open the black door, muttering to himself. As I passed I saw him crank the dial all the way to off. He slammed the furnace door, walked down to the first guy's door and kicked it three times, screaming that he was some kind of asshole for screwing up the heat.

A dozen or so pairs of trailers were butted end-to-end like dominoes and connected down the middle with a several centuries long hallway. Farther ahead the main hallway cut across. Beyond it an identical wing ran on. The hall was narrow and nothing was quite finished, with exposed pipes running overhead and a generally ratty look. Every four rooms there was a cranky furnace. A bathroom with too few showers and a laundry room were at the far end. That wing, like all the others sprouting from the main hallway, housed fifty-two workers. That was fifty-two union workers, because they kept the nonunion crowd in the next camp over.

I walked down and turned into the main hallway. Fourteen hundred construction workers lived in Parsons and the horde was roaming the halls. Two official Teamo heavies were coming the other way. The smaller one was only five-ten, but he was grim and went two-sixty. I knew them from a dark day in the past. We nodded as we passed.

A twenty man gang of 798ers just coming off shift clogged the hall ahead. They were very hardcore, red neck pipe layers, always from Oklahoma or Texas, always wearing Jesse James bandanas around their necks and always in noisy, aggressive groups. They worked in crews of a couple hundred, so you always saw a lot of them together. They liked to mess with anyone at all, but especially with the Teamsters. Nobody in their right mind messed with the Teamos, but the 798ers had a lot of guys definitely not in their right minds. I knew one of them who taped a .357 into his hand before going to sleep. He said he had enemies. No surprise there. I didn't want to be his roommate.

A stream of middle-aged carpenters, various long hairs, indeterminate stray humanoids and occasional ladies filtered cautiously through the clot of 798ers. Three of the 798ers changed course to get in my way, pushing me toward the wall. I stood aside, let them pass, then stepped the other way to get past the next group.

A block party in a side trailer boomed loudly I walked past. A superior fiddler and a plausible banjo player had two couples dancing and fifty men crowded around drinking and smoking dope. Two or three security guards in gray Wackenhut uniforms were walking around with walkie talkies, looking for trouble so they could go the other way. Attila the Hun could have strolled down that hallway without causing a stir.

I did pick out Wayne Tyson. He was surprised to see me, since the troops really weren't supposed to be floating around from camp to camp after work.

"Hi, Wayne."

"What are you doing here?" he asked, automatically critical and displeased as ever.

"Livin' fast. How about yourself?"

"The movie." he mumbled with a slight nod and immediately pushed past without a good-bye.

I took a left into trailer fifteen and knocked on a door. It opened and Annie Melling was standing there. She had a cabin close to mine, in the woods outside Fairbanks. Annie was a good friend and a great neighbor who had bailed me out more than once. She was pulling a startlingly long run on the Slope, getting out of debt like I was trying to do. She was a short, powerful, dark-haired woman, about thirty, who was also one of the better jocks I'd ever come across. Her face had an unusual look that went back and forth between severe and attractive.

"Nick. Great to see you. Come on in. How're my dogs?"

"Still howling, Annie. How're you holding out?"

"It's tearing me up to miss the best mushing weather. I guess they figured out my price. Anything less and I'd be out running the dogs."

She was completely dog nuts, even to the point of having an armchair in her cabin formed out of fifty pound sacks of dog food. And she was tough. I liked her a lot, though I didn't understand how an otherwise sane person could be so hopeless over huskies, especially when they destroyed your quiet by falling into vast howling sessions at the least provocation. Not even teenagers were supposed to be that crazed over their means of transport.

Part of me wanted to stay and visit, but mainly I was hoping that things would still work out with Jeanne. I caught myself feeling very driven to score some thrill powder and go meet her. So, I stayed on that point. Annie liked cocaine, and she would surely be scoped into the local scene. Fortunately, her roommate wasn't around to inhibit the conversation.

"Any toot around?" I asked her.

"It was pretty dried up, but you're in luck. Remember Spacey Acey from Galbraith last year?"

"Yeah, he was a Teamo expediter for Arctic."

"He just opened up his store again. He's down in Twelve, about room twenty or twenty-one. You can't miss it. He's got 'Din of Iniquity' written on his door with a felt tip. It's some sort of Zero wit."

"Thanks, Annie. If I connect, I'll get back by later."

I went back along the main hallway and turned into twelve, another wing of trailers, empty except for a woman in an Air Force parka, hood up, hurrying through the door at the far end. Her pocket got hung up on the door latch and she stopped to free it. I thought it might be Jeanne, but I wasn't sure. I called out "Jeanne," but she jerked her parka free and continued through the door without looking back. I thought she must have heard me, but then again she may not have recognized my voice. Anyway, she was gone.

I went halfway down and found "Din of Iniquity" scrawled on the door of room nineteen. Loud Hank Williams was pouring through a partly open door. I knocked. No answer. I pushed the door open slowly. "Acey?" No answer.

These rooms were divided into identical left and right halves, with a shared desk in the middle of the back wall. The left half was plain, with little gear around. I pushed the door open a bit further and could see that at the very center of the desk the decor went overt. A solid wall of centerfold ladies began at that point, relieved only by a lurid framed panther-on-velvet that pretended to be a painting.

Acey and his roommate were gone, but Phil Dalira was there, a bit difficult to recognize. He was sprawled on the floor next to the bed, a pool of blood spreading around him. He was completely dead. I knew the look.

I stood suspended on the doorstep. The smart thing would have been to yell as loud as I could and draw a crowd. I knew if I did that how bad it would look for Jeanne, if it had been Jeanne who had just gone through the far door. I like to mull the tiny decisions of life, worry them back and forth and get them just right. The big ones I'd rather make in an instant. I took a breath, concluded that she hadn't killed her brother, then stepped inside and shut the door.

Phil had been knifed down in a bad way. Blood seeped out from several wounds in his chest. Any of those might have killed him. His face also had two long, deep slashes. One ran right through his left eye. That was something extra, more than killing, the culmination of a frenzy. His remaining eye stared up, empty and tired. I had to make myself look. I didn't want to, but I had to know.

Broken mirror fragments lay on the floor beside him, along with a razor blade and an awful lot of coke. He must have been sitting on the bed chopping coke on a mirror when someone had started in on him.

A couple things were missing. His wallet was not in his pants. Four or six grams of coke were on the floor, but nothing it would have been wrapped in. There were no baggies, folded papers, bottles or anything else. I checked his pockets. Keys, but nothing that could have held cocaine.

I knuckled open the desk drawers and the wall lockers, to avoid tagging them with prints. I wasn't exactly confident

I could keep out of it, but I was always careful when it didn't slow me down. Nothing special in any of them.

Altogether, it looked like Phil had just copped an ounce or more from Acey and the killer had taken off with the goods. Only why did Phil have so much on the mirror when he went down? However much he dealt or tooted, he didn't have an advertising budget like that.

There was also no knife. The razor blade had been strictly for fluffing up the powder. Maybe it could have done the slashes across Phil's face, maybe, but it was dry. And, in any case, it would have had nothing to do with the chest stabs that had taken him down.

I had to check something out and saw only one way to do it. I opened a matchbook, thumbed it into a scoop and loaded up out of the coke on the floor. I checked for glass and lifted it up to my better nostril, my right, and snorted up. When the rush came on I found myself fighting against it. It affected me, but I felt bored with the sensation. And then I had to forget about that because the door opened and a tall, skinny, over-dressed speeder in a gold velour pullover and shiny blue slacks stepped in. Spacey Acey himself, stopping in mid-stride, still holding the doorknob.

"Rezkel," he said quietly.

"Was there a knife in this room, Spacey?"

"N-n-no," he said, backing out the door.

He was scared, but I thought his first impulse would be to secure his stash. He didn't even look around. He must have kept it in another room. Good move for a high-profile ounce dealer. He shut the door behind him and started shouting. He was surely being smarter than I was.

I scooped up another hit and tooted it, to be certain. The rush was decent, but had a burn to it. The cocaine was passable, likely cut with speed and definitely cut too much. Still, it wasn't stepped on to where it would provoke the typical customer into pulling a knife to even up the deal.

Acey was going to reappear with security in short order. No way around that. I looked around the room, still keeping my fingerprints off things. I didn't figure on much credibility with the cops, but I didn't want to complicate their work. Then I sat down on Acey's roommate's bed and waited for them.

I cheered up half a click by reminding myself that Jeanne didn't have a knife on her. I remembered that I had direct evidence on that point. Then I just stared at the cocaine dissolving into the blood and felt very sad.

Footsteps pounded down the hall and I brought myself back to attention. The door opened slowly and three Wackenhut guards came in. Acey peeped in the door behind them. I stayed where I was, sitting down with my hands on my knees. They shut the door.

Two of them were sizeable guys, but soft. The third one was smaller. He was boss. The bigger two stood close to me, unsure what they wanted to do. The guy in charge looked over Phil, then turned back to me. Name, rank and service number time.

"My name is Nicholas Rezkel. I'm a Laborer for Randolph-Lightner at CC2, and I didn't kill him."

"Bullshit," snapped the smaller guard.

He pointed to the pile of cocaine on the floor slowly turning red.

"The occupant saw you taking that narcotic."

"That proves a lot about nothing."

He knelt over Phil and poked him half-heartedly. He seemed to think that was his duty, though there was no doubt how dead Phil was. He straightened up and moved toward the desk, stepping into the pile of cocaine by Phil's side.

"Hey, don't touch anything. I know you're not a cop, but haven't you ever been to the movies. Christ."

"Yeah? What do you care?"

"I didn't kill him, that's what. I found him dead and I don't want you trampling the evidence that's gonna clear me."

"Right, asshole. Why were you breathing that stuff?"

"A lot of coke dealers get dead peddling bad shit."

"That's why you killed him, eh? Because you didn't like his narcotics."

"His coke was fair. Nothing special either way."

The noisy rumble of a crowd was suddenly loud in the hallway outside. One of the bigger guards turned to the boss guard and said, "Maybe we oughta get him out of here."

"Yeah. Let's seal off this room."

"Hold on. Search me first. There's no knife in here and I don't have one on me. I want that in the report. And send someone outside to find there's no knife under the window either. I want that in the report, too."

The smaller guard tried out his hardest look on me. I gave him a cheery smile.

57

"Stand up, asshole"

I got up. He lined up on me and then did a quick search of my nuts with his knee. I doubled over before it quite got there and tossed in a grunt for effect. He liked it.

They patted me down in a half-ass way that would have turned up a machete but not much else. Then they opened the door and we walked out into the hall. Three more Wackenhut guards were waiting outside. A crowd of two hundred or more pressed in on us. They went silent, eager for something to happen.

The Wackenhuts formed a phalanx around me and we walked toward the main hallway. The crowd parted for us, except for the Teamo muscle, standing in place, staring at me. The Wackenhuts squeezed me around those two mountains.

The bigger Teamo's eyes were burning. "Dalira was one of ours," he said in a flat voice. "If you beat this, Rezkel, we'll be around to see you."

I saw Jeanne for an instant through the crowd as they hustled me along the corridor. Her head was tilted, wondering.

"Nick. You didn't do it, did you?" she said so softly I barely heard her.

"It wasn't me, Jeanne."

That started up the crowd. Jeers and outrage poured out.

"Must've been his foreman."

"A frag. Beat him to death with bunny boots."

And then I saw Lori standing off to the side, looking at me with great hostility. She was wearing jeans and she was carrying one of those ubiquitous Air Force parkas, exactly like Jeanne's.

They marched me down to the Billeting Office for interrogation. As farce, wasn't bad. I stood around with four guards in a windowless office, waiting for the camp manager.

Eventually, the door opened for a doughy-faced toad with a permanent sneer ironed into his upper lip. He was excited about having an actual murder come up, but he was afraid of the bureaucratic consequences of failing to cut in the big timers. So he made a phone call and then we started waiting for his boss. No questions, just waiting.

Half an hour later a tall, lean and smooth man turned up in the full executive splendor of a suit. Very off-key clothing behavior. Five thousand people worked at Prudhoe Bay and maybe a half dozen wore suits. This one had a bland manner, a neat gray moustache, trimmed to the finest tolerance, and the heart of ground glass that is required of Barner Oil vice presidents.

After hearing a third-hand rundown of the situation, Mr. Oil Slick tranced for several minutes. He evidently decided that there was no immediate danger of plummeting oil prices and told the camp manager to call the cops.

I got a break there. The Alaska State Trooper assigned to Prudhoe wasn't around. He was down the pipeline at Coldfoot and couldn't get back for hours. Even better, the troopers couldn't get anyone up from Fairbanks until morning.

I wanted to talk to Jeanne before I left her out of any historical fiction I was going to give the man. Plus, I needed a chance at the Randolph-Lightner files. There was plenty of time to make a move, so I sat tight and talked to Slick until the enemy lines thinned.

We went over my story a few times. I told it leisurely and overloaded him with detail, omitting any mention of Jeanne or my stolen truck idling outside. Slick wanted to know how I got over to Parsons from CC2. I spoke abstractly of Prodlick Bay hitchhiking, then descended to the particular with considerable praise for the Northern Lights which had cheered me as I was supposedly standing in the wind with my thumb out. He wanted to know who had given me a ride. I did a ten-minute description of Woody Allen and said he worked on a drill rig. Slick suspected my bright, helpful attitude of being sarcastic.

He brought in Spacey Acey and went over his story. Spacey was covered. He and his roommate had left Phil in their room and gone off to watch the movie in the Rec Room. He was with people right up to when he found me in his rooms. No, he had absolutely no idea where the cocaine came from. He wasn't even sure what cocaine was. I volunteered to Spacey that he shouldn't be ashamed of his toot, that it was stepped on but was still an alright snort. That got me looks of massive displeasure from around the room and Slick did a fast resume of all the rules against cocaine that they had managed to think up, to restore the proper mood.

Several local residents of trailer twelve were interviewed. Most knew from nothing. The neighbors in room twenty, for instance, went out of their way to point out that the furnace room between them and Spacey's room made it unlikely they'd hear anything. But an electrician in eighteen, on the other side, said that although the music from Spacey's was quite loud, as ever, he did hear someone go into Spacey's room three different times, a few minutes apart, just before the uproar. After each of the first two visits, footsteps hurried down the hall toward the outside door. The third visitor turned out to be me.

I was cheered somewhat by that account, though I had to consider someone other than Jeanne or Lori. It gave me more reason to avoid any mention of Jeanne at all.

About eleven, Slick got Barriss on the phone and did a formal rendition of the dirt. Sounded like Barriss loved the news. From his perspective, Dalira and me going down together was optimum. Judging from what came up later, he'd even extemporized that he'd heard Phil say he was worried that I was going to try to rip off his cocaine.

That last bit sold Slick. I leaned back in my armless plastic chair and kept them entertained by playing to their image of me as dingy and callous. They were relaxing steadily. The situation was gradually maturing.

The room was connected to another windowless room which had doors leading to the security station and to the hallway near the main camp entrance. That adjoining room was empty every time the door was opened.

The graveyard shift came on at twelve and they changed out my guards. The Wackenhuts were not normally armed, but they had dug up a .38 from somewhere. Slick was reassured and he cut back to one armed guard in the room with us. I decided to give them a half hour to settle down.

61

The guard had the .38 in a holster on his right hip. The way he was sitting in an armchair, the pistol was as useful as a crossbow in a closet.

I avoided smirking as Slick continued asking me questions, playing the tough prosecutor for the benefit of the others. He was behind a desk, facing the door. The guard's chair was beside the door. The camp manager and me were in the two corners furthest from the door. It was alright.

When I was ready, I said, "I've got a confession to make."

It pleased him to hear that.

"I never read *Don Quixote*, not a single word."

"What does that mean, if anything?" he got out in an irritated voice, his face clouding.

"It's the best I can do. You're so horny for a confession, but I didn't kill anyone. In some circles that's a rather embarrassing admission."

"Well, this isn't one of them," Slick bit off, denting each word.

His temper was slipping away from him. The camp manager and the guard were entranced to see him thrown off-stride. He wanted to reassert his will over them. His lips pursed as he thought of something apparently vicious and executive.

I was out of my chair and on top of the guard in two steps. He started for his gun but realized mid-motion that he didn't have time. He thought I was going to punch his face and threw up his left arm to block. I knocked it away. He tried to punch from the chair with his right. I snapped it away with an inside forearm block. I was right in front of him, both hands ready.

Nobody else moved, but behind me I heard Slick pick up the phone. I grabbed a handful of the guard's hair and bent his head back. He went still, waiting to be hit, afraid to move and hurry it up. I held his head back, reached down and took the .38 out of his holster. Then I turned around, holding the revolver. Slick put down the phone.

"I'll be on the morning plane. I didn't kill him."

I closed the door, went through the empty room and out into the hallway. I ran toward the main hall, shouts and footsteps behind me. The .38 was a handicap. I wanted them to converge on me, but as long as I had it they were going to hang back. Once I heard them in the hall I tossed the .38, making sure they saw it hit the floor.

I turned right into the main hall and kept running until two more Wackenhuts showed, coming from the opposite direction, holding walkie talkies to their ears. I slowed and let them all get closer. When they were within fifty feet I cut into the nearest trailer, number eight, went out the fire door and down the steps into the snow under the trailers.

Everywhere else on the Slope they put down a gravel pad and then built on top of it, in order to keep things from sinking into the tundra in the summer. Not Parsons Camp. They had put the trailers on long wooden posts and got by with a cheapie gravel pad laid down around the buildings. Summers, the hole underneath filled with incredibly grungy swamp water that bred mosquitoes by the ton. Winters, it made a great place to lose an indoor crowd like the Wackenhuts.

I ran off between the pilings. A flashlight beam blossomed, but it didn't pick me out. They found the snowy footing tricky for Oxfords, but I could move easily in my gym shoes. Something about being outdoors in twenty-odd below without a coat also tended to discourage them. I didn't want to disappear too soon or the whole point of the exercise would be lost, so I showed myself for the flashlight and pursuit got on track again.

I went toward the lower number trailers, counting them as I went, staying away from the road side of the camp and taking care not to get too far ahead. Looking back I could see that they had got themselves nicely stacked up in a pack behind me so it seemed the moment to double back toward my wheels. I put on a surge, stayed well away from the beam of light and cut through the pilings, this time toward the road side of camp.

They didn't catch on to the change in direction until I'd crossed under the main hallway. I blasted back through the pilings, counting off the trailer wings as I went under them, heading toward the road, no flashlight in view anywhere behind me. When I hit wing eleven, I went straight away from the main hallway all the way to the end of the trailers. I scrambled up the bank exactly in front of my lovely stolen Randolph-Lightner pickup, unlocked the door and got in. I ducked down as a Barner Oil security crew cab rolled past and turned the corner toward the rear of the camp. Soon as the pickup was out of sight, I cranked my rig around, pulled out of the parking lot onto the road and was gone.

Nothing much moving as I drove back toward the other side of Prudhoe. The ice fog had thinned enough that I could make out the wrecked plane lying in the snow beyond the end of the Deadhorse runway. A season before, thieves had stolen a wad of drill bits. Those things were the size of parking meters and went for five grand apiece. The crime was perfect, except for the part where they overloaded the DC3 and botched the takeoff because they couldn't catch enough altitude. No one was hurt in the crash, unless you call getting five to ten getting hurt. The oily companies left the fuselage where it landed, right where everyone drove past it all the time. Maybe they thought it was a message. I thought it was littering.

I got back to the other side with no encounters, turned in to CC1 and parked behind C Wing. Then I went inside, trying not to think ahead of time about what I was going to hear from Jeanne, only hoping I was going to like it.

She'd said her room was C219. I went up to the second floor and walked along a deserted hallway toward that. There weren't any locks on the doors. I turned the knob and stepped into the room. In the orange light leaking through the shade from the mercury vapor lights outside, I could make out a figure in each bed. I looked back and forth between them. Two men. Then it hit me. C Wing wasn't the women's wing at CC1. This couldn't be her room. I stepped out and shut the door, wondering at first if I'd misremembered the number.

I walked down to the front desk. The clerk wasn't around. A sign propped on the desk announced that he'd be back in a few minutes. On the night shift, that meant next year, so I hopped over the counter. A large board on the wall had a slot for each room, with a card in it for each occupant. I scanned the cards for all the women's rooms. No Jeanne. Her name wasn't in the mezzanine section for culinary workers either, nor in the central card index.

Several slots had blank green cards. I'd cracked that code the year before when I lived at CC1 and had an impossible roommate who wouldn't clear out when a certain lady came to visit me. I had to figure out how to find an empty room to move into for the night and those blank green cards took care of me. Loveflex. I knew they were going to be looking for me at CC2, so I got the number of one of the empty rooms before I took off.

I drove the rest of the way back to CC2, turned into the camp and nosed the pickup around to the far side. Two men were standing in front of the Randolph-Lightner shop. I stopped and backed away from them, as far as the front of D Wing. Then I parked it, put on my coat and pulled my stocking cap down over my face. Turned out to be unnecessary as I didn't run into anyone on the way to Phil's room.

I walked in without knocking and turned on the lights. No roommate. Phil'd had enough boss stroke to manage that. His wall locker had a padlock on it, but it wasn't serious because the door simply came off the hinges when I jerked on it. That was more noise than I wanted to make, but nothing especially unusual and the neighbors didn't stir.

Inside was the expected clothing and stuff, plus several empty little glass bottles that would each hold a gram of coke. Four cases of booze were stacked on one side. A half dozen Alaska maps cut out of forty-eight inch pipe were shoved in the back. They were strangely popular. Phil had needed inventory to keep the store open.

Behind a pile of socks and underwear I found a three-beam balance scale, a lot more tiny glass bottles and a leather notebook. On one page was the number 66A6139. I took the notebook and borrowed Phil's alarm clock. He wasn't going to need it. I wiped my prints and then went looking for Lori.

I wanted to minimize my exposure, so I went outside, walked to the center of camp and came back in the front doors, only a few steps to the front office. Nobody was around to see me. I got Lori's room number from the camp roster, then went outside and around to her wing.

I opened the door quietly and went into her room, leaving the door ajar. In the light coming in from the hallway I saw a woman there.

"Lori, wake up," I said quietly.

The woman woke quickly.

"Lori?"

"I'm not Lori. Which one are you? Can't you see she's not here?" the roommate answered, pointing to the empty bed.

"I just want to look at her parka, if that's OK," I explained, moving to Lori's wall locker and opening it.

She looked at me with grave suspicion.

"Well, go ahead. But wouldn't you rather look at her stockings?"

"No. You don't understand. Just her parka."

"Oh, don't I understand?"

There was no parka. I moved to the door. "Nothing there. Sorry to wake you."

"Don't be concerned about that," she said, her syllables drowning in sarcasm. "Come back anytime. Try her panty drawer next time."

I wanted to correct the impression, but it was hopeless. I retreated, properly mortified, and went out to my truck. As I drove back to CC1 to get some sleep, I replayed it over and over, wondering if it had been Jeanne or Lori I'd seen.

Chapter Five

My desperate youth forced me to learn the art of sleeping in any stray circumstance, so when Phil's alarm clock went off after two hours I was ready to go. I got up, showered, grabbed a cup of tea in the Rec Room and drove the time-keeper's rig back to CC2.

The wind had shifted around to the south, coming straight up from the Brooks Range. Walking to the front doors it felt warmer out, maybe only a minus-fifty factor. The front office clock read five. Several men were in the halls, but nobody paid me any attention. I walked past the mess hall, past absolutely do not enter signs into the kitchen area, then past totally absolutely do not enter signs into the transformer room where large, gray paneled machines hummed electrical chants. I went outside at the far corner of the building and was a few steps from the rear of the Randolph-Lightner shop. I felt especially visible walking alongside the sheet metal building.

The shop doors opened to my touch again. Barriss' truck was inside with the hood up. I looked around inside it. His Buck knife was not on the seat. I hung the truck keys back on their hook and opened the door to the office. Lights were still on. A desk was right inside the door with another in the back. Along the left wall were three chairs and a copier on a small table. On the other side was a filing cabinet and shelves with small tools Barriss grudgingly parceled out to the troops.

Monday's timesheets were in a basket on the rear desk. I poked through them and found my crew. There were eight of us out on the line, counting Huey and Theo, but the timesheet listed nine names. The extra name was Dave Marshall, down as another Laborer getting in ten hours a day like the rest of us. Another name I didn't recognize was on one of the other sheets, an Operator named Morris Thompson. I liked it, feeling comforted to find water on the payroll. I turned on the copier and shot all the timesheets.

The desk drawers were low grade trash. I had a long, dry run through the filing cabinet looking for anything with Phil's name on it. He didn't rate a mention and the Arctic Wrap folder didn't have a thing about heavy foam. Finally, in an unlabeled folder at the back of the middle drawer, I came up with the Arctic Wrap letter to Randolph-Lightner covering its corporate ass for having barged twenty crates of defective insulation to Prudhoe. Their out was to order it destroyed. The letter had a careful and contrite tone as it announced that the excessive water content of the foam reduced its insulation properties to substantially below par.

It didn't mention that the stuff was also unusually heavy and an awkward bitch to work with. I shot the letter and went back for more.

Huey suddenly filled the doorway, making a mean little slobbering laugh. He had likely come by the shop before breakfast to start up all the rigs. My first thought was that he had shown up way too early, then I remembered the rumor that the crew was going to twelve-hour shifts. After that, I realized that I had focused in too tight on the immediate task, again, or I might have heard him come in through the outside doors.

Huey was the sort of guy who'd like an excuse to see if gravity made blood run downhill. That is, if he'd ever heard of gravity. He didn't say a word. He just kept on with a strangled laugh. He should have come right at me, but he made the mistake of stopping to reach for a hammer off the shelf. His left cheek began to twitch.

I shoved the copies into my coat pocket and came out from behind the filing cabinet.

"Huey, how are you going to hit me without a crane?"

That pissed him off, but it didn't distract him as he took hold of the hammer. He was a mountain and he filled the narrow room. There was no space to get around him or come from the side. I glimpsed a figure behind him and wanted to even things up fast. I grabbed a clipboard off the desk as he was turning around with the hammer in his fist. I back-handed it at him, putting in the least bit of curve for control. His face was still turning toward me. The clipboard crashed into his black horn-rimmed glasses and knocked them to the floor.

The impact slowed him half a count. As he shook it off I took two steps across the office and was snapping a kick with the third step, getting my hands up to deal with the hammer which was starting down. My left foot connected and drove into his nuts. That didn't end anything. He was numb to start with and football must have taught him something about that sort of pain. The hammer was still coming down. I reached out my left hand and guided it past my head. Stepping inside its arc I caught him in the nuts again with my right knee. He felt that one, but he twisted and threw his huge left fist at my face. I wanted to beat that punch with one of my own, but there wasn't time. I was close to him and had to block it.

He was quicker than I expected and I didn't get it completely blocked. His fist glanced off my cheekbone and jolted me. He wanted to start another punch, but I got ahead of him, grabbed his shirt, jerked him toward me and kneed him twice more, fast. That finally got to him. He bent way over. And then I had all the time there ever was. I sank down into forward stance and fired a counterpunch to the point of his jaw. His head snapped to the side and Huey came down. I stepped aside and let him fall.

Barriss was standing outside the door. He stepped back and bumped into another man. That guy was wearing completely clean slacks, a blue wool Pendleton jacket and a wolf fur parka that had probably set him back a thou. He was mid-forties, a little under six feet, pudgy, pouty, slightly decrepit in his immaculate clothes, the class creep who made a bundle. His face was smeared red and blotchy, definitely from the best booze. I knew him from Thalman's poker game. Harold Scanlon. He ran the Randolph-Lightner operation in Fairbanks. He was back-peddling from us.

"What are you doing here?" Barriss demanded.

"I came by to get in a free call on the company phone. Dufus tried to take my head off, only he missed again."

"Didn't you see that 'Authorized Personnel Only' sign?"

"I'm just semi-literate. I don't read signs."

Barriss jammed a hand into his parka pocket. I stepped in close to him. He pulled out a pink slip and handed it to me.

"You're fired, asshole."

"Oh no, please boss, say you don't mean it," I groveled for him. "It's too cruel. Where the fuck were you at nine o'clock last night, anyway?"

"Don't give me any of your lip. I'm going to get the cops down here," he said plowing straight ahead.

"Where were you, Barriss? And where was your Buck knife? It's not in your pick up over there, like usual. Were you showing it to Dalira?"

Scanlon whipped his head around and stared at him. Barriss brushed past me and went into the office. He picked up the phone.

"What about you, Scanlon? Where were you last night?"

"I was back in Fairbanks. I only got up here an hour ago," he said, edging away from me.

"You must care a lot about Dalira to charter a flight up here in the middle of the night."

Unsteady resolution crept into Scanlon's face. The skin around his mouth wrinkled and his nostrils flared.

"You wait right here. We're putting you on the next flight to town," he said primly and walked into the office, holding his fancy parka to keep it from rubbing against anything dirty.

Huey was trying to stand up, moaning with the effort. Scanlon went around him without offering a hand and stood behind Barriss.

"You can tell them I'll get to that plane by myself. And by the way, Scanlon, how's your lo-ball game? Bad as ever, I trust? You still trying to beat pat hands by hitting the deck for two cards?"

No point in hanging around for the appearance of uniforms. I had to secure my goods because my next encounter with officialdom was likely to become prolonged and would surely open with a search. I trotted around to the rear of B Wing, keeping out of the wind. Straight twenty below was balmy. Thinking about how quick Scanlon had been to suspect Barriss was also warming. I considered that a wholesome development.

I went quickly through the crowd in the halls and ran into Allen by the theater as he was on his way to breakfast. He was tall, thin and gangly, but he moved with a coltish grace. A gentle smile played across his high cheekbones and full, rubbery lips as he saw me. He'd been a friend for a long time and I knew he wouldn't buy the talk that had to be going around without hearing me out. As it turned out, he didn't believe any of it to start with.

"I knew you hadn't done it when they said Dalira was stabbed twenty times," he told me right off, smiling gently. "Twice, I might have gone for, but not twenty."

Two electricians who lived across the hall from me stopped talking as they walked past. One nudged the other and he nodded in return. Then Paddy and Jack came up and after them several men gathered around. The man was going to show anytime, but I had to run down the story for them. I gave them the quick version, without any mention of Jeanne. They started believing me when I got to the fight with Huey. Finally, I was able to pull Allen away and get in a word with him.

"There's a guy I want you to check out for me. Harold Scanlon. He's maximum leader in the Randolph-Lightner front office. Slacks, blue wool jacket, leather boots, a silly, extravagant parka. The bottle has got to his face."

"What do you want to know about him?"

"Anything, but especially when he got to Prudhoe last night."

Three Barner Oil security guards appeared next to the commissary, asking questions. One of those in the crowd I'd just explained myself to edged toward them. Allen and I moved into C Wing, out of their sight.

"Call me in Fairbanks tonight. At Tommy's, at seven."

"OK. Expect comprehensive rumor coverage. And Nick, that's a nice-looking eye you're going to have. Purple by sundown, I imagine."

I went up the stairs two at a time and hurried back along the second floor hallway of C Wing to the front of the camp. Outside, it got easy. A Barner Oil security crew cab was parked by the front door, idling. I got in and drove it the twenty miles over to Atwood Camp, which was a parking lot away from the Deadhorse Airport terminal. There were a couple hours to kill, so I had breakfast. It wasn't too bad, though the cook broke all three yokes. The main item of conversation had Phil getting stabbed with a broken mirror.

Fifteen minutes before the morning flight was due in, I got a Red Zinger tea bag out of my coat pocket and made one to go, two Styrofoam cups, to keep it from cooling too fast. I zipped up and went outside. I walked across the parking lot toward the yellow and blue terminal building, feeling quasi-indistinguishable from anyone else with my face mask down. A cluster of security vehicles were parked by the main entrance, but nobody was outside.

I walked down to the end of the terminal and went into a minute air freight office. The small-parcels clerk was too harried getting it all sorted for the next flight to even look up when I handed him a manila envelope with the Randolph-Lightner copies in it, addressed to Quentin Compson in Fairbanks. He went through quadruplicate paperwork at escape velocity. When the Red Zinger was exact, I fished out the tea bag, squeezed it for the last drops and flipped it into a wastebasket behind the counter. The clerk's head jerked up, but he saw it was a hit and went back to his forms. I sipped the tea and paid him an outrageous $21, that being the flat rate. Then, I went to turn myself in.

I went outside, then back in through the main terminal entrance. No hassle, until I took off my face mask. Then they were on me. Slick and four armed guards pushed me against the wall. I went with it. They patted me down, a lot better than the first time. Then Slick directed us into a small office behind the ticket counter. Slick wasn't talking to me anymore. He left.

The Wien Air Alaska 727 landed and shortly afterwards four State Troopers came into the room. They cuffed me, hands front, and read me my rights. Nobody actually said I was under arrest, so I considered myself a volunteer.

We went out and I was paraded through the lobby before a group of subdued citizens. The electronic doorway went nuts over the cuffs as we walked through. That struck me as funny. I stopped and asked, "Do you want me to empty my pockets and try again?" No laughs. The trooper behind me snarled and shoved me through. The mood of the citizenry turned hostile and the stares directed at me were a palpable pressure.

Then all that faded away as I saw Jeanne coming toward me across the waiting area, giving me a very tender look. She had come in from outside and her parka was still zipped up. There was nothing like bloodstains on it, but the right front pocket was torn.

"Nick," she began.

"You can't talk to the prisoner, lady," the head trooper said, leading me away.

She put her hand on his arm and looked at him, eyes moist.

"Please, only a moment."

He gave her a long, appraising stare, then said, "Alright, but make it quick. And I'm staying right here."

She looked at me and flashed a brief smile that receded into a wounded expression.

"It's so sad, Nick. I don't know what to say."

"I didn't kill him. You should know that."

I was looking into her eyes. She seemed very hurt and almost lost as she answered, "I want to think so." Something in her tone was off, but I couldn't sense exactly what. Her face lost its pain and faded to neutral, her expression becoming still. It flashed to me that maybe she did want to think exactly that. I started a question. She surprised me by knowing immediately, before I'd barely begun it, that it would be a hard one.

"Where did you tear your coat? Didn't you hear me call?"

Her eyes followed mine to her right side pocket which was hanging loosely. She didn't react at all. I was surprised again because she didn't seem to understand. I thought that maybe she hadn't heard me call to her, after all, as she was going out the far end of that Parson's camp trailer. And then she was suddenly sad again. She threw her arms around me and kissed me, intensely, like on the tugboat.

"I never really thought you killed him. I only thought I saw...," she trailed off.

A flight attendant opened the waiting room door to the boarding area.

"No more, lady. You can see him in jail," the head trooper cut her off.

Then they led me out to the plane and put me on board before the real passengers.

Fairbanks, Alaska

Chapter Six

A state car took me to that squat little building on Cushman the troopers had as headquarters, with large squares of plastic, white alternating with an impossible disc jockey aqua. Perhaps that splash of atrocious color on the outside was sound design because the inside had nothing but blunt gray and a lot of cops sitting around. Two photographers started firing as we came in the door and reporters surrounded us.

"Why'd you kill him?"

"I didn't."

"How much cocaine did you rip him off for?"

My escorts loved it. They moved in closer and firmed up their grip on my arms. Mainly, they tried out the dedicated, sincere cop look for the cameras and made sure the newspaper crew got their names straight. Gradually they pushed me through the crowd and around a corner to a long bench against a gray wall. The only other customer was a wino working on arrest number three hundred.

They shoved me down on the bench next to him and stalked off.

The wino sat there clawing at the air in slow motion, looking like the idiot son of Ivan the Terrible. Considering the ancient sea of booze he was moving through, the slow motion was fairly quick. He clapped his hand shut, making a loose fist.

"Got'im."

He looked over at me and slurred, "Kill the first one and there ain't none the whole year."

He pawed the air again.

"So that's why we didn't have any mosquitoes last year, Pops. Thanks."

"Yeah. Drunk trapper told me that."

A city cop turned up and went off with the wino. They didn't bring any more criminals in. The arrest rate falls off a cliff at lunch time. The only action came when a slack trooper growing balder by the hour took me over to a counter to get printed. He was real tight with the hand cleaner afterwards and I couldn't get all the ink off my fingertips.

After that I sat. It figured Forzano was going to keep me on ice for a couple hours, maybe to improve my moral fiber, while he waited to hear more from Prudhoe.

I went over the reasons why I didn't want to call in my lawyer. Forzano was a plausible cop to deal with and the astounding fact of my innocence might lead him to release me if I didn't force his hand. Since I lost my ticket in the Arthur case none of the real lawyers in town would touch me, anyway. I ran through my appeals of the suspension with a freshman lawyer who had just hit town and didn't know any better. He majored in smash-the-state at law school in Berkeley and that didn't particularly help. I didn't especially want to smash the state. I would have been content to kick it a few times. Above all, there was nothing I wanted to tell my feeble counsel about Jeanne. In the end, the equation worked out that I should try Forzano on charm alone.

Eventually, quite eventually, the trooper who printed me got a buzz on his desk intercom and came over to me.

"This way. The man wants you."

I followed him along the corridor, around a corner to a door with Lieutenant Forzano on the nameplate. He knocked, then opened the door. Forzano waved him away without looking. I went in and the door was pulled shut behind me.

We were in a small office with a neat, emptyish desk and a filing cabinet on the right and two hard backed chairs in front of a window on the left. At least it wasn't gray. The walls were a reclusive ice blue that matched Forzano's pale blue gaze. He was a strongly built man, about six feet, perhaps forty-five, in a pricey blue suit, leaning back in a swivel chair. His smoothly featured face tapered too quickly from his thin blond hair to a chin so sharp he'd punch a hole in his tie if he nodded his head yes, only he didn't ever nod his head yes because he didn't ever agree with anything. Might have been genetic. His skin bunched beside his eyes in a measuring, skeptical way like he was a trifle bored with the lies you were no doubt telling him and he was about to pick out one of them to run through the shredder. I usually fed him one or two to keep him at bay.

He was fiddling with a black felt tip pen, popping the top off and snapping it back on. He stopped abruptly and pointed the pen at the chairs. I sat down. The room was warm, but right in front of the windows I felt a draft. That went well with his eyes too.

"Tell me, Rezkel, once he was dead, why did you waste all that time cutting him up before you snorted his cocaine? Did that help you enjoy the experience?"

"He was dead when I got there."

"Really. And what were you doing there?" he asked, punctuating the question by tapping his pen on the desk.

"What do you think? I wanted to score a gram."

"So, you found Dalira dead and did his stash for thrills?"

"The thrills were bonus. I wanted to know who killed him and why. The basics. Bad coke might have been a reason."

"Was it?"

"No, though the coke wasn't any too good."

"That's some sort of expert criminal opinion, I suppose. You should have let our lab make the determination."

"I'll remember that the next time someone turns me on to a line. I'll bring it down here and have you check it out for me."

Forzano leaned back in his chair. He toed open the bottom drawer of his desk, then stuck his left foot on it for support.

"Tampering with evidence, obstructing. That can get you a steady five to ten in this state."

"Come on. Save that for the outlaws. You got no case against me. I haven't even been arrested."

He shifted his chair a little and gave me a disdainful look.

"That changes whenever I say. I could chew you to pieces on this. Where were you from nine until we caught you with a felony in your nose?"

"Right there in Parsons Camp. I was in room 15, talking with Annie Melling. She's a friend of mine, and a neighbor. I asked her who was holding and she steered me to Spacey Acey. I left her room less than five minutes before Spacey walked in on me and three minutes of that was walking from her room to Spacey's."

"That's rich. You got about half an alibi and you think you're clean."

"I got the right half. And Annie can tell you I was going down there to see Spacey. I didn't know Dalira was going to be there and she didn't know it either. Ask her."

"I did."

"Well?"

"You look dirty and you feel dirty. Real dirty."

"But I don't look very guilty of murder, do I Lieutenant? I didn't have any coke on me when security searched me and there wasn't any in that room except what was on Dalira. What was that, four, five grams? He didn't have that much coke on a mirror at one time. Not even Teamsters chop up five grams at a time. When he went down he knocked the mirror over and broke it. That spilled some on the floor and some on him., but the killer dumped more on him to make it look like a drug burn, somebody who didn't know much about cocaine."

He was listening, letting go no sign of conviction, but still listening. I went on.

"There weren't any bottles or papers or baggies or anything you'd ordinarily keep your cocaine stash in. There has to be a big stash, a few ounces probably, that was carried off. What'd I do with it if I did Dalira? Tell me that."

"Maybe you threw it out the window and it got scattered in the snow."

"Then what did I do with what it came in? They didn't find anything like that outside or inside. I know because they ran that so-called investigation right in front of me. And, they didn't find any knife either, on me, in the room or outside."

"So? Maybe you're a sword swallower, Rezkel. Maybe you shoved it up your ass. You aren't innocent in this borough until I say so."

"You mean I don't have to double check with Elkin?"

"Huh," Forzano snorted. "Our DA always signs off on my stuff. You might be part right," he continued. "Those fools I sent to Prudhoe are telling me that the cocaine was definitely poured on him after he was down, but the only thing completely clear is that they don't know shit about anything."

On the wall behind him was a photo of a dog sled racing along a frozen river and two framed certificates from some sort of FBI cop school. I pointed at them and asked, "You mean everyone around here isn't an industrial grade cop? And you sent the lightweights out by themselves."

"That's all I got. The old help quit to work security on the pipeline. That trooper who flew you back, we found him asleep in a patrol car in Dufur, Oregon, and he's just marking time until he can get out with the Teamsters."

Forzano paused, then kicked the drawer shut and leaned over the desk.

"Give me reasons to kill Dalira. Start with your own."

"He smoked cigarettes on the bus along with all the rest, but I didn't want to knife just him. I was hoping for mass executions."

Forzano slowly reached into his shirt pocket and pulled out a pack of cigarettes. He lit one with extreme delibera- tion. I didn't catch the brand, but it looked like one of those organic, health food, low tar types that were supposed to hold off lung cancer an extra month or two. I started over.

"He was into a lot of things. Coke, booze, lottery tickets, anything that sells. Even pipe maps. Maybe a customer got greedy. Plus, he didn't get along with his boss. You take a look at Barriss yet?"

"Pipe map? Those dumb Alaska maps torched out of pipe? Who would cut lose a fifty for that tourist junk?"

I shrugged in cultural agreement.

"Never mind. Who else was in that room?"

"Nobody when I got there, except Dalira."

"The man next door heard someone hurry away two different times a little before they found you there," he said snapping the pen open and shut again, staring at me.

Jeanne flashed before me. I didn't have any clearer take on what she'd been doing there than before, but I knew I didn't want to talk to Forzano about that. I didn't have anything to give him except sarcasm, so I got right into that.

"You think I sliced Dalira with two guys, then let them run off with the stash while I tooted up off his body. Can the DA can deliver that theory in court without blushing? The *Tribune* is going to love it."

"Look, I don't care about court. I do things for my own satisfaction. I can hold you until I get someone better. And if I get a hot foot from on high, I can feed you to Elkin and let him put Draino in your milkshake. I wouldn't want to have to try and prove you didn't cut him. And if you really want your rights upheld, we could ship you up to Barrow. Prudhoe's in their Borough. The Eskimos do just fine at putting on a first class trial. They could do you better than Elkin."

Forzano gave me the look and snorted with disgust. I didn't like his manner. He wasn't bothering to smoke his cigarette and only had it running to annoy me. I decided to lie to him as soon as I could, so he could take it apart and step on it. I thought that might make him feel better and trust me a little for having done the predictable thing. An opening came up shortly to repeat one from the night before.

"What were you doing at Parsons last night, anyhow?"

"Magnum living. Cocaine. Maybe women. Getting out of camp and cruising."

"How'd you get there?"

"I hitched. I got a ride with a roustabout."

"What roustabout?"

"He said he worked on a rig for Carruthers, on N Pad, I think it was."

"Carruthers doesn't have a drill rig on N Pad. That's a certain fact. I like to be educated on your horseshit, Rezkel."

"Well, I didn't believe the guy either. I thought at the time that he'd borrowed the truck and was a little shy about it."

"Uh huh," he muttered, "and how'd you get back to that camp you were assigned to, CC2?"

"Right, CC2, Construction Camp Two. I hitched."

"Really? Who with?"

"A night mechanic. He was just out cruising and..."

"Bullshit. You boost a truck and call it hitchhiking. And later you stole another pickup from Barner security at this CC2."

"Alright, Lieutenant. It was an emergency. I had a plane to catch. Sort of borrowing. Besides, crew cabs are not pickups."

"It's borrowing until charges get pressed." He was quiet for a few moments, snapping the pen, then he started in again, "What were you doing at the Randolph-Lightner office?"

"OK. I confess. I had their pickup. The Randolph-Lightner timekeeper's pickup. I was returning the key."

"Why bother? You knew they were going to fire you."

"I thought I might come across something about Dalira. I took a pass through their files, but there didn't seem to be much there. You should look into it though. They're a

89

construction company hustling the pipeline. How can they be clean? You really ought to check out their insulation contract and the water on their payroll. And who they were bribing? They must have been bribing somebody. Dalira might have been caught up in a fast play."

"You got a lot of theories, Rezkel, for someone who doesn't know nothing that adds up to anything."

"I'm naturally mathematical."

Forzano stubbed out his cigarette and lit another with deep drags. The office air was hopeless.

"I don't think you killed him, so I'm gonna be dumb and let you go. Only I want you right here in town where I can put the arm on you if this thing keeps growing."

"But you don't mind if I look into things?"

"Stir up anything you want, but bring it to me if you do. One rule, don't go back to Prudhoe. Barner Oil wants to have this get very peaceful quite suddenly. I don't need you up there creating problems. I'll make sure of that right now."

He picked up his phone and pushed buttons. I tracked it—452-8201.

"Peter Jensen, please"

"Pete, this is Bill Forzano. Yeah, fine thanks. Hey, I want you to do me a favor. You know Nick Rezkel? Right. That one. Well, I'm releasing him. Maybe some public spirited Teamster will run him down and save the expense of a trial. What I want, Pete, is Rezkel here in town. He gets excited, forgets he's not a PI anymore. I don't want him charging up to Prudhoe and screwing around. Can you make certain, completely certain, he doesn't fly up there on your planes?

Great. You know what he looks like? Good. You'll do that personally? Thanks, I like things to be certain." He hung up.

"Now get out, Rezkel, and have something to feed me the next time I see you."

On the way I detoured past the fingerprint counter and helped myself to some more hand cleaner. No one caught me, so it must not have been a criminal act. The press had abandoned the lobby. I stopped at the pay phone and looked up Wien's airport number—452-8201. I always followed up on Forzano.

Chapter Seven

The cloudy sky looked about like Prudhoe, but, with no wind, the minus twelve was easy comfort. I walked down Cushman, unzipping my down coat after a couple blocks. I picked up on the tail at Tenth. He was on foot in the next block behind me. His partner with the car didn't show. I let it ride.

The buildings downtown were mostly two stories in drab colors with an occasional eight story office building/hotel combination. A lot of them were bars since Alaskans tossed down masses of booze while dealing with the extremity of it all. And since the pipeline had turned up, there were a whole lot of banks as well.

I turned left on Third. A drunk was lying in the snow outside Lindy's Grocery. They've got North America's toughest winos in Fairbanks. All-weather winos.

The Laborers Hall at that time was mainly a big empty room in a graceless commercial building. Plate glass windows across the front let in a soft light. A guy in jeans and a parka was standing along the left wall examining the out-of-work list, looking for his number, probably hoping it was better than he damn well knew. Three other men were hanging out in folding chairs in the far right corner, next to the Coke machine. The offices were barricaded against the back wall. The duly-elected officials worked back there out of sight behind many closed doors.

I went up to one of the windows and got out my termination slip. A woman behind the counter put aside an account book and took it.

"Nicholas Rezkel, Randolph-Lightner Construction, fired," she said looking up on that word, and continued, "ineligible for rehire."

She looked up again and then she placed me. She gave me a small smile and walked off to check out my hours and general Laborer credentials in the books. You had to have 800 hours with the local to get on the A List and that was the only list to be on. It took 100 hours to hit the B List. Some picked-over jobs filtered down there, giving them hope they'd get in enough hours to move up. Three or four thousand guys were paying five bucks a month to be buried alive on the C List and wait for a dispatch that was never coming. And there were others below them on the D List. Pity them for they didn't even exist.

A ragged hippie in brown Carhart coveralls got in line behind me. He had dirty blond hair and a bristly moustache that wished it lived on a porcupine. We nodded hello. He seemed familiar. I thought maybe I'd seen him at call. Then the counter lady came back. No hassle. I'd worked fewer than seven days, so I got my old number back instead of going to the bottom of the A List. That made me number A 169. I walked away from the window and the hippie moved up and turned in a pink slip. As I was walking to the bulletin board I heard the woman say, "Dave Marshall, Randolph-Lightner, RIF, eligible for rehire."

I cruised the posted A List, then went outside. He came out the door in a few minutes and turned left. I caught up to him and said, "You're not Dave Marshall." He kept walking. I placed my hand lightly on his elbow. He stopped. "That's bad karma, turning in somebody else's pink slip. Your dope might change into oregano."

"What do you want?" he challenged me, tensing himself.

I edged a bit closer to him, deliberately making him uncomfortable, but wary because I didn't trust him not to explode.

"I was on that Randolph-Lightner job and I know who you weren't. Don't worry about it, though. Tell me who gave you that pink slip and I won't tell the Hall."

He was quiet. He stood there looking down, wishing none of this was happening. I didn't give him any room.

"You don't want me to mess you over with the Hall. What list you on? The C List? How much did he pay you?"

He hesitated, not far from trying to get rid of me with his fists. I sank down into stance, cautious. He had to be in the depths of the C List and had never gotten closer to the pipeline bonanza all around him than turning in someone else's termination form. Then he no longer wanted to jeopardize even that.

"A guy gave me twenty bucks," he said picking out the question he least minded answering. "He told me he didn't want to show his face because somebody looking for him. There's no harm done, man."

"Who was he?"

"Christ, I don't know. Dave Marshall, I guess. He came up to me in the Cottage Bar."

"What did he look like?"

"Well, he was a big guy, not so tall, but very hefty. Short hair, expensive clothes."

"How old?"

"Forty or something. He had a scar like this," he said tracing a finger along the right side of his jaw.

"And after he paid you, he acted like he had lifetime rights to your body and soul?"

"Yeah. If I didn't need the money I'd have told him to shove it."

I cut him off sharply. "What'd he say about the Operators?"

"How'd you know that?"

"Just tell me."

"He gave me a twenty for doing that one too."

"You supposed to meet him afterwards?"

"No. He already paid me. He said he'd be watching to see that I did it."

I looked around the street, keeping this guy in view. No Barriss. My tail was meandering through the parking lot across the street.

"You said you wouldn't tell them at the Hall."

"And I won't. I'm even gonna buy you a drink next time I see you in a bar."

"That's where I might be, too, going back to the Cottage, look that guy up again. He didn't treat me right."

I left him and circled the block away from his direction. No need to make it easy for Forzano's boys. I was wondering why Barriss didn't stay at Prudhoe and keep the insulation thing rolling. I guessed that Phil had gotten the original dispatches for the Laborer and Operator payroll ghosts. There would be one less split now. The timekeeper had to know, but that marshmallow was never going to stand up to Barriss, especially not with extra bucks coming his way. Maybe Scanlon knew, but not necessarily. It had to take some nice footwork to hide two mirages on a hard dollar job. So, it appeared that the Inspector General was coming and Barriss was spit-shining the paperwork. What I couldn't figure was what this had to do with Phil catching a knife.

Second Avenue had a lot of action going, but then Fairbanks has always had a rowdy crowd on the street, especially downtown in bar central. The locals were mostly loaded and throwing money around almost as fast as the merchants were raising their prices. Plenty more were dead broke and getting itchy around all that green. Thousands of aspiring union hands had hit town looking for their chance to help peel the Big Banana. Half the cops had heard the call of the pipeline and the ones that were left had abandoned downtown, except for the sporadic appearance in force.

An unreal number of beautiful black hookers had come up from Seattle and LA. They were stopping traffic right on Second, two to a car sometimes. One would hit up the driver and the other would open her parka and flash a super tight jiggle dress at the passengers. Only a hundred bucks. The hookers renamed Second Avenue *Two Street*, and it fit. You expect a city to be cooking on Saturday night, say, but Fairbanks was one of the few places where a riot might kick off at 4 a.m. Wednesday morning.

The usual half dozen natives were lounging on the window ledge in front of the Co-Op, laughing at the strange people going by. A drunk oil persona in sun glasses and Stetson hat was offering a foxy sixteen-year old Eskimo girl a ride to Barrow in his private plane. He was wearing cowboy boot-shaped rubbers over his cowboy boots and he only looked at ease when he was fingering his wallet. Her aunt was doing the talking. She said she went along or no deal.

Inside the Co-Op I bought the *Seattle PI* and the *Anchorage Times*, both from the day before. That was $1.15. I liked news well enough, but the sports pages were a matter beyond life and death. I walked back to the lunch counter and booths. The place was a tacky drug store/semi-department store combo, short on quality, but an obligatory stop on any Fairbanks search pattern.

Daniel Callahan was holding down a booth by himself. He was a tall, rangy fellow Laborer, distinctly Irish, cosmopolitan, clearly ready for desperate acts. He projected himself well, especially to women. The man secreted a confidence that his pleasures were manifold and were just about to be met. He knew exactly what he liked in the way of bodily thrills and comforts and could focus in on them so well that most everyone was drawn into the expectation that he was verging on immediate fulfillment. I'd heard many people say that he was vainly wasting his life, as though throwing it away was proof that it might have been something. I knew better. He was a seeker who took chances. He was very good at people research and during his spermier episodes he could move in any social circle at all. We'd been friends for years. I liked bantering with him and I trusted the guy.

Callahan had long, dark hair and a meandering scraggly beard. He was wearing a bright red flannel shirt, a subdued gray vest and jeans. His bunny boots stuck out into the aisle as he leaned back against his parka stuck in the corner of the booth. He looked up well before I got to him and started clapping.

"Got another one. Give the man a hand," he boomed out in a deep rolling voice, still clapping.

A cozy couple in the next booth glanced around at the volume. I slid in across from him. A quick interior glimpse of Jeanne and me together in the tug came to me, then faded into a white obscurity as I thought of some research I wanted Callahan to do.

"Haven't they been treating you unkind at Purdue Bay, accusing you of mercy killing and drug theft," he chortled and stopped clapping to pound his fist on the table.

"I see I gotta fire my PR man. How'd you hear about it?"

"You're all they talked about down at call. This fiend of a Laborer. An ax murderer who uses a shovel. I liked the part where you threw a pound of coke in his face to blind him before you moved in with the chain saw."

"It was two pounds and I cut him with my fingernails."

"The worst part, speaking of your distorted image in the public eye, was that you were still snorting when they came

98

to bust you. I can get into it though. Freedom in the moment. Very sixties and touching."

Callahan dropped the sarcasm in an instant to ask seriously, "Well, who did it?"

"I don't know. They'd love to audition me as fall guy, but Forzano released me over a small matter of innocence."

"That makes probably three, four people in town who don't think you killed him."

"That's manageable, but there is a beautiful woman who is now ambivalent toward me over this, which is intolerable. I want you to check into her for me."

Callahan pawed the table and did a broad leer.

"Down with that lust in your heart, but learn anything you can. Her name is Jeanne Dalira, as in Phil Dalira, only a sister. It's going to be easy. Her roommate does travel clerkship at that place in the Northward Building. I don't know the name. Especially find out who Jeanne works for. She passed herself off as a Teamster for Livingston at CC1, but it doesn't wash."

"Is the roommate also beautiful?"

"If she is, that's your bonus."

A very down blonde waitress came over and asked what I wanted in a tired, whiney voice, disgusted with it all. I ordered an egg salad sandwich—silently praying for edible bread—a glass of orange juice and hot water.

"Hot water?"

"Yeah. Hot water, in a cup."

She stood there waiting for me to go on. I fished out a Mo's 24 tea bag and showed it to her.

"This is the good stuff."

"What's wrong with our tea?"

"You got Lipton's, right?"

"Yeah."

"Well, there you are. All I'll need is hot water."

"You trying to beat the price for tea?"

"I'll pay the price. Just don't put a teabag in the water."

"I wouldn't anyway," she sniffed and walked off.

"Nice touch you got with waitresses," Callahan snickered.

I maligned his prowess and we traded insults over lunch as I filled him in. We agreed to meet later at Tommy's, and then each of us went into a trance over the sports pages.

Somewhere in the account of an NBA squeaker that went into overtime I stopped tracking the basketball story line and my mind strayed to replaying the night Floyd Arthur got killed. He caught a couple .45 slugs and I caught the killer. It didn't stick. What was worse, I never did nail down who was really behind it. Those thoughts reopened an old sore. I got no further with it than ever before. I forced my attention back to the game story, making it catch up to my eyes, which were still scanning ahead. Inevitably, they reported that one team finally lost and I found myself very pissed, once again, that they took away my PI ticket.

An anger rose up in me, driving another part of my spirits down. Two images flicked past. The silent drive afterward with Jeanne. Allen licking the rug. Then just as fast, I felt embarrassed that I had so little control over what I was feeling, and over the self-pity that had worked its way into it. The embarrassment woke me. I shook off as much as I could and went back to reading the sports pages with a sullen rankle coiled beneath my attempted good spirits.

After his twenty-ninth cup of coffee, Callahan surfaced to ask me, "How could two Big Ten teams get to the Final Four the same year?"

"I've been laughing at Big Ten football so long," I told him, "I'm astonished they play basketball at all. In football they think the forward pass is a commie plot out of the West Coast. So how can their basketball teams even run the fast break?"

"I love it. They'll probably bring in Adolph Eichman and Charlie Manson to referee. But the pros suck, no matter what you say. The NBA is strictly a minor league for retired college players."

"Ah Daniel, there will be transcendence yet. Someday Walton will lead Portland through the Great Hoop."

"It's all rather suspicious, Nick, knifing Teamsters and rooting for ex-UCLA heavies."

We paid the check and went into departure behavior. My tail was browsing the magazine rack. His partner was studying a phone book by the front door.

"Is your truck functioning?"

"The Orange Delicious is freshly ransomed from the shop. Runs with grace."

"Perhaps. It's time I shook those two cops over there, so they can get back to work."

"Where?"

"Pick me up in ten minutes on Fourth, just past Nerlands."

Callahan left and I strolled over to the Third Avenue exit. Both tails moved my way. I stood by the cash register and did postcards. They found objects on the shelves to ponder. I went outside, stopped on the sidewalk and looked around the street, staying in a leisurely rhythm. I angled across the street and went in Nerlands' Third Avenue entrance, took a quick right and walked into the window display where they could see me from outside. I fondled an armchair, displaying abstract materialism itself. One of them left for the car. The other went on hold on the sidewalk. I moved back away from the window, keeping in view. I played customer until I saw Callahan's orange former Highway Department pickup truck roll past the Fourth Avenue entrance across from the store. I eased slowly around a couch and soon as I was out of sight of the street, hurried across the store and out the other door onto Fourth. I swung into the truck and ducked down on the seat.

"Right on Lacey," I said and Callahan tromped on it.

Chapter Eight

Callahan gave me a ride to my cabin a few miles out of town on Esther dome. The view was grand, with spruce, birch and aspen sweeping down the valley. Annie's Huskies started up a vast howling session as we rolled past her cabin. I could never, ever come home without their uproar.

After we got my occasionally reliable Toyota started by means of deep battery cable massage, Callahan left to get a line on Jeanne's roommate. I went inside and grabbed a change of clothes. I didn't bother firing up the stove. I only got out my binoculars and took off down the hill.

The heater was still broken. I had to get that fixed. The bad part was that no heater meant no defroster and I had to roll the windows down a couple inches to keep my breath from icing the windshield. I pulled the hood down over my head, leaned away from the inrushing air, and drove toward town. On the way I exploited the gym at the university for a free shower.

At the Wien air freight office they gave me my manila envelope with no hassle. The *Tribune* had taken more pictures of me than Sirhan Sirhan, but they weren't out on the streets yet so I was still partially invisible. I drove out to Old Airport Way where Randolph-Lightner had their headquarters in a cluster of trailers.

Inside the front door was a small anteroom with two chairs and a table with magazines like *Contractors' Digest* and the *Heavy Equipment Quarterly*. I walked up to the sliding glass windows and stopped at the counter.

An interesting woman presided over the desk, watching me very carefully as I walked toward her. The Friday before I'd been to the Randolph-Lightner office to check in and fill out forms, but she had not been there that day. I was struck by how alert she was, most especially how she seemed to have a very clear sense of me before I even said a word.

She was tall, slim and lanky, with long dark hair. She had on a blouse, jacket and skirt combination, in golds and browns, with a gold necklace. And she was pretty, though I didn't observe that as carefully as usual because I was intrigued by an odd sense that she had already figured out who I was.

She tapped a finger by her left eye twice, then pointed at mine and asked, "A gift from a certain Randolph-Lightner cretin?"

"Indeed."

"Then you are Nicholas Rezkel." She tilted her chin to the side, her left eyebrow levitating in sync with a rising voice as she said my name, emphasizing her deduction, "The one they're all so pissed at."

"The very same."

She glanced around the office. Two older ladies and an under-assistant junior executive sort were working quietly at desks. Nobody was paying us any attention. She turned to me with a wondering look, and I knew exactly what she was going to ask.

"Did you?"

"No," pleased and surprised that we had been able to communicate that so easily.

"What they were saying sounded off to me, so I started out not believing that you'd killed him. Anyway, congratulations on flattening that disgusting giant. How'd you do it?"

"I hit him with a Frisbee."

"Come on," she scoffed.

"Well, a sort of Frisbee. I might have kicked him, also."

"Who did kill Phil?"

"Don't know, but I'm working on it."

"You should do just that, because otherwise they'll find you irresistibly convenient. I'm surprised you're not in jail as it is."

"I was, for a while, but the Head Trooper wasn't too interested in pretending I did it. He'd rather have me out agitating the waters so he can see what floats by."

She smiled and cocked her head to the side again, then remarked with the friendliest sort of sneer, "So, now you're back here, trying to get requested out on another Randolph-Lightner job?"

"No. The only reason I came here was to meet you and already I almost know your name," I said, catching myself flirting with her without meaning to.

"Yes, almost," she said, smiling and making me wait.

I had a flash of Jeanne, how gorgeous she was, how attracted I was to her, much more than to this woman. I carried on anyway, not knowing why, maybe because she made the by-play so easy and light. "Well?"

"Sharon Groves."

We looked at one another without speaking for a delicious little interval. Then she broke that off and reached into a drawer, asking "Do you want your last paycheck?"

"Charmed."

She handed it over to me. "Scanlon wanted to hold it up, but he was afraid the Laborers would get tough. Scanlon doesn't like tough people."

I checked over the statement. Three governments and the union took their end off the top. I got $637, which wasn't bad for four days on the job, but it wasn't completely straight either.

"They shorted me four hours travel time."

"I know. Scanlon said it was because you traveled back under arrest," she said, laughing in disdain at the reasoning. "Also, the company is sending your stuff back from Prudhoe. I'm supposed to bill you for it," she told me seriously, pausing as I gathered a response, then beating me to the punch by asking, "Perhaps you have a special address for bills like that?"

Her timing broke me up. Then I saw her studying my reactions in exact detail, pondering me. I liked that sensation. I also liked her sarcasm. I had lots of questions I wanted to ask her. I postponed the interesting ones, though, and stuck to business.

"Can I get in to see Scanlon? Is he back from Prudhoe?"

"They're all coming back. Scanlon, Barriss, two guys who quit, you, the timekeeper."

"The timekeeper?"

"Uh huh. He flew out to Cleveland on emergency R&R today. A death in the family, or so he said."

"Must have been some shirt-tail relative of a Teamster. Those other two, they're Dave Marshall and Morris Thompson, aren't they?"

She turned over a couple pieces of paper, nodding and said, "They couldn't be friends of yours. You don't seem to have any."

"Those two are only names to me, but I do have a few friends left, though I could always use another one."

"Oh," she said, an eyebrow rising, questioning and inviting.

"Only she'd have to be beguiling, exciting and at Tommy's tonight at seven. Could that be you?"

"Maybe, it depends on how beguiling and exciting I am at seven."

"I bet it's somewhere between very and extremely," I told her, though I didn't really believe she was going to show up, or know what I'd do if she did.

She looked at the lights on the telephone console. "The boss is off the phone now."

"Let me at him. Say, isn't he a lot skinnier lately?"

"Yes, anymore he looks like he just got back from the Auschwitz tour. It's that door," she said, pointing to a door across the office. "Don't hit him, he's much more fragile than that disgusting Huey."

I stuck my hands in my pockets like I had to keep the closest watch over them. Sharon laughed and waved me through the door.

Scanlon was sitting at his desk, rumpling his gray suit with its subdued pink pinstripes as he reached something out of a bottom drawer. When he saw me he reversed field and put it back. I heard a gurgle as he shut the drawer.

The office was crammed with unnecessary chairs, filing cabinets and too many pictures of seascapes and mountains. The desk was going down for the third time in a sea of papers. He was looking very antsy when I stepped in, shut the door and sat down in the best chair.

"What are you doing here? I thought you were under arrest."

"Scanlon, you're as lousy at calling in the troopers as you are at poker. Besides, I didn't kill him."

"We'll have you arrested for breaking and entering and assault."

"Save that shit for the cops. It'll be a good distraction when they ask you where you were last night at nine o'clock."

"I flew up there quite early this morning, at three a.m.. I told you that before."

"You speak right up, don't you. Were you expecting to get asked again?"

"Don't talk to me like that."

"Yeah? What are you going to do about it? You already called the cops, remember. And Huey made his move with the crane. And you fired me. What are you going to do next? Pout?"

Scanlon fidgeted around in his chair. He reached for the phone and then pulled his hand back. His booze-red face was turned slightly away from me. Then he got his mind made up. He opened a drawer and came up with a .38 pointing vaguely toward me. He didn't look me in the eye, even with a gun in his hand.

"It's too soon to shoot me, Scanlon, I've just begun to scare you."

He looked quizzical. The nose of the pistol floated around. He had it aimed at me every now and then.

"Since you aren't going to fire that thing yet, why don't you put it away and pour a drink instead. For you, it's a tougher front."

He decided to change gears and lowered the gun.

"I was only kidding. Let's have one."

He put the pistol back in the top drawer and got the bottle out of the bottom drawer. He poured two stiff slugs of Chivas Regal and slid one of them over to me. I don't much care for Scotch, but I like toasts, so I tried one out on

Scanlon. I waited until he had the glass tipped and had just started to swallow.

"Here's to the water on your payroll."

Scanlon's throat tightened, but he held on and tossed down half his glass. He glared at me, taking back his friendly overture of a moment before.

"Did Barriss cut you in on his straw men, Marshall and Thompson?"

"What do you mean?"

"What do you think I was doing in your office, Scanlon, stealing pencils? Dave Marshall and Morris Thompson are phonies. They don't exist. I got copies of your timesheets right here. Look at this fiction."

I slid the papers out of the manila envelope and waved them at him, so he could see they were as advertised.

"That's just Barriss. I don't know a thing about it."

"Really? I'm curious, naturally, but it won't matter either way to your Baltimore head office. When they hear about the soft water on their hard dollar job, it's bound to explain a few things. See, if you did know, you were left-handing them. If you didn't know, you should have. Either way, you're playing another damn dead hand."

Scanlon finished his drink. His reddish face purpled around the edges.

"Dalira did the impersonations down at the Laborers and the Operators. He was a triple threat, getting three dispatches out of three halls for the same job. Did you get tired of covering for Barriss and stick Phil a few times to simplify things?"

"I wasn't there, remember?"

"You could have hired it done. The newspapers are going to love it. You'd rate about forty-eight point type for the headlines, I'd say."

"Now, wait a minute. We don't need any newspapers. We don't have any big problems here. What do you want?"

"That's better. You sound like a guy who can help out a poor Laborer."

"Sure. You want a request. We need a Laborer foreman at Chandalar."

"Save it, Scanlon. It wouldn't work out. Just you don't throw any cops at me and I won't throw any reporters at you. You got it?"

"Sure."

"And you tell someone out front to make me out a check for the travel time you shorted me. Four hours pay."

"Alright."

He picked up the telephone and gave the order.

"And don't take out any goddamn deductions."

"Uh, Sharon, the full amount. No withholding on that."

He hung up the phone, eased out a tinny little smile and patted the air in a conciliatory way.

"The difficulty here is Barriss. He held your pay and actually called the police. He gets a little out of control at times. None of this has to go any further than my office."

"And where was Barriss at nine o'clock last night?"

"I don't know. He was in his room, I think, working on our bid for the insulation maintenance contract."

"Who around this company wanted Dalira dead?"

111

"I don't know. Not me. I liked Phil."

"What did he ever do for you?"

"Nothing. I just liked him. He told a lot of jokes. He drank good liquor. We got along."

"That why you flew up there at three a.m., because you liked him?"

"He was an important employee. All this was a shock."

"Tell me something. How much of that excessive water content insulation got put on the pipe?"

"What? None of it. Arctic Wrap shipped twenty-one crates of that stuff to Prudhoe for no good reason. A blunder. It all had to be scrapped. We back-charged them for the time and equipment to bury it at the dump. None of it was installed."

I believed that's what he thought. His nostrils were flaring open a little, and that was always the tell that let me read him at the poker table. Scanlon pissed away chips steadily on bad hands and we all loved him for it, but when he got a hand he liked, one that he was sure of, out puffed his nostrils and he got reckless. He didn't merely lose a chunk then, he lost everything, because he couldn't tell the difference between good tickets and the absolute nuts. I pinned him down on the topic anyway.

"Not true. I was putting it on myself for three straight days on that job."

"Impossible, Barriss told me he dumped it. He turned in the time for it two weeks ago."

"Remember this, Scanlon?" I said, showing him the Arctic Wrap letter. "We worked crate 63 yesterday. It's on this list."

"I know the letter," Scanlon said, waving it away. He looked at my glass, still about full, then tipped the Chivas bottle and poured himself another. "If that Barriss..." he muttered.

"What were you going to say?"

"Nothing. Only that if Barriss put that stuff on the pipeline, Randolph-Lightner could be in a lot of trouble."

"And so could you. Baltimore isn't going to like this one any more than the other. Anything else you don't know anything about?"

"Hey, we agreed. You weren't going to tell anyone."

"As long as I got this Peruvian Death Grip on your throat, Scanlon, just answer the questions. You ever snort cocaine?"

"Me? I've got a position to think of. I wouldn't touch cocaine. It's very dangerous, and certainly immoral."

His nostrils were widening again.

"OK. Let's leave it at that. No cops, no reporters."

He nodded, keeping his eyes fixed on the Chivas. He was lifting his glass as I went out the door.

Sharon looked up at me and smiled when I got back to her desk. She handed me a machine-signed Randolph-Lightner check for $72.

"Did you get blood on your hands?" she asked, one eyebrow arching by itself in emphasis. I liked her questions. They were amusing. And I liked the amazing control she had over her eyebrows.

I held my hands up. She was skeptical, so I turned them over for her to inspect the other sides. "See, completely clean."

"Then how'd you get him to pay you?"

"I told him it was only fair."

"That impressed him?"

"Maybe something in my choice of phrase." Another little pause. This time I ended it, asking "Uh, do you know where Barriss is?"

"He's likely out at the S&B development on Old Nenana."

"S&B?"

"S&B Enterprises. Him," she chuckled, crooking a finger toward the boss' office, "and Barriss."

"They must make great partners."

"It's good for laughs around this place."

"Hard as it is to go away, I must evaporate."

"Pamper your eye," she said, and as I turned to go, added, "See you at Tommy's."

Chapter Nine

I stopped at the College Inn and got Toby Vinson on the phone. He was a washed-up California adman who drifted north in the sixties and floated in and out of a series of obscure government jobs in Fairbanks and Juneau. Toby had a bad reputation, but he never cheated me while I was watching him. He was adept at making deals, but not consistent at keeping them because he couldn't help working both sides of the handshake. He wasn't in solid with the big timers, but he did have enough momentum that he was surfacing as a Democrat to run for the State House. Toby was especially expert at extracting information from the government. Tracking politicians was his hobby. I asked him to get a line on S&B Enterprises, at the usual rates, and then I went out to take a look at the site.

Took Old Nenana Road, cut through the Goldstream Valley a few miles north of Fairbanks. Fine stands of trees lined it, although there were many patches of swart, scraggly little spruce trees attempting growth on permafrost. Occasional driveways led off to houses or cabins. After a few miles I came to where S&B Enterprises had cut a dirt road through the trees, with the snow plowed out of it. I went on around the next bend and pulled over.

Snow covered the undergrowth and had drifted through a grove of thin, straight birch trees. The woods looked very open close at hand, but by the middle distance the birches melded into a gray haze. I walked in tire tracks along the curving road and heard the roar of a Cat a quarter mile ahead. The road straightened and ran down a gentle slope. A half dozen pickups were parked ahead in a clearing.

I cut off the road and slogged through the snow. I stayed away from tree trunks, but the snow was waist deep anyway. When I came over the ridge, I brushed out the snow that had gotten up my pants and down my socks.

Downhill another road curled around the side of the valley. Along it were eight almost finished houses with a few trees separating them. Visquine hung in the windows. There would definitely be electricity here, unlike up by my place, but no power poles had been put in yet. A hundred yards further along, another road cut across.

A D9 Cat with a ripper was snorting and grinding out there, grading another site. I remembered thinking the summer before when I had seen this development from up on Esther Dome that the work had been proceeding rather slowly. That was changed. It looked more like the pipeline with that machinery tearing at the frozen ground, fighting winter to get the work done.

The operator was getting maybe an inch at a pass. It made a terrible sound. I was content to allow the Operators to have the extra bucks for running those things. Work life as a Laborer may have been often menial, but it was far advanced beyond bouncing around all day on something horrendously loud that was gradually pulverizing your kidneys.

I got my binoculars out of the case. At least I had some good equipment, Bushnells, the kind that are focused by fingering a little butterfly tab instead of twisting a dial and losing track of what you wanted to see in the first place.

I put the glasses on the houses along the first road and saw that the work was concentrated on the last house on the right. No one was visible, but a compressor and a generator were chugging away outside the house, with lines from them running in through a side window. A few stacks of material were sitting beside the door.

Like the others, this house faced squarely on the road, which had turned north at that point. Most of the windows faced the east and would get little heat from the winter sun. I panned the Bushnells around the valley and up the hill. Stray log cabins were nestled into the woods. They all faced south, naturally, for whatever warmth the sun would yield. Scanlon and Barriss weren't concerned with matters like proper orientation. They were putting up a little bit of suburbia out in the forest.

Two men with carpenter belts came out of the front door. They walked quickly over to a stack of paneling, peeled off two sheets and carried them back to the house. Another man came out of the house. He was wearing down coveralls. He stepped off the porch and looked back. A burly man came out of the door after him, wearing a heavy brown wool coat and red stocking cap. I focused in tighter. Barriss and no surprise his face was clenched with rage.

Barriss came stamping off the porch and kicked at a mound of snow. He pointed across to where the Cat was working and then stalked off to a green Randolph-Lightner pickup, the other man following him. They got in the pickup. Barriss kept talking and pointing around the site. I was sure no rock 'n' roll was playing on the truck radio.

The other man figured to be the job foreman. He nodded a lot and spoke little. Barriss stabbed his finger at the Cat again. I could see his face in three-quarter profile, angry that more work hadn't been completed. He pointed to the Cat two more times.

Then Barriss suddenly stuck a mediocre little grin on his face. The foreman shifted around in his seat to face him. Barriss patted him on the back and said something softly. That insincerity meant the interview was about over. The foreman got out and Barriss drove over to the D9 and waved the Operator over to him.

I made my way back through the snow to the development access road, going quickly and ready to step off into the snow if Barriss came along. On the way, I paused long enough to note down the license numbers of the workers' pickups. I had half an idea teasing the back of my brain, heating up in my inherent suspicion of Barriss. Then I hurried back to my car.

I was slouched down behind the wheel of my Toyota when Barriss came steaming onto Old Nenana and turned toward town. I followed him from several hundred yards back, since there weren't many ways he could go. He drove fast, and well enough, but he was pressing. I caught up as we neared a point where he might go in more than one direction.

Barriss swung left on the University of Alaska road system, went around the campus, did another left and burned off a fast five miles along Farmers Loop Road. I stayed back and then closed up again when he turned onto McGrath Road. Then I had to keep up because there were several dirt roads off McGrath and all of them were plowed.

Barriss didn't notice me. He got out of shape on one turn and almost put it in a snow bank. He turned left onto a road near the top of McGrath and rolled into the driveway of large expensive house, stained cedar, all sharp angles and assorted planes meeting abruptly. It had two stories and enough glass to lock in a thousand dollar heating bill every winter month. There was an enclosed porch out front. Barriss went straight in without knocking.

Beside the house was a small cabin with a large dog yard filled with fancy dog houses. Huskies were chained to each house. As ever, they were stirred up by a new arrival.

Barriss was back out of the house before I got turned around. I let him get ahead and took the opportunity to check the mailboxes at the corner. He'd been to see Roland J. Kirby, a certified heavyweight politico. Barriss blasted back down McGrath and kept his foot on it. I gave him a big lead, especially when we hit the freeway. He drove right to the Randolph-Lightner office, parked the company truck and trooped inside.

I went in the office after him, not exactly sure what could be accomplished, telling myself I was doing it out of basic snoopflex. I was barely through the door when I saw that Barriss had stopped by the front desk to talk to Sharon. I held back to be sure he didn't see me.

Her face was turned to the side as she spoke with him. She was concentrating on Barriss and didn't turn around to see who had come in. Suddenly, it struck me that she was much better looking than I had noticed before. Then I turned around and went back out before she could see me. I let it lie at that and drove to a pay phone at the University Center Mall, thinking about her, hoping she was going to show at Tommy's.

I tried Toby again at the office equipment joint he was using as his primary pretext. It was a superior gig for him. He was downtown all day, making a certain amount on the job and plenty more on the side. He had lots of time off to run for office. He didn't have enough money for his campaign, but he scared the pros with his energy, though he also intrigued them with a charming lack of scruples. Office equipment meant access everywhere and Toby made certain to keep current with the typewriter life of any and all secretaries. When I had something for him, he charged me pipeline wages, plus expenses, but he dropped everything else while he was on the payroll. His office told me he was off to the Mecca Bar and I got him on the phone there.

I asked him to come up with names to match the license plates I'd collected at the S&B development. He gave me a surprise. He said that he'd already run down the stuff I'd asked him for earlier. I told him to wait for me.

I cashed my paycheck at a bank branch. On the way out to my car I saw that the *Tribune* had hit the streets and I was news, complete with a lurid headline. The photo was lousy, but certain to make me highly visible, especially since there were snide remarks in the lead paragraph about Forzano releasing me.

The Mecca Bar was a changeable place, right on Two Street, so anything might wander in. That didn't make it an exclusively rowdy bar, like the Chena or Savoy, but the quieter crowd stayed away at times. The Irish did a lot of their drinking there and they seemed to need fist fighting to properly absorb their whiskey. But, late afternoon, the place was still peaceful, waiting on the night.

Two men were coming out as I entered. We met in the space between the double doors. The one in front was soft, fleshy and smooth. He was putting on an expensive parka over an expensive blue herringbone suit. He had a permanent smile which oozed confidence and bucks. Roland J. Kirby, local fixer. I knew him from some poker games.

The other was Michael Elkin, our ascendant local DA. He even had a plausible knowledge of his job. The guy was startlingly cautious in court, but he made up for that with all-state arrogance on the street. Kirby nodded. Elkin glared. Kirby stepped aside politely. Elkin permitted his shoulder to bump mine as I passed.

Then I saw the face of another guy walking behind them through the inner door. He was short, with sharp features, bad skin and a lump pushing through the left side of his flashy green blazer. I knew him also and I didn't like the feeling. A burst of ancient history flashed before me, in particular an image of him smiling a nasty triumphant smile a certain day long before.

We got to the door at the same time. I wasn't polite. I kept walking right at him with strong crescent steps. He tried to stand aside. I turned into him. He moved back and I walked him into the wall. He stood there glaring at me with hard, hard eyes. I turned slightly to keep Kirby and Elkin in view while staring at the small man. His dark eyes suddenly lost focus and went flat. They hardly seemed to shine and then they turned in until he was looking at me cross-eyed. His right hand fluttered and wanted to reach inside his coat.

"Go ahead, Devery. Try it. It might go off while I'm taking it away from you. What is it? Another .45?"

"He was only getting out of your way," Kirby said easily.

"Keep on getting out of my way, Devery."

His eyes uncrossed, flicked toward Kirby and then looked down. They had a bit of light in them again.

"We'll see," he said a deep, froggy voice.

I stepped back and let him go. He followed Kirby out the door, hitching his shoulders. I decided that instant to get my gun out of hock. And I started recalibrating some old equations, seeing if they added up any better with Kirby or Elkin on the same side of the equals sign with Devery.

Lou Devery had gunned Floyd Arthur. He was the one I

122

served up to the cops on a platter afterwards. But the cops weren't hungry. They rolled over on it and a fancy Seattle lawyer got Devery off. He'd blown it with others around town and I'd thought at the time that he'd never show his face in Fairbanks again. That wasn't any particular consolation since I was the one who got burned in the deal. Next time I wasn't figuring on handing him over to any cops.

I saw Toby sitting at the far end of the bar. As I walked back one of the customers nudged another and they both took a close look at me in the bar mirror. Growing up I always knew I'd be famous, but I thought I'd enjoy it.

Toby was also smallish, a handsome sort of hustler with a thin moustache and movie profile. He smiled steadily, but he always seemed to be wondering why it didn't work better than it did. He was wearing a tan sport coat over a lime shirt and dark slacks, which didn't quite fit his legislative campaign.

I sat down on the stool beyond him and swiveled around. I've always watched doors, especially doors Lou Devery has just walked through.

"You pick on all us short guys, Rezkel?" he asked me.

"Only the helpless ones, Toby. What you got for me?"

"First, I've been on this since two-thirty. That's three hours, so that's $90. I made $5.65 in phone calls and bought three rounds of drinks for two at the Northward and that's $13, so the bill's $108.65, but I'll cut it down to a twenty if you'll give me a little help on the campaign."

"I'll give you the whole $108.65, Toby. It'd ruin my aesthetic perspective on guys like you to hand out leaflets."

123

"Nick, take it easy on yourself. You're gonna want to know a state representative who's five or ten percent indebted to you. Let's call this a freebie. And you know there's no leaflet crap. Just a little looking around."

"Forget it. Your installment plan is too steep."

The bartender appeared, looking sour and even more disappointed in humanity than the last time I'd seen him.

"Nick, I don't like you bothering the customers."

"Joey, you know Devery's a special case."

"Was that Teamster on the Slope also a special case?" he asked, looking too tired to do anything except ring up the cash register.

"I surrender. How about a brandy, Joey. Your best."

Joey moved off real slow. I looked back at Toby and got no sympathy at all.

"What do you expect? With your ass hanging out the way it is, of course people are going to shoot BBs at it. You'd do better helping me get elected."

"What I should be doing is docking you for trying to recruit me for your lousy campaign while you're on my payroll."

"Alright, OK. I'm only trying to do you a favor."

Joey came back even slower than he left, set down a snifter and went off with the money. Toby turned toward me and lowered his voice.

"S&B Enterprises used to be a limited partnership, only now it's an empty shell that has been sold to another limited partnership called Arctic Diversified. Their assets are wholly given over to a firm registered in Seattle called Associated

Investors. That's so much smokescreen for these two developers, Scanlon and Barriss, and their partner."

"Who's that?"

"Couldn't find out. I can work on that through a guy in Seattle, but it'll get expensive fast."

"Later. Does that imply that if S&B Enterprises gets caught cheating, Associated Interior doesn't have to pick up the tab?"

"It could work out that way."

"What else?"

"I checked the former owner of that parcel they're converting into money, only there wasn't exactly any former owner. You see, it was a mining claim until it got patented. At that same instant, it passed from state ownership into private hands and was sold to S&B Enterprises, with the purported mining operation driving the deal separated from the land where they're building. Six months later, which is a discrete interval in these matters, S&B mated with Arctic Diversified and gave forth Associated. They seem to still go by the name of S&B Enterprises, except when it comes time to sign papers and then it's always Associated.

"There's a trapdoor clause in their charter. If a partner dies, his interest passes to his heirs, but as nonvoting shares. Whoever thought that one up must not trust his partner's wife. Anyway, the surviving partners assume control."

"And I got something else for you. Mining claims are one of my hobbies, so I did some extra-curricular work, Nick, and talked to the miner who worked that claim before. That's what those drinks at the Northward were about."

125

"I didn't think you were corrupting civil servants with alcohol."

"Right. Money works much better during office hours and sex at night. You're lucky, this one didn't cost you any bribes at all."

"I'm sure you're going to tell me exactly how lucky, aren't you Toby?"

He put in a pause to finish off his drink and order another. I sipped mine and concluded that Joey had gone with his worst brandy instead of his best. Toby nodded Joey over to me to collect for another Scotch on the rocks. I got out a couple singles and handed them over. That was a fair sign. Toby wouldn't order a drink after he'd delivered the load, so more had to be coming. He didn't cheat, when he was being watched.

"This miner wouldn't say much beyond ordering doubles. He hinted that he might have something to say next Wednesday. There's a big payment due and if his bank doesn't receive it, he's going to get his claim back, only this time he'll own it and those houses sitting on it. He did let go the nugget that getting the land patented was a condition of the sale. For an uncommunicative sort he leaks a lot of information."

"Does he know who the hidden partner is?"

"No way."

"How'd he get his claim patented? That's tough these days, isn't it?"

"Impossible, ordinarily."

"Well?"

126

Toby shrugged. He sipped his Scotch, put a finger on an ice cube and pushed it under, saying, "With these partnerships too much is out of sight to know for sure. You can never tell who the commissioner of mining might decide is a worthy applicant."

"Who was the commissioner at that time?"

"Two years ago? That should have been Tom Rizoner."

"Wasn't it?"

"Oh, it was, but Tom had a bad heart and he spent months Outside getting treatment. The man who ran the show was the deputy commissioner, Kirby."

"Kirby, as in the esteemed Roland J., who just walked out that door?"

"The very one."

"Were you talking to him?"

"Kirby doesn't talk to me."

"The man has some good points. What was he like as deputy commissioner?"

"The usual. He was for anything the people would fall for."

"OK, Toby, are you ready to tell me the big secret now? How'd you come up with this so fast?"

"It's my trade. I know people. I don't understand how you can get along without knowing the people I know."

"Right. Now tell me."

"Well, I was even pretty surprised myself when this guy I called told me he already had all this stuff on his desk. He wouldn't tell me who he rounded it up for. He gave me this vague crap about some sort of media researcher from

Fairbanks. I thought he got a bit poetic on the topic. Like over a female, maybe. That mean anything to you?"

"Hope so."

I paid Toby off. On the way out I confirmed with Joey that Toby hadn't spoken with Kirby or Elkin. Toby saluted me with his drink, to honor having his character temporarily reaffirmed.

Chapter Ten

The pawn shop was closed, so I had to defer getting my Ruger until the next morning. The tails hadn't picked me up again or they were doing a much better job. I didn't bother with any shake plays. I walked over the Cushman Street Bridge to a buff colored building from which the *Fairbanks Tribune* emanated. A thick facade ran around it like heavy eyebrows, giving it a frowning Neanderthal look. I went in the side door, down a short corridor and took the stairs up to the newsroom on the second floor.

I pulled my stocking cap mostly down and walked between the desks. There were three men typing, phoning and reading, including a photographer who had shot my picture about forty times that morning, but they were too preoccupied to notice me. I slipped past their attention and walked into Dave Babcock's office. He was reading and didn't look up. I sat in the best chair.

Dave was a big shambling man with sloping, bearish shoulders and large hairy arms. His face was swarthy and fifteen minutes after shaving his whiskers were out in force. He had round features and shiny dark eyes. His ears stuck out and were pointed in the middle. He told me once that he was Armenian, but all I believed of that was that his family used to sell rugs. Now he was peddling a rag. There wasn't a major difference. Finally he finished what he was eyeballing, or maybe he figured I'd waited a proper interval. Anyway he looked up and got excited right away, booming out greetings.

"Rezkel, my favorite headline. How kind of you to drop by. Didn't you like the photo we ran? We really should have done something better with that black eye. Want to give us a better one?"

"How about me standing on a scaffold? You do keep your own rope around here, don't you?"

"You might volunteer a statement. Or maybe we could reenact the moment they caught you with Dalira's toot in your nose?"

"Using *Tribune* cocaine, of course."

"No, it'd have to be yours. Us here in the newspaper biz, we don't actually make the news. We only goose it."

"Dave, slow down a minute. I need a favor."

"These days it better be a small, quiet favor."

"Is Jeanne Dalira working for you?"

"That's not small or quiet."

"I'll take care of the quiet part. Tell me what's so tough about the question."

"Christ. She's not on the payroll. She is working for us, but it's not precisely official."

130

"What's that mean, freelance?"

"Well, it's more like security. I don't know why I'm telling you."

"Yes, you do. I've brought you a lot."

"Let's say I fed her a storyline, but, uh, do you know her? She gets erratic. She hasn't been checking in with me."

"How long's she been on it?"

"I could tell you that, I guess. A month. She came up from Anchorage with plausible recommendations. I thought I'd let her do what she could before she got real well known around here."

"What's the story?"

"It's tricky. Could make the wrong people look bad."

"Like what wrong people?"

"No way you get any of that."

"Listen, I can't dodge this Dalira thing. I've got to beat it. I have to find out who killed him, because I don't think anyone else is going to."

"You saying Jeanne is involved?"

"That's exactly what I'm not saying. I didn't kill anyone and I need a shot at proving it. All I really need is for you to confirm it for me if I can name the general topic. Will you do that?"

Long pause. He looked at me. "I don't know. Try me."

"I will. Mining claims. Patenting mining claims. Real estate angle behind it."

More pause. "Close enough. That's all you get. We pointed her at something and she went after it."

"How far along is she?"

"You get no more. But she's not checking in. I don't like it. I really don't like it when you come in here and tell me it connects to murder. That's why I confirmed it for you, because I don't like not knowing what's going on. And I'm not sure I like her talking to any more public officials."

"Thanks."

"Next time bring in some hard news. A sodomy or something."

Outside, it was nearly dark and the air was murky. Steam coming out of the power plant downriver was not dispersing. It made a ninety-degree turn at the top of the stack and lay in a wide band over the town. A temperature inversion was containing exhaust fumes under that layer. Frozen smog. Summers, Fairbanks air was good, but winters you'd breathe better in LA.

Over the bridge I went left and walked down First Avenue. When I got under the street light at Lacey I heard a flat whack-whack sound. A moment later a Frisbee skipped off the icy street climbing toward me over the hood of a Volvo parked at the curb. I tracked it, moved back some, twisted and jumped enough to catch it behind my back. A Wham-O All American. I knew it had to be Callahan, but I couldn't pick him out at first in the dark. He didn't wave his hand for a return toss and three people down the block were on the other end of possible trajectories for the skip shot. And then I knew which by that curious walk of his that concealed its grace behind a loose, toes-out shuffle.

I threw a slicing curve toward the Polaris Building. A light breath of air retarded it at the high point and then dipped the front edge steeper and steeper as it came down to Callahan. He sidestepped across the sidewalk and snagged it behind his back, that most artful catch.

We moved into the street and tossed a few. Callahan was bending high curves around a telephone pole. I worked on my side whips, high curves first and then, as my arm got warm, the hard flat ones. Jeanne kept floating into my mind and my game got a bit wild, butchering the odd throw. She hadn't been to the cops, which was clear from Forzano's questions. Did that mean she was protecting me, or maybe herself, or was it the other way around? I couldn't accept that she'd killed Phil, but I didn't have the right goods on Barriss or anyone else. Acey's neighbor said there had been someone hurrying down the hall two different times, just before I got there. Jeanne was on to the S&B left-handed claim patenting. I wondered if because of that she could be covering for Scanlon, or maybe for Barriss. Or, for someone else entirely. Finally, I blew a catch outright, so I shook all that out of my head and just threw and caught, threw and caught, threw and caught.

We worked our way up First and into the parking lot behind Tommy's Elbow Room. Callahan was ahead, walking backwards as we tossed the friz. We shortened up the throws and played right up to the rear door.

I made a wild throw at the door. Callahan picked it up and we made another set of throws. A Frisbee game has to end on two catches. You wouldn't let your basketball team walk off the floor at the end of practice until they rip one

133

through the cords. If you miss that last shot in practice, you might miss the last shot in the game.

Tommy's bartender was getting a huge stick of birch off the back porch as we came through the double doors. He maneuvered it past the jukebox and shoved it into the fire, flames blazing up. There was a crowd by the bar up front, but most of the tables in the back were empty. We picked out a choice spot by the fire and sat down. I couldn't see everyone at the bar, but nobody in view was interesting. Callahan launched right into a report and I turned to listen.

"The roommate was a washout for both of us. No charms at all on the physical plane and no hard info," Callahan said slowly. 'She's only lived with Jeanne a week and knows nothing much about her. We had a beer after she got off work. The woman does not know how to start a topic. Can only answer. Was a struggle to do an hour with her. The only maybe interesting thing that turned up was that once she perceived I was not in fact intriguing toward her flesh and I then mentioned Jeanne, she assumed that I was trying to score a gram. Jeanne equals toot in her mind. What this mysterious Jeanne would want with her as a roommate I don't know, unless it's someone to watch over the stash. But," he hesitated for effect, "there was the roommate's friend, the fair Nancy, who appeared at the last minute."

"Nancy? How can I believe you've met yet another Nancy? This becomes excessive, Daniel."

Callahan shrugged.

"There's a lot of women named Nancy. Anyway, she was a win for both of us."

"That means she's beautiful, but what else?"

"She knows Jeanne from other times, in Anchorage, only we didn't get any genuine tete-a-tete due to the extreme presence of the roommate. I am seeing her tomorrow, however, and," he said, stopping to shake his head at the immensity of what he was about to say, "I shall ruthlessly subordinate all my base animal drives to the higher purpose of spying on Jeanne. May she be worth it."

Callahan was in a grand mood. He regaled me with amusing talk about his terrible sacrifices on my behalf. He was clearly in form and was going to have a superb time that night doing something. I listened along, saying little because too many partly connected images were floating through my mind. Jeanne and Phil Dalira kept coming back to me, and Barriss, and Lou Devery. I tried out different explanations to relate the recent to the ancient. Then I was remembering a small episode when I caught up with a guy I was hired to find because his nose couldn't handle all the toot he put in it. He had burned a hole right through his septum. It did something funny and nasal to his voice that people remembered and I was there waiting when he went in for the operation. I'm not sure I could call that thinking, but sometime the best way to connect the disparate is to stop concentrating and allow everything to mingle together.

Callahan saw that I was distracted and excused himself to go and check out the crowd. Pretty soon I brought myself back to the present and meandered up to the bar in the front. As usual, Tommy's was two shades more peaceful than any other joint downtown. Two clean-cut troops from Fort

Wainwright were playing Foozball in an alcove off to the side. Most of the seats around the bar were taken up by a mixed crowd having a few and talking quietly.

There wasn't much going on, except in one certain place. Way around toward the front I saw Sharon, wearing a creamy yellow dress with black zigzag stripes. I looked at the long chestnut hair flowing down over her shoulders and realized that I was very pleased she had shown up.

Men on either side were trying to capture her attention, but she was swirling liqueur in a snifter, deliberately looking nowhere in particular. I came up behind her and caught her eye in the bar mirror. She swiveled around with an incredible smile that reached right inside me. I turned, and sweeping my hand toward the fireplace, offered, "A table by the flames?"

She flowed off the stool as smoothly as the amber liquid in her glass, saluted me with it, and said, "Lead on."

A barmaid followed us back to the table. I ordered two more of what Sharon was drinking and told the barmaid that I was expecting a phone call. I only gave her my first name, but she hit me with a look that could inspire a lynch mob, so I figured she had me placed from the *Tribune's* front page.

"You should have come back to the Randolph-Lightner office this afternoon. You would have liked the scene."

"I bet so," I said, recalling standing there in the anteroom, secretly looking at her. "Let me guess. Scanlon got mad and threw paperclips at Barriss."

"They did get into it. Barriss was steaming before he even saw Scanlon. Hilda and I could hardly keep from

136

laughing. Those two used to get along, at least until they formed their partnership. Now their arguments are the main floorshow in the office. We even moved the copier over to the table next to Scanlon's door last month, so we could listen in better. Told Scanlon that the light was better there and he thought nothing of it. It used to be funnier, but now it's gotten old. I knew you'd be interested, so I went over and played copier. I cupped my hand toward the door and Hilda cracked up."

"I always knew office workers were subversive," I accused her.

We were still, not speaking.

"I learned a dirty secret, just your type," she resumed, turning toward me, shrugging her shoulders despairing over my depraved curiosity. "They hiss when they're mad, so it's sometimes hard to make it out, but I did hear Barriss telling Scanlon that he better come up with fifty-thousand dollars by next week or he was out. Lotta money, isn't it?"

"Yeah. Especially when you're throwing it away like crazy at the card table."

"You know about that?" she said surprised.

"I have reached out these very hands to catch some of his chips as they roll away from him," I said, cupping my hands, reaching them out to mirror my words, deliberately moving them just slightly too close to her.

An eyebrow slowly raised.

"The dread Mrs. Scanlon used to raise holy hell about his poker losses. About that and his one true love, the bottle. They're separated now. I used to feel sorry for him, living with that phony old witch."

"No more?"

"He's too nasty anymore to feel sorry for. He's become a joke. An unfunny joke. Maybe they deserve each other."

The barmaid arrived with two Drambuies. I paid. She put Sharon's down neatly and halfway dropped mine so that some of it slopped over the rim onto the table. She didn't even pretend to count out my change while waiting for me to tell her to keep it. Then she stalked off.

Sharon laughed softly.

"I guess I'm better at being a wise guy than making new friends."

"Maybe you're doing OK."

We sipped our drinks and I was starting to feel very good. Sharon leaned forward and said, "Before the subject gets too changed, there's something else you should know. When Barriss stomped out of Scanlon's office he went into his own and made a phone call. I could tell by the lights on my phone. Soon after that, about quitting time, close to five, a call came in for Scanlon from the guy who's the acting Randolph-Lightner superintendent at Prudhoe, filling in for Barriss."

I nodded, listening, but also tracing the zigzags of her dress with my eyes and savoring the rock pouring out of the jukebox.

"Well, I listened in on it. We have strange phones and I can do that on incoming calls. He told Scanlon that Barriss had just phoned and told him to lay off Luke Evans and get him on the next plane to town. He was calling to confirm. I heard Scanlon sigh. Then he said that Luke wasn't laid off, only a mix-up by Barriss, thanks for calling, good-bye. That's all you get, Nick. No more shop talk. Hilda and I went home and left the bosses there to hate each other without our help."

We sat quiet briefly, looking at each other for a vibrant instant. I noticed that we were nodding our heads together, just slightly, but nodding in rhythm.

"So, where are you from?" I asked her.

"Arizona."

"This place must have been a transition."

"The people were, for a while. But I got used to that. Now Alaska seems very like other places to me. In a strange way, the snowfields even look like the desert I grew up in. And you? Where are you from?"

"Oregon, once."

Callahan appeared walking back to our table with a young lovely he'd discovered by the bar. No one understood the depths of his power over women, but they were clearly resonant. He was walking in that insolent slouching glide with his left hand hooked behind his Red Army belt buckle, looking down mock seriously at his blonde companion as he made a point by gesturing with the beer bottle in his right hand. She was smiling in a reserved way like she was about to take a flyer and believe, say, half of what he was telling her. They sat down and we went through introductions.

Callahan picked up where he'd left off, explaining, "Allison, you should run off with me tonight and I guarantee you'll live in a state of spiritual ecstasy."

"I'm already living in a state of spiritual ecstasy," she replied.

"Ah, but it's not guaranteed," Callahan answered, still not convincing her to do anything but smile.

Some small talk and a few jokes later, Stephen Plumb came in the back door. He was a handsome hippie, tallish, strongly built in a slender way and graceful. He wore dark horn-rimmed glasses that gave a peering quality to his intense face, which was framed by long brown hair and a high-amperage beard. He was wearing jeans and a green chamois shirt, open an extra button to show off his hairy chest in the mistaken delusion it had something to do with sexual powers. He called greetings from across the floor and brightened when he saw Sharon. She scooted her chair toward me to make room and Plumb sat down at our table.

"Howdy, Stephen. Meet Sharon and Allison. Sharon, this is yet another reprobate. It's going to ruin my reputation to be introducing you to such people."

"Listen, Nick, according to the *Tribune*, you have no reputation left to ruin. Why'd you off that Teamo, boy?"

"He claims it's another frame-up," Callahan put in.

"Come on. We're not innocents here. Least of all Callahan. How many times can you cop that plea?"

"In this town it could get to be habitual. I thought all that was on the shelf when the pipeline came to Fairbanks."

Callahan laughed expansively and said "So you signed up with 942 to get on the dole with the rest of us and figured you'd never have to deal with fiscal reality again?"

"Right. Looked perfect. Suffer the camps, collect

petrobucks and work on my Frisbee game. Then I opened the wrong door and found a dead Teamster."

"Nick, knowing you it could not have been that simple," Plumb laughed.

"You were at Atigun too long, Stephen. It's made you irreversibly cynical."

"Actually, Atigun was a tiny monastery in the far north where the brothers meditated on the job ten hours a day and did without women."

Plumb gave an exaggeratedly careful look around the bar. No one was particularly looking at us. Then he whipped a tiny bottle out of his shirt pocket.

"I wasn't at Atigun quite long enough, however, to put down all my humanoid vices," he informed us.

Callahan cheered, cleared a space on the table and confided mock seriously to Plumb that, "it's the trivial state of your inner enlightenment, son, that keeps you thinking this elixir of the yogis is a vice. Ask any woman."

"That's nearly true," Allison replied. "Cocaine is a vice, alright, but only for men."

Plumb dumped a mammoth load of white powder on the table and began loosening it with fast, loving chops of a razor blade. He worked it back and forth, slid it around, made piles, combined them, finally laid out five impressive lines, thick, but mainly distinguished by their great length.

And there it was again right in front of me. I felt that old pulse toward the fun, sharing a hit with friends, but the thrill powder looked like so much ground turnip. Seemed like it was just the memory of past highs that was so exciting. Sharon's expression was puzzling. For the first time, I couldn't quite get a read on her reaction. Maybe she wanted to do some lines, but was hesitating because I was hesitating. I was confused about her. We looked at each other again. Everyone else was getting into it, keying in on a quick rush, their excitement flaring up.

"There's an old Aleut saying," Plumb was carrying on, "that you can tell the size of a man's cock by the size of his lines."

"I heard that one," Allison affirmed. "It goes something like the longer the one, the shorter the other."

Plumb snorted his disdain, though I knew he loved playing the straight man. He rolled up a hundred dollar bill, did a line and handed the tube to Sharon. She paused a count, then shrugged her shoulders, bent over the table, whiffed up and passed it to me. And so I put aside my questions and got in on the white magic tour. We launched off into enjoying fine toot, but it felt a bit like swimming against the tide.

Then the barmaid came by and told me I had a call. She didn't notice Plumb finishing off the last of the lines because she was trying so hard not to.

I walked up to the bar phone and heard Allen calling in from Prudhoe. He didn't have anything definite about Scanlon and he reported abysmal failure in an effort to seduce Lori. He told me she did no work of any sort and just rode around in the same Randolph-Lightner Teamster foreman's pickup all day, a position now held by Luke. And

Luke, of all cynics, had lost his cherry and plunked down a thousand to get in the Denali. Now the two of them were promoting it full speed. Allen cheered me somewhat by mentioning that the troops had demoted me from my former rumor mill eminence, the better to discuss the huge checkpool.

Going back to the table I saw Jeanne walking toward me from the back door, her hair gleaming in the dim light. Under her open parka she was wearing tan cotton pants and a fluffy bronze sweater. She was more beautiful than I'd ever seen her, especially at the moment she saw me and hurried forward. She threw her arms around me and kissed me. I felt her warmth against me, but I didn't want her. I wanted to know why she hadn't gone to the cops. An image of her half-naked in the tugboat flashed before me. It stirred me for an instant, but at the same time I was searching my memory of that night, of touching her silky flesh and all her clothes, and concluding again that she had had no knife and little time to get one. I didn't think she could have killed Phil Dalira and I didn't think she had a knife to do it with. She sensed that I was resisting her embrace, but she pulled me closer and kissed with more feeling.

As we separated, I saw the barmaid pointing me out with a nod. I looked back and saw Sharon looking at us, her face in neutral. I hoped she'd seen that I didn't return the kiss.

"Come over here," I said, leading Jeanne toward the front of the bar, out of Sharon's sight.

"Nick, it's wonderful that they let you go. I was afraid they'd be hard on you. I didn't know what to do last night.

When I was walking down to that room where...where..." she stumbled, "where Phil was, I saw someone just then going out the door at the far end."

"Man or woman?" I asked, imagining Barriss and Lori as possibilities.

"I couldn't be sure from so far. I just got a glimpse. Then I got to that room and saw," she said, hesitating, "saw Phil like that. Horrible. I knew he was dead. I just had to get out of there so I ran after the person I'd seen."

"Did you catch up?"

"Sort of. I saw someone tearing off in a pickup. I saw it very clearly in the lights. One person in it, no passengers. I couldn't make out the driver. It had that Randolph-Lightner logo on the door, just like yours. I couldn't believe this was happening."

"What'd you do then?"

"The pickup drove off real fast and went around the corner of camp, out of sight. I went into the next trailer and ran all the way across to the main hallway, then down to the far end of the opposite trailer. I went outside and your pickup parked there, idling. I didn't know what to think. So I went back to where Phil was. They were taking you away through that crowd in the hallway. I didn't know who called to me when I tore my pocket going out the door. I was in a hurry and didn't hear the voice well. I was afraid you'd killed Phil. I cried it was so terrible, but later I understood, Nick. Because you saw me tear my pocket, it couldn't have been you who killed him."

"How come you didn't go to the cops?"

"I was afraid they wouldn't believe me. It would sound like we had contrived it to get you off. Then I heard they let you go and I wanted to talk to you before I did anything. I had to talk to you first. Did you tell them about me?"

"No."

"Nick, there's something else. Don't hate me, but I have to ask you something."

She cupped her hands over mine on the table and looked up at me. The gold fleck sparkled in her eyes.

"Where were you at five-thirty today?"

"Having a brandy at the Mecca. Why?"

"Lyle Barriss was shot and killed at this housing development he was a partner in. The killer got away. I just heard about it at the *Tribune*."

I looked at her and felt slightly set up. A hardness infiltrated her features and I felt things fleeting away.

"If you had told me that first, then asked me where I was, I would have told you the very same thing. Now tell me where you were."

She pulled back. A burst of anger and betrayal raced across her face, then was gone just as fast. She lowered her eyes.

"I guess you have the right to ask. I was home."

"There's a State Trooper named Forzano who is going to ask you that same question, as soon as he finds out you've been investigating how Barriss and Scanlon patented a certain mining claim.'

Ice crystals formed in her look.

"That's none of your business. I'm amazed my boss would have told you anything about that."

"He didn't need to. Would it be better if I still thought you were a Teamo expediter for Livingston at CC1?"

She started to walk off, then relented and smiled again.

"Jeanne, there are dangerous people in this."

"Nick, I'm glad they aren't holding you. I can't talk about the rest of it. I have to go."

She turned to leave, then stopped and looked back at me.

"Should I tell this Forzano I was there?"

I nodded.

She kissed me again, but put nothing into it. Then she walked away and out the front door.

I stood there a moment, breathing quietly, calming down from her, noticing that everyone in the joint was looking at me. It had to be checked. I walked to the phone, past a solid wall of hard stares and silence. I dialed the *Tribune* and got Dave on the line.

"Did Barriss get taken out?"

"So she found you already. Yeah, a lady musher had the dogs out and heard shots, just about five-thirty. She didn't think much of it until she saw Barriss in a snow bank. They're guessing a .38. Now, lad, where were you?"

"I get asked that too much. I was drinking at the Mecca Bar at that time, with Toby Vinson."

"Christ, Nick, sometimes you keep the most miserable company."

"I can't help it if everyone likes me."

146

I called the Staters and told the trooper who answered where I'd been at five-thirty, asking him to pass it on to Forzano. I needed to maintain diplomatic relations with the Lieutenant.

I went back to the table by the fire. Plumb was bent over. As he straightened, Callahan's head bobbed down.

"Have a jolt," Plumb said, blading out another line.

I felt only one single thing about that. I simply didn't want it, no matter how much fun my friends were having, no matter how much it might possibly make for a sexy vibe to share with Sharon. I looked at her. I wanted her, but I didn't want any toot. It hadn't been that long, but it seemed like ages since I'd wanted any of that white powder. I didn't want to inflict any of my resolution on them, so I smiled and waved it off. Plumb handed the snorter to Sharon. She turned it down also.

"A pipeline romance?" Sharon asked, a sharp edge in her voice.

I sat down and spread my hands to plead nolo contendere. "It's over," I shrugged. "You could see that, I hope."

It seemed to take forever, but then Sharon smiled and nodded that she had seen. I felt a great relief.

Then she said, "That woman came in to see Scanlon last week. I don't know what they talked about, but I do know I didn't like her. She's got a pair of pliers for a heart."

Sharon looked so beautiful and clear. I wanted to stay with her, but I had to leave. If I didn't take care of some things I'd get flattened by a storm.

"Our beloved ex-boss," I said nodding to Sharon, "the former Randolph-Lightner Superintendent at Prudrude Bay, one Lyle Barriss, just got shot to death out at his housing development. Cops are going to be swarming all over me, but I have too much to do just now to be talking to them."

They were silent in surprise. Sharon put her hand on my arm in sympathy. Callahan reached into his pocket and tossed his truck keys on the table. "They're going to be onto your car. Take my truck. It's parked in back."

"My ride?" I asked him.

"No. I don't think I want to be driving that damn thing tonight."

"Be careful," Plumb said.

Sharon was writing numbers on a piece of paper. She looked up at me, quickly pursing her lips into a crooked little pout, then raising an eyebrow and smiling, she continued writing. I noticed that she was left-handed. It seemed that I had known that for a long time. Everything about her was wonderfully new and intensely familiar at the same time. She put her hand on mine and passed over the paper, saying "Call me."

The touch was electric. It passed right through me. I looked at her eyes and then couldn't resist tracing my glance over her zigzags one last time. I got up. I felt her eyes pulling me back. I had to go that second or I wouldn't have been able to leave at all.

Chapter Eleven

Callahan's Orange Delicious fired right up and the cassette player came on at full torque with "Wild Horses," that Stones tune aching to cut loose and rage away which instead they play slow and teasing. As I let the pickup warm up, I wondered if I had been wrong about Jeanne early on, if perhaps I shouldn't have pursued that strong initial flash. I was uncomfortable playing back Tuesday night, imaging a knife in her hands, but I did it. I came away from that exercise unpersuaded. I knew I hadn't been wrong about Sharon at all, though looking back I felt I was slow to appreciate her.

Then trucks started playing tag in my mind. Randolph-Lightner had green Ford pickups assigned to Barriss, Phil Dalira, my foreman Theo, that pompous Arctic Wrap person, Tyson and also the timekeeper. Barriss' had been in the shop all that night with the engine pulled, but that didn't let him out since it might have been him I saw drive off in Theo's truck. Even getting dead didn't say much one way or the other about whether Barriss killed Dalira. Phil must have driven his truck over to Parsons that night. I wondered if Lori had driven it back. Tyson had probably used his truck to get to Parsons, though that wasn't confirmed, but I didn't see how to tag him for Phil. The timekeeper's truck, well, I had that one. And then there was Scanlon. I wondered what he'd been driving around in the incipient ice fog up there.

I turned up Lacey, past the Northward Building parking lot where I'd put the Toyota. A blue Fairbanks police car was stopped right behind my car. The passenger cop was talking on his radio. Went on by, face averted. After taking a right on Fifth, I swung over to Cushman and then came back down Fourth. I parked a half block past Thalman's card joint and got out. Bundled in winter clothing, hood up, I figured to be anonymous on the street.

A skinny, fidgety man bounced down the sidewalk ahead of me. He had on Florida clothes, a light sports coat, slacks and patent-leather shoes. His nervous, springy walk was his only protection against the ten below. He was a cardroom bum named Triangle Bill and no doubt had just walked the three blocks over from the Polaris to catch the evening action. He turned into a two-story office building and I went in the door after him. He half turned and snuck a quick look at me over his shoulder. His bulgy eyes peered out of a ferrety face with lots of freckles and twitchy lips.

Triangle got his nickname from his inexhaustible supply of little green triangular Dexedrine tablets that he popped to keep going. He had plenty, but he didn't sell them. They were some old model pill that he'd had for ten or fifteen years and they were just perfect, for him.

If Triangle had the bucks, he'd play lo-ball. Otherwise he'd shill or tend bar if they needed him. His lo-ball game was good, but not sound. He played three times too fast. Triangle loved the action and you couldn't keep him out of any pot he had a remote chance to win. He'd be in there hitting the deck on anything and then giving it a decent play. You could be sure he wasn't going to go broke calling that last bet with the second-best hand. He could kill you on those nights when the cards were sweet to him and he was catching lightning in a bottle. Usually, he was busted.

We were standing in a long thin lobby that served a dress shop and an insurance office. An elevator came and we took it up to the second floor. The door opened on a small anteroom with a tired, bent-nosed hulk slouching in an overstuffed armchair. He looked up from a skin magazine and checked us out between puffs on an obnoxious cigar. The steady faint click of chips came purring through the inner door. The hulk nodded and buzzed us into the game room.

There was a blaze of crushed-velvet scarlet wallpaper setting off several green card tables. A craps game was thrashing to the right, four plungers and a house man. Another empty craps table was beyond it. Half a dozen poker tables stood around the left side of the room. They had a lo-ball game and a draw poker game, both full but partly with house shills, and a blackjack table with three live ones.

Most of the card players were going on a stack of $100, though it only took a twenty to get in. The dice fans had a lot less or a lot more. Back in the left corner was a small counter with a bored bartender polishing glasses and waiting for the next tip to show up. Through a doorway at the right rear was another room, smaller and intimate in a garish way, with a thick black cord hung across the entrance. It had orange wallpaper, but Thalman called it the Gold Room. Only high-rollers were allowed in. The Gold Room was for lo-ball, $500 take out, no limit table stakes and watch out for your own self. Triangle Bill cut away from me soon as we came in the door. Not even cardroom bums wanted to hang out with me those days.

Thalman had a fair crowd for an early Wednesday night. That made it a bad time for Triangle to be tapped out, since Thalman wasn't going to need any more shills to keep the games alive. I cased the crowd for familiar faces. No Scanlon.

Thalman went strong on the trade, but the pipeline kept it coming like never before. The dice and blackjack took care of themselves and he raked the poker and lo-ball games heavily. Thalman advertised a five percent cut of the pots, which was steep enough, but if you kept a count on the house man, you'd see that over time it always came to more. The breakage they called it. Plenty of pots they were going double the five percent, especially when a rookie in off the street won a big one.

The cashier's cage was in the wall behind the dice games. A big fellow leaned against the wall beside it. That was Pinky. His sloping shoulders and large gut wouldn't fool anyone. He was still about the right size to play the defensive line for Southern Cal. His boss liked size.

Pinky wore bright green pants and a lime green shirt. Unfortunately, he also had on a shiny vest in a brilliant and completely wrong shade of purple. His reddish face sported a constant smile that had all sorts of shark in it, but with charm. Everyone liked Pinky, unless they got into a beef with him and saw how fast the charm slid right off his face and left only the shark. He managed the joint and might be able to come up with a couple items they wouldn't sell you over at the Co-Op drug store.

I started across the floor toward the Gold Room. Pinky detached himself from the wall and cut me off halfway.

"What you doing, Rez, coming round here bringing heat," he said in a voice a little too high and thin.

"How could I get any to bring, Pinks? Didn't your boss buy it all long ago?"

"You ain't getting no play, Rez. We gots to get along with the man."

"That's fine. I'm only taking a quick look around. Trying to find a friend."

"I like that eye of yours. You could maybe use another one. Have a nice matched pair that way."

Charm was steadily evaporating from his face, but a noisy dispute sprang up at the blackjack table behind us and Pinky went off to settle it, directing me an eyeball warning as he departed.

I walked over to the doorway of the Gold Room and stood in front of the black cord. There were three locals in

153

the game who I knew were tough players and tight as well. Barney was in the game and he rated as the best poker player in the state. The houseman was Vero. He was back from the bottle and played a strong game. A tall, thick man in his fifties was also at the table. He looked soft and had small, fleshy hands with long droopy fingers, but his face wasn't soft. His sharp nose stuck out too far. His lips were so thin and sharp he could use them to shave. He was hard to read in a card game because he was always angry, and always in the same way, except when he was dragging in a big pot, and then he wasn't not angry but only less angry. That was Thalman. He was so good at what he did that he probably hadn't personally pulled the trigger on anyone for years. He had a lot of help to take care of details.

I stepped over to the far right side of the doorway. That brought another player into view. Scanlon. He was looking very red in the face, short in the chips and out of his class. He was the only fish at the table and he wasn't going to get far with a short stack. He was keeping his eyes on the table and was most definitely not looking at me. I stared at him until he relented and looked up at me. I pulled out my notebook, swiveled my head around at the clock and elaborately wrote down the time. Scanlon turned away and reached for a cigarette. Seemed funny to me, but Thalman didn't appreciate it. He got up and walked out the back door of the Gold Room. A few seconds later Pinky appeared at my shoulder.

"He's gonna talk to you," Pinky snarled and jerked his thumb toward the door Thalman had gone though.

154

I didn't like that because I didn't know how Thalman had gotten the word to Pinky so quick. His communications were too good to feel comfortable being around. I went. I always wanted to know where Thalman was at. Where he was at was trouble, but trouble you could avoid. When you didn't know things about him, he got a lot more dangerous. And he was mostly willing to tell you what he wanted, because his wants were simple. They were mainly "gimme" and "more."

Pinky held open a door for me in the wall beside the cashier's cage. I waited for him to go through it first. He led me down a short hallway with two doors on each side. He knocked on the first door on the right, paused a moment and went in.

It was the office. Thalman was sitting very erect in a soft chair behind a huge maple desk. Pinky went over to the right and slouched against a liquor cabinet. Two armchairs were parked in front of the desk. A couch and filing cabinets framed a door to the left. Thalman had two pictures on the wall behind him. Winter Alaskascapes. One picture I could figure. It would cover the wall safe. Two pictures threw me, because gratuitous art didn't fit. The walls, the chairs and the couch were all in earth tones. The room was far more relaxed than the vivid cardroom, but it didn't appear to have any effect on Thalman.

"Sid down, asshole," he muttered in a rumbly, raspy voice and pointed at the chairs in front of him. That would put Pinky behind me. I sat down on the couch instead.

155

"How'd you get in here?"

"Through the roof."

Thalman snapped a look at Pinky. Pinky straightened up and started explaining. "Tony musta fell asleep on the door again. You gots to keep on him all the time."

"You do that. Now, asshole," he said turning to me, "why'd you come here?"

"Nothing special. I thought I'd take a peek at what kind of phony alibi Scanlon was setting up for himself after bumping his partner."

"Lay off Scanlon."

"Why? Can't he pay the vig so good when he'd getting his nuts squeezed? I thought that's how it was done."

Thalman was quiet for a few moments. I didn't like the sensation as I watched him making up his mind about me. It worked out alright though, because when he resumed talking he was explaining.

"He's been here since a quarter after five. Anybody in the Gold Room game that long can tell you that."

"Busy guy like you, where'd you find time to get them rehearsed?"

"Rezkel, you got that same problem you used to have. Too much lip. You might need a lip specialist flown in from Seattle."

"I might. The locals are no damn good."

Pinky tightened up. Thalman didn't have much color in his face to start with, but all drained away. He sat there completely still. He wrapped his long, bony fingers around the edge of the desk and squeezed hard. His face clenched as tight as I knew his heart was.

"You're eighty-sixed. You got told. You stay told. Keep out of my joint."

I stood up and walked toward the door. Pinky's right hand eased toward his belt.

"I saw Lou Devery in town today," I said.

"I heard he was back," Thalman said.

"He got told too."

"He stayed that way, until today, and he stayed healthy, until today."

"Maybe somebody who doesn't like you brought him back. Maybe you're crowding the wrong guys these days."

"You see Devery, you give him a message from me."

"Save it, Thalman. I got my own message for him."

Chapter Twelve

As I pulled into the parking lot, two city cops came out of the Big I. I waited until they drove off before getting out of the pickup. My profile felt entirely too high going through the door, but luckily two drunks were getting into it at the bar. Wasn't much of a fight. The best blow was a glassful of beer to the face. The crowd cheered them on anyway and I walked anonymously through the tables, past the bar to the most obscure booth in the back.

Liz Clarke was working her way toward me with a tray of drinks. She was short and blonde, about forty, but she'd leveled that barrier with full tilt living so she seemed a lot of different ages. Her face was plain and hard, because Liz never took any shit, period.

A prominent Fairbanks doctor was sitting with his back to me two tables away. He was writing a check when Liz arrived with drinks for him and the two other men at his table. He handed her the check. Liz glanced at it and belted out in a loud voice for half the place to hear, "A hundred bucks! Not bad for a nooner."

The good doctor was mortified, but he tried laughing along with everyone else and then made some explanation that nobody listened to. Liz came back to my table with the immediate crowd still laughing.

"Hi, Nick. The man was just in here looking for you. They change their mind about letting you go? Like maybe that was a mistake?"

"They're working on a new mistake now. Lyle Barriss got shot dead a couple hours ago and they want to talk to me about it."

"Who's that?"

"A Randolph-Lightner superintendent. A former boss."

She sat down next to me and nudged me with her elbow.

"Well? You can tell me." she whispered in a playful, conspiratorial way.

"Neither one. I didn't kill Dalira and I didn't kill Barriss."

"That's good enough for me, Nick. I'll buy you one to prove it."

"Thanks, but what I really need is a better take on Hal Scanlon. You know him don't you?"

"Yeah, I know him, that miserable little old dick of a drunk. Listen, he's falling to pieces from Scotch. There's not enough left in his bottle to keep him from bottoming out the next time he dives in."

"It's worse lately?"

"Much, and now he's two-timing his wife, sanctimonious horror that she is."

159

"Who with?"

"Lori Jennings."

"Lori Jennings? And that wreck?"

"It's not a shock. Her sex drive is controlled by her dollar bill gland. Remember that old fart she was going around with at the bridge sectional in Anchorage last fall?"

"I didn't know she was there. I didn't play against her."

"That's because she spent all her time in the hotel hustling two-penny-a-point side games."

"She's vague by me. What's her bridge game like?"

"About as mediocre as yours. She doesn't do anything well and her bidding is pedestrian. I mean, she normally can't get to slam without using Blackwood as a crutch."

"Then what was she doing working the side action?"

"Right, Nickaroonie, and what was she doing winning a chunk at it? I talked to two guys who played her. They're quite good, but she beat them like a drum, for at least a thousand each. Lori had a very good partner, but they still should have creamed her, except they kept running into slams. And Lori's bidding was odd. Usually she's very chicken, but she kept jumping into slams, and they were making. Probably neither one could keep his eyes off her tits long enough to concentrate. I can't stand the way she waves those bazookas around. It makes me want to beat her to death with a bloody Kotex."

"Christ, Liz, what do you do all day. Sharpen your tongue with a file?"

"I just don't like her."

"Anything else you don't like about her?"

160

"Yeah. It'd take major surgery to remove her make-up."

I stood up and pulled on the parka.

"Thanks, you gave me ideas."

"Are the cops going to shoot you on sight?"

"No way. On a cold night they prefer Napalm."

I walked quickly to the front with my head turned away from the bar, covering the awkwardness of that with a long, slow adjust of my stocking cap. I felt quasi-invisible and figured I was getting away with something until I looked up at the mirror over the door and saw the bartender staring right into my face.

I got Callahan's truck out of there quickly and drove back over the Cushman Street Bridge, hoping the bartender didn't pick up on my wheels. I knew Barney could answer the questions I had, but I couldn't go back into Thalman's and even a phone call would be pressing it. I could have gotten Plumb or Callahan out of Tommy's to deliver a message, but I wanted to give my luck some play before I fell back on lesser powers like reason or planning.

Fourth was dry, but as I went past Lacey I clicked. Triangle Bill was walking toward the Polaris, dry night for him and he was likely trying to stir up someone to lend him a few bucks. I went around the block and back up Lacey. I eased the pickup over to the curb and rolled down the window as he got there.

"Hey, Bill," I called and waved him over to me.

He stopped and then edged away half a step when he recognized me. I motioned him over again. He looked up and down the street and didn't move. I got out a twenty and held it up for him to see. He cocked his head a touch to the left and came over to the truck in these minute movements you could have called steps if he'd been about a foot tall. His lips twitched and by the streetlight I could see his perfect, straight teeth and how they were stained nicotine yellow to the roots.

"Thalman eighty-sixed me, Bill, but I got to talk to Barney. I want you to take him a message."

He retreated at that proposal, but not far.

"You get this Jackson. Go over to the Co-Op and get him a milkshake. Strawberry. All anybody will think is you were tapped and ran an errand for him."

"I don't know. What's the message?"

"Tell him I have to talk to him right away. I'll be in this truck. It's an orange Ford pickup, right? I'll park it right up the street. Tell him to go down Fourth, turn up Lacey and I'll be right there."

He wanted to reach for the twenty, but he hesitated.

"You sure about this, Rez?"

"You'll be OK. You know about Barney. He'll know something's up. He's smart and careful. He always gets up from the table to take a break when you bring him something. Tell him then. No one will hear."

Triangle looked up and down the street again and fidgeted.

"Bill, take this twenty and you'll be back in the action." I fished out two singles and put them with the twenty. "This is for the milkshake."

He nodded his head a half dozen times real quick, then took the money and scurried off.

"Make sure it's strawberry," I yelled after him.

I pulled forward across Fourth and parked. Fifteen minutes later the door opened and Barney climbed in with a milkshake. He saluted me with it and said, "I came because you got the flavor right." I put it in gear and drove off.

Barney was balding and puffy around the cheeks, with a jolly expression and happy brown eyes that I could never read in a poker game, though most any other time they let you know exactly what was on his mind. He had quite a presence, particularly at the card table, and a smooth way of doing things that told you here was someone not to mess with. He was in his thirties, but he got age guesses ten years either side of that. He had a phud in statistics from MIT, but that stuff was only recreational. His business was poker, with occasional side bets.

"You got me out here for a chat about Scanlon, didn't you?"

"Reading my mind again, are you, Barney?"

"I could never do that."

"Then how do you beat me so bad at lo-ball?"

"That's privileged information and you're not that privileged."

He laughed and started again. "Scanlon figures from that psych you ran down on him. I like the way you gave him the needle without saying a word."

"When did he get to Thalman's tonight?"

"Funny you ask that. I don't exactly know. I've been there since late afternoon myself, but I didn't know he was around or I would have jumped in the big game right off. Can't pass up a softie like Scanlon, especially when he's

163

been drinking. See, I checked out the Gold Room periodi-cally, but they didn't have enough high rollers to get much of a game going. Thalman, Vero and one of those hard rocks were playing. I like short-handed games, but not against Thalman and his houseman."

"So, I played at Table Two," he continued. "We had a fair lo-ball game going. Small, but soft and I did OK. Then later, about six, I took another look. I still didn't think I wanted to bother because all I could see were hard rocks. Didn't look like much. Then I went right up to the cord to see if anyone was in that inside corner seat. Well, that's when I saw Scanlon. I don't know how long he'd been there, but I felt silly for passing up any of his action. I jumped right in."

I calculated the drive time from the S&B site at about thirty minutes, best case.

"Alright, Rez, my turn. Why do you want to know this?"

"Scanlon's partner, guy named Barriss, got wasted about five-thirty. They didn't get along real well."

Barney whistled and said, "Scanlon's way into Thalman for cards and I hear things sound like Thalman's his shy. If Scanlon's hot, Thalman has plenty of reason to alibi him."

"Thalman could come up with easier ways to do that without involving himself. Maybe Scanlon didn't give him the chance."

"Huh? Oh, I get you. The back door to the Gold Room leads to the back stairway. That would be just like Scanlon too, to do the half smart thing. He gets dirty and then barges in on Thalman through the back door asking for cover. It could be, Nick. You know how Thalman usually doesn't say

164

one unnecessary word about anything to anyone. Well, tonight he's been needling me, low key like, for not getting in the game sooner. How'd he put it? Yeah, he said twice they had a four-way game going for ages, waiting for a live one like me. That would have been Thalman, Vero, a rock who owes Thalman, and Scanlon, if you believe Scanlon had been there all along."

"Do you believe it?"

"Doesn't matter. Those others work for Thalman or owe him. They'd stand up for Scanlon as long as Thalman told them to."

"Scanlon playing on paper?"

"Yeah, and that's not kosher anymore, unfortunately. Scanlon hit the cloth drawing dead to an eight, bless him, and Thalman gave him two yards on account. Nobody liked the short buy, but who's to bitch to Thalman about how he runs his game."

"There's something else, Barney. You know a girl friend of Scanlon's, dark hair, very built and..."

"And heartless and named Lori. Yeah. We met."

"Can she move with a deck?"

"Very well. She used to work the joints in Gardena. She's got all-around hands. She can do bottoms and seconds fairly well. Actually, real well. I saw her move in Anchorage two different times. But I just know from that flourish and the way she waves those tits around that her strong move has got to be a cold deck. She'll get them checking her out and then ring in a deck set up just right."

"What's the best way to stop a cold deck?"

"Dump your hand and wait for the next deal."

"What if you got to play it, for your whole stack and never mind why? What's best?"

"A shotgun might not be too bad."

I was quiet, but Barney knew I was still asking. He said quietly, "The only thing you got going against a stacked deck is that you know it's coming in just when the real deck is supposedly being put back together after the cut."

Chapter Thirteen

Scanlon's wife lived close to downtown, by Kellum and Birch in an attempted upper middle-class neighborhood. The house was a dark blue ranch-style. Lights were on, including an unobtrusive off-white electric cross discretely hanging right in the middle of the front window. It had the feel of a neon beer sign, only more subdued because it didn't blink on and off.

Callahan had the accumulation of several extravagant episodes scattered around his Orange Delicious. The prize was a railroad conductor's cap. It had a shiny black brim and a soft top, with a Red Army star pinned to it, gold hammer and sickle inlaid in red enamel. There was also a black leather notebook. They looked about right for giving Mrs. Scanlon a bit of bad theater to critique. Sometimes they never trust you more than right after they expose you.

I crunched through the snow up to the porch. A large color TV shone faintly through blue curtains. I rang the bell.

Fairly soon the porch light came on and the curtain was pulled back. An overweight frowsy woman in her forties wearing a bright blue robe peered out at me. Then she turned her head back to snatch another look at the TV.

"Captain Reynolds, ma'am. Salvation Army."

She looked back at me again. I held the black notebook piously in front of my chest and eased it forward like I was showing her a Bible.

"Salvation Army. Captain Reynolds."

She fiddled with a chain and then opened the door half way. "Yes ma'am, we like to help our Christian neighbors on a personal basis."

She flicked another quick glance at the TV and then turned back to me, leaning forward, inspecting my cap.

"What's that star?"

I whipped the cap off my head and held it down by my side. "Actually, Mrs. Scanlon, I'm Tony Reynolds of the Trib. I was afraid you wouldn't want to talk to a reporter."

"The *Tribune*?" She shifted her attention to my cut cheek and black eye. "You look familiar, almost like that man in the paper."

"You must have seen the picture of me questioning Rezkel. I know we're supposed to be unbiased, but he's a mad dog. He punched me and knocked the camera out of the photographer's hands. That's what I've come to ask you about, anything you might know about that death."

It wasn't going over. She didn't like the idea of knowing anything about it and she kept looking back at the tube. I changed front.

"I'm working on another story also, about how unscrupulous elements are interfering with the land developers who are trying to build our community. Un-Christian parasites, you might call them."

"You mean that bloodsucker, Thalman?"

I recognized an entry line. "Exactly the one, Mrs. Scanlon. Could we discuss this indoors?"

She stepped back and let me in. The house was crammed with a mishmash of overstuffed furniture and too many end tables, all with the worst available kitsch figurines crowded on them. A Nativity scene was arrayed on a small table by the kitchen door. A sideboard stood against the left wall, holding forth another mob of plastic statuettes. Starting with the robe over her amorphous body and the faint tint to her hair, the entire place was blue. The walls were a startled peacock. What little could be seen on them between twenty-odd Christian prints and Alaska scenes was painted velvet. I felt abused by unart, as though Nixon was addressing remarks to me.

The tough part was the air, so stale and musty that the thermostat must have been set on mildew.

She motioned me to a lumpy ultramarine armchair in front of the tube and I made my way there through a thicket of standing lamps.

Mrs. Scanlon plopped down in a matching armchair and was immediately reabsorbed by a medical melodrama. I think the patient had leukemia and the doctor had a hard on, but more action played out on top of the TV where a Seal point Siamese was dozing on a newspaper. A bottle of

McNaughton's was standing on the floor next to her chair. It was no virgin. I pretended not to notice as she slipped it out of sight beside her.

In front of us, at the other end of the living room, a fat kid of about twelve with pasty skin was bent over a butterfly collection in a glass case. He snapped a spiteful glare at me, checked that his mother was engrossed and slid a screen off the top of a terrarium behind the butterfly case. He was putting it back on when Mrs. Scanlon surfaced and caught him at it. She hopped out of her chair shouting at him, flicked off the TV on the wing and arrived in full feather at his stool.

"I saw that, Billy," she shrieked at him. "I told you never again. They're going out the door." She picked up the terrarium, hustled to the door, fought it open and tossed it right out onto the snow. Then she was back at him. She grabbed him by the hair and dragged him through a short hall to a bedroom. On the way he made an obnoxious face at me from under his arm. The bedroom door banged shut. I couldn't make out what she was yelling at him, but it sounded terminal.

The first buzz I completely ignored, not even bothering to interpret it as something else in March in Fairbanks, Alaska. Then one of them landed and sank the shaft in my forehead. The old mosquitoflex, the one you never lose, jolted my hand up to squash it.

That gave me a bad feeling about Billy and his terrarium.

I brushed another one off walking over to the case. When I got there, I saw that it wasn't a butterfly collection.

The little bastard had mounted a dozen different kinds of mosquitoes on a white mat. He was neat. None of them was squished. They stood rampant, ready to drill and he had them labeled with their scientific names, like Mosquitus Humongus.

The kid had to be sick. He must have hatched out frozen spores. Three other escapees from the terrarium buzzed me. They were half-grown, but they knew the whole kamikaze routine.

I brushed them off, pissed to have to contend with those demons in late winter. On the way back to the armchair, I noticed that the half of the paper the cat wasn't on sported my crimo photo. I started to move the cat and turn the paper over, but the bedroom door opened, so I settled for dragging the cat's ass over enough to cover my picture. It let out a whiney squawk and nailed me with a swipe to the hand. I gritted out one of my several imitation smiles and sat down again.

Mrs. Scanlon didn't seem to notice the cat by-play. Her attention was deeply buried somewhere behind her dull brown eyes and leaden features. She trudged stiffly to the other TV chair and sat down heavily. Then she put on a smile as tinny as mine and we sat there talking, looking at each other sideways over our shoulders.

"Now, what did you want to know, Mr., uh, Reynolds?"

"We've heard, down at the paper, that Thalman has some sort of power over your husband. Is he trying to work his way into Associated Interior Investors?"

"Into what?"

"Associated Interior Investors."

She gave me a blank look.

"I'm sorry. I meant S&B Enterprises. Is Thalman trying to move in."

"The answer is no. He could never be a part of S&B, never a man like that. S&B is a Christian endeavor. We have the Baptists and the Methodists with us. Do you know what Thalman is?"

"What is he?"

"Are you going to print this in the paper?"

I automatically shook my head no. Wrong answer. She just sat there. I waved off another mosquito attack and adjusted. "Of course, when we get the story developed we'll run it. The more you can help, the sooner we can do that."

That was what she wanted to hear. She was a little drunk around the edges and ready to talk. She took off in a voice too high and shrill and laid it out for me. She slurred words occasionally, especially when her attention wandered.

"Thalman is a loan shark. He's a bloodsucker. My husband, my foolish husband, borrowed fifty-thousand dollars from that man when S&B was in a bad spot this fall and the banks wouldn't help us. He mismanaged all my money and then right in the middle of our development he borrowed from that gangster and S&B has been a disaster ever since. Thalman makes him pay ten percent a month. A month, can you believe it?"

"Definitely. Has Mr. Scanlon been able to repay any of the loan?"

"No. None of it. He sold my car to pay the interest and he's lost thousands more at poker at that same man's place, at Thalman's. He won't tell me where they play that poker game or I'd go there and denounce them before the Lord. They were very sympathetic to me at my church when I made a public confession of my husband's sins. I didn't tell them who Thalman was because I just found out his name for the first time last week. Hal would never tell me his name. I told him I would cry it aloud on Second Street and let the entire town know what was in our midst."

She caught herself carrying on and paused to pull a pack of cigarettes out of her robe. She lit up. The air was already so bad I hardly noticed, but I gave up politeness to smokers long ago and she saw it in my face.

"You don't approve of tobacco, Mr. Reynolds?"

"Well, it will kill you."

"You think tobacco causes cancer, don't you? When Christian love blooms in your heart throughout the year, your body sanctifies all it takes in. Genesis 1:29. 'And God said, Behold I have given you every herb-bearing seed, which is upon the face of all the earth.' The Lord didn't exclude tobacco, Mr. Reynolds. He said every herb-bearing seed."

She leaned forward and fixed me with her shallow, dull eyes. "Tobacco doesn't cause cancer. Sin causes cancer."

"Oh, I didn't know that," I said, perhaps without conviction, and changed the subject. "Mrs. Barriss must be active in the Methodist Church to support you in making S&B such an example of Christianity in business."

"No. They're Baptists."

"My mistake. I thought you were Baptist. You're the Methodist."

"No. I'm of the Pentecostal Lighthouse of God. Mr. Kirby is the Methodist."

"He is? I didn't know that. Roland J. Kirby?" I exulted over the bingo, helping her confirm.

"Yes. He has been our angel. He saved S&B. We took him in as partner last month and he brought the money to finish the first houses. He is much better at dealing with the government than my husband, or that animal Lyle Barriss. And he got us a fine attorney."

"Has Thalman interfered, except with your husband?"

"No. Only that way, but he's destroying my husband. Poker and that insane drinking and…," she trailed off a moment. "Hal has all but moved out of here. He doesn't even give me money. I have to call the bank to find out if it's been deposited in the checking account."

"Mrs. Scanlon, before I came over here I found out at the city desk that Lyle Barriss was murdered tonight. He was shot. They found the body at the S&B development."

Big pause, then, "That's terrible. That poor Mrs. Barriss, living with him all these years and now this. It's awful."

"Can S&B survive this? Is there insurance covering the partners?"

"What? I don't know. About the insurance. Of course, S&B will survive. That Barriss was only a foreman. We've actually been making do on a shoestring the whole time. Now Mr. Kirby will have a larger role. We'll manage so much better, though I'm terribly sorry for Mrs. Barriss. We should have had that insurance. Hal wouldn't know about that, but Mr. Kirby would. We must have that insurance."

She was starting to ramble and I was afraid she'd dry up at any moment. I hit her with the harder questions while I still could.

"The police are looking for your husband. He is the main suspect. How would he gain by killing Barriss?"

"No, Mr. Reynolds," she snapped at me way too loud, startling the cat into abandoning the TV. "You're like that other one. My husband certainly never killed anyone. That would hurt S&B."

"What other one?"

"That snippy blonde reporter who was here last week. She was making insinuations just like you."

I felt a flash of anger, first at the sanctimonious old witch and then at Jeanne. She'd been this far along before I'd even met her and she hadn't clued me in to any of it, not even when I'd gone so far to cover for her. It put bite in my voice when I asked, "Like what did she imply? That S&B pulled something crooked to get that land claim patented?"

She jumped out of her chair steaming and started walking around the living room, enraged but very self-absorbed. On the second pass by the TV her attention lit upon the front-page photograph of me in full criminal persona. She jerked her head at me, then looked back at the photo. I knew it was over and stood up. She didn't back off. She put it on automatic pilot and shouted at me.

"You tricked me. You talking about my husband killing that Barriss. You're the killer. You get out of here. I'm calling the police."

I put on my cap and coat and maneuvered back through the maze of standing lamps. She turned the TV back on and marched over to the front door to show me out. She pulled it open and got out another cigarette.

"Do you smoke marijuana, also, Mrs. Scanlon? It's an herb-bearing seed."

Chapter Fourteen

They were waiting for me outside. Three of them got out of a plain, dark car when they saw me in the porch light. Big men. City bulls. They stood by Callahan's truck. I walked out to them. Two were new to me. The third one was McGarrity. He'd been a detective for a long time and knew his job a little better than you'd figure a dummy would. The only thing McGarrity really wanted was respect. Respect was what you gave him after he hit you with the blackjack. You were supposed to lie there quiet and bleed. That was respect. I didn't have a lot of it.

"Well, well, so we got an ex-PI creep getting out of line."

"You wearing your badge tonight, McGarrity, or is that your face? I can't quite tell."

He shined a light in my eyes. He liked my black eye so much he poked it with his flashlight.

"Where'd you get that, punk? Goddamn PI punk."

The other two drifted around behind me. They grabbed me and pushed me against the truck.

"Spread'em," one snapped at me.

"Wider," McGarrity snarled and kicked my right foot out.

McGarrity frisked me. I knew how he liked to go about it. He didn't slap you down. He checked out a pocket by punching you there. I braced for the shots, but they didn't come. He ran his hands over me and satisfied himself that I had no iron. Everything was off, way off, and the alarms started ringing in my head.

The two I didn't know walked me over to their car. They both pulled at me so I couldn't walk straight. I was shoved into the middle of the back seat between McGarrity and one of the new cops. We took off.

Nobody said anything. McGarrity didn't even threaten me with resisting arrest. The car stopped at Cushman and Gaffney. The cop next to me got out and walked over to a pay phone on the corner. He opened the door, looked around and came back to the car.

"Nothing there," he reported.

McGarrity gave me a shove and I went with it out onto the sidewalk.

"We gave you your rights," McGarrity announced and looked around at his help. They seconded him on that point. "Since you want to make a phone call, we'll let you make a phone call right now."

"I don't want to make a phone call."

"Get in that phone booth. We're holding you for the troopers. Forzano wants to talk to you."

The driver picked up the car mike and called in our location.

They shoved me over to the phone booth. As I pushed the door open and stepped in, I kept my head forward, but slid my eyes back toward McGarrity. He palmed something and slipped it into my left-hand coat pocket as I went past. I shut the door behind me.

I took the receiver off the hook with my right hand and twisted around to my right to where I could see McGarrity. I mouthed "Fuck you" at him and used the distraction to search the pocket with my left hand, out of his sight.

It was a small glassine envelope filled with a white powder. Coke, smack or maybe something else with even a stiffer hit in court. About a gram. Say five years worth. I'd just turned down some stuff and now the cops were giving it to me.

I put the receiver down on the shelf and, while I went through a charade of fishing change out of my pants, I managed to tear open the plastic and dump the powder on the floor. Forzano would get there soon. I knew that if I came out of that phone booth clean, McGarrity would take it apart to find where I'd dumped his dope. Looked down and there the little mound was, waiting for a McGarrity evidentiary discovery.

McGarrity didn't notice that I faked putting money in the coin slot. I dialed seven numbers.

The phone booth was one of those jobs with clear plastic panels on the top and solid blue panels on the bottom. I spoke my opinion of McGarrity into the empty phone and unzipped in the grand tradition. Americans have been taking a whizz in phone booths since the middle ages. I know because in a past life I used to clean them.

I had a lovely time playing my flow across the floor, watching dope dissolve into a yellow puddle, insinuating itself out under the door as I smiled brightly for the man outside the booth. I especially enjoyed whipping it back and forth, dissolving away incrimination, holding the glassine envelope beneath the lower blue panels and dosing it thoroughly with several lovely exculpatory splashes. Once I was dry, I placed the former evidence on the phone booth shelf, zipped up with my left hand, and then kept on remarking insightfully upon *Little Gidding* into the phone until Forzano pulled up in an unmarked white Chevy.

"Come on, Rezkel. Hurry it up," McGarrity said, banging on the door.

I hung up and stepped out of the phone booth. McGarrity had been about to search me, but then he saw the torn envelope on the shelf.

"Hang on a minute, Lieutenant. He left something in the phone booth," McGarrity said to Forzano, and the first smile I ever saw played across his rough, wrinkled features. He pointed and Forzano saw it also. McGarrity reached into the phone booth and picked up the envelope.

"Torn. He dumped something," McGarrity snorted. He was still smiling as he bent over to look for a pile of white powder on the floor.

McGarrity took a hilariously long time to assimilate the yellow puddle he was looking at. He stood there confused, knowing he was angry, but unable to focus in on exactly what. He straightened up and looked at the envelope he was holding. It was still wet. He flicked it down.

Forzano had it figured and was laughing at him. He asked, "What did you do? Plant a wet envelope on him? Need to wash up, Sergeant?"

McGarrity bent over and cleaned his fingers in the snow. His eyes were raging. He took a step for me. I settled into back stance and brought my hands up.

"Come on, McGarrity, try it. All you're gonna be eating is soup, cream of aspirin soup."

He wanted to, but his partners grabbed him and held him back. Forzano took my arm and pointed his thumb at his car. I went, but I kept my eyes on McGarrity the whole way.

"It's gonna be your ass, Rezkel," he rasped at me as I slammed the car door shut.

Forzano didn't head for his office. He turned onto Airport Way and floated along with the traffic. He looked worn by a hard day, but McGarrity's play had relaxed him. He was even chuckling over it. I didn't think I'd have to lie to him to make him feel good.

"You know," he said, turning to look at me with a nasty grin on his face, "I'm going to be asking that asshole for years if he's got his fingers wet lately."

"Yeah, what a phony frame job. Couldn't get me for murder so he tries smack."

"What do you mean couldn't?" Forzano snapped, changing back to ice mood in an instant. "You want to try out one of the juries we can get together around here?"

"Do we have to go through all that again? I didn't do it."

"Maybe."

"Maybe? I don't know about you, Forzano. Do you even believe the basketball scores they print in the sports pages?"

He gave me a disgusted look but kept quiet.

"Did you get my message about where I was when Barriss gained all that weight tonight?"

"I got it. That's the only thing you've done right today. Why'd you hold out on me about Dalira's sister?"

"Because she's beautiful."

"Come off it."

"Because we're close."

"Getting laid's got nothing to do with nothing. Tell me."

"How can I tell you when you don't believe anything until it comes in the third or fourth revised edition?"

"I'm waiting."

"Because I didn't think she did it. I still don't. And she didn't talk about me either. That works with me."

I remembered the night Floyd Arthur got it. I was convinced of something then and acted on it. I was right, too, only it didn't work out very well for me.

"Give me your latest version of what happened at Parsons."

"When I got to Dalira's hallway, I saw her going out the door at the far end. Her parka got hung up a second on the door latch. I called out to her, but she didn't give any sign she heard me. Then she pulled free and was gone. Everything else is exactly as I told you before. She said she saw..."

"I know what she said she saw," he interrupted. "Why don't you think she did it?"

"I believe her. And we were together earlier. We arrived at Parsons after sweet dalliance. No way she was planning to kill him. She couldn't know he'd be there alone. She couldn't know when we were going to get to Parsons. And she didn't have a knife on her."

"You know a lot about what she had on, huh?"

"Like I said, Lieutenant, we're close."

"I thought you met her for the first time the night before."

"Some of us have that gift, you know, for getting acquainted."

"You're doing great with McGarrity."

"Listen. Why do you think he ran that down? The frame wasn't just to hit me. They wanted you to look bad. You let me loose around town and here I am doing smack right under your nose. That was the play."

"I owe you a favor, you're saying, like you weren't saving your own ass, but mine," Forzano said with maximum sarcasm.

"OK. I'll give you something you can use. Scanlon's alibi for Barriss is as pathetic as his lo-ball game. Why don't you grab him and shake his tree? Thalman'll forget about backing him up if you push it, really push it."

"I'm looking plenty close at Scanlon, as close as I can. I got a casual hint from up there in the sky to keep it informal unless I get something better. That's natural with his juice. It's a funny thing, though, I got mixed signals from the big boys. Seems someone wants Scanlon sweated."

"Who?"

"Never mind."

"You got anything on the other end, where Barriss got it?"

"Maybe. You tell me something. Why did the Randolph-Lightner timekeeper at Prudhoe skip before we could talk to him, or didn't you know about that?"

I didn't even pause. I figured Scanlon to have had a hand in taking McGarrity off his leash. That meant any agreement between us was beyond the do-not-drink date.

"I heard. I don't know for sure why he left, but the guy's a jellyfish. Touch him and he quivers. Barriss and Dalira had a scam going where Dalira tripled as a Teamster, a Laborer and an Operator. He got dispatched to the Randolph-Lightner insulation job under three different names from three different halls. That's two extra pipeline paychecks a week to cut up. You might call it genuine money. But nobody can water the payroll without a tame timekeeper holding the hose. He had to be doing pretty things to the timesheets. Then Dalira turned up dead. That wasn't in the deal. The jellyfish got shook and ran."

"Why didn't you tell me about this either? You pick this up when you went through the Randolph-Lightner files?"

"That's when I stumbled onto it, but I didn't know what was what until I got to town and got a break down at the Laborers. I ran into the guy Barriss hired for a twenty to turn in a termination slip for the phony Laborer. Barriss was reducing his defensive perimeter because he saw bad weather coming. I didn't think I had to tell you about it. The tail you had on me was right across the street, wandering around the parking lot, sort of, and he saw the whole thing when I braced the guy. He did report it to you, didn't he?"

Forzano muttered something to himself in dismay. I didn't catch what he said and I didn't ask because I already knew what he thought of his help.

Forzano made a sharp turn and looped back toward town along College Road. We passed Kathryn, Rosella, Bonnie and all the rest of those side streets named after Gold Rush hookers.

"I don't think I'm arresting you tonight, Rezkel, but there is one more thing I want to know. What were you talking about with that goddamn Liz Clarke?"

The anger in his voice broke me up.

"What's so funny about that?" he demanded.

"She didn't insult your stick, did she?"

"She kicked me in the nuts is what she did and then she tried to get the city force to arrest me. Goddamn woman."

"You can't bust me anyhow because I'm doing your whole case for you. Liz told me all about the pink elephant safari Scanlon is in training for. That, and what a rat he is for running out on his wife. Want me to get you an appointment with her so she can fill you in?"

"Don't press me, Rezkel. And remember, stay in town. You aren't going back to Prudhoe, period."

By the time he dropped me downtown it was eleven-thirty. I cabbed back to Callahan's truck and drove out to the S&B development. No snow had fallen all day, but the wind was blowing ground snow into drifts across the dirt road into the work site. I hit the gas and rolled through them.

The crime lab team was done. Nobody was around. I drove right to where the D9 had been working and stopped with the headlights shining on the Cat. I pulled on my parka and got out. The temperature was down a few degrees from daytime. As I was climbing over the tracks and into the cab of the D9, the zipper pulled open letting in a swirl of cold air. I didn't bother with closing it up. Sometimes, when I get intent on things I'd rather feel the cold than let myself do anything about it.

A pack of wolves burst out howling somewhere up the Goldstream Valley. The savage cries carried a great distance across the frozen snowfields. In a thin winter for wolves, they come closer to town for food. Frightened answering howls started up from dog teams chained at several cabins on Esther Dome. Then more dogs took it up and the night was filled with their cries.

Huskies were always chained separately to their own doghouses so they wouldn't run their chains together, foul them and fall into a noisy fight. When the wolves were really starved they went after dog teams. Since the huskies couldn't reach one another, any one of them was alone against all the wolves. A pack would pick out one dog and that dog had no chance. The wolves would make the kill, grab the hind legs, stretching the dog taut against the chain, and jerk it out of its collar. Then they'd drag off the body. The wolves were fast at this because all the other dogs would be going absolutely crazy and the racket was sure to bring someone out of the cabin firing a rifle as he came.

I ignored the howls and poked around the D9. A small plate was welded to the frame next to the steering clutches. Stamped on the metal was the serial number 66A6139. I got out Phil Dalira's leather notebook and cross-checked. The same number.

That made clear how Scanlon and Barriss were pulling off their cheapo development, but I went back to the house the carpenters had been working on anyway. I burned through a deck of matches taking down the serial numbers of two generators, a compressor, a big twelve inch table saw and anything else around there that had a number on it. Those serial numbers were redundant. Asking Sharon to check them against the Randolph-Lightner equipment log was not.

I left the S&B site about twelve-forty five and drove back along Old Nenana in a quiet frenzy. Sharon lived on the other side of Fairbanks, on Gilmore Trail, a half hour drive at least. I turned left on Sheep Creek Road, right on Miller Hill, and headed toward her place.

Then the second thoughts started in. I wanted her so badly, but I was afraid to screw it up with a silly, impulsive move. I almost turned around at Yankovich, but I kept on going. I was torn between the drama of a late, late arrival and thinking it might be more prudent to be cool. I almost turned back again at Farmers' Loop, but by then I was thinking that maybe I could just be discrete, only wake her up and ask her to check all the numbers I'd collected. I drove on, alternating between entertaining conclusions based on what Sharon might turn up relating to those equipment serial numbers and playing out images of the exquisite flesh under her zigzag dress.

As the miles went by I realized that Prudhoe was a mandatory move, first thing in the morning. I tried to conclude I was doing the right thing in going to see Sharon on the night before leaving town. Didn't seem smart, but somehow inevitable. That thing she'd done with her eyebrow as we said good-bye at Tommy's came flashing back to me. It had to be an invitation.

Going out the Steese I was thinking that since I wanted her, therefore I should go knock on her door and try. I thought about the intensity of Jeanne in the tugboat. That thrill had found its moment, but hadn't worked out so well. Then I remembered how awkward it had been trying to check out Lori's parka after a spontaneous late night arrival. I almost turned around again. Almost, but through what I considered to be cold and stark analysis I concluded that only Phil's death that had tangled everything up.

So I kept going and made the turn onto Gilmore Trail, asking myself why had I taken down all those equipment serial numbers if not to have Sharon check them out for me. After splashing the headlights on several mailboxes I found hers. I turned part way into the driveway and then stopped. I didn't want to blow it by turning up way late. I started beating up myself for not having tried a phone call. I could have told her I was sorry to wake her, told her how interesting she was, asked her to check out those serial numbers, then told her about these rare sensations she produced in me and then maybe someplace right in the middle of that she'd invite me over, right then. It seemed so discrete.

I turned the pickup around and drove back to Fairbanks, calculating a route to the nearest pay phone. At one-forty I pulled up to a phone booth and took another look at the slip of paper she'd given me. I read it and then just sat there, my heart out-revving the engine, wanting to call but afraid it would be too stupid. Finally, I put the truck back in gear and drove home, perfectly miserable.

I got there well after two. Wolves were howling again and that started up Annie's dogs. Anything and everything started them up. The stove hadn't burned for days and inside my cabin the temperature was fifteen below. There was no point to building a fire. I undressed and hit the sheets. They were fifteen below also. I thrashed and kicked about, warming up one small part of the bed. It was cold wherever I moved, so I lay still and slid down the long spiral into sleep.

Chapter Fifteen

In the morning I rolled the Toyota down the driveway to get it started and headed for town. It was warmer overnight. The First National Bank read minus nine. After a plateful of the Arctic Pancake version of blueberry waffles and four cups of Matte Orange Spice, I went and phoned Sharon at work.

"Why didn't you come see me later? I was hoping you would," she said.

"Well, I almost got there," I told her and kicked the phone booth door in frustration, wondering why I got those things wrong so much of the time.

"So, when?"

"I want to, but I can't right now. I have to go to Prudhoe today."

"I thought that trooper had you grounded."

"Don't take that too seriously. I have to go and then I want to see you when I get back."

"Mmmm," she hummed into the phone.

190

I savored that a moment, then shut out such thoughts and launched into an explanation of my theory about the serial numbers, read them off, especially the D9 number, and asked her to confirm whether Scanlon and Barriss had been using Randolph-Lightner equipment that Scanlon and Barriss were using for a bit of private enterprise. I told her I'd call later and then we lingered through good-byes.

I drifted over to the Laborers Hall for nine-thirty call. The place was packed. Four hundred men and a few ladies. Old-timers told me that there used to be zero women. The Equal Opportunity laws did wonders for 942 social life.

In '74 the pipeline had gotten off to a delightfully bumbling start that created the impression easy money would last forever. Megabucks seemed a permanent fact of life. If you were on the A List, any day at all you could take a job paying fifteen hundred a week, maybe better. If the job wasn't spiritually suitable or if the cook couldn't get your poached eggs right, then you could drag up, let them pay you another four hours travel time back to town and get another job the next day.

Construction went straight on, but by the second winter Uncle Oil had learned how to assert its power. The calls turned to trash in November. People started remembering how tough it could be to be broke in Fairbanks, especially with snow on the ground. The Hall was filled with Laborers down to their case bucks and looking for a soft cushion, or even any sort of cushion. The place was itchy. That's why an outdoor insulation gig at Prodrude had looked good enough the week before to burn my number on.

191

I worked my way through the crowd and nodded hello to a dozen of my fellow union hands. I was getting pointed out by nods and whispers, so I didn't stop to talk to anyone. Callahan was standing in the back with two friends. They were laughing at a tall blonde lady who was swearing at the Coke machine and kicking it with her bunny boots. I gave Callahan back his truck keys and arranged communications with him. Several guys moved in around us and I did a brief exposition of the Theory of Rezkel's Innocence.

Sam Whitaker appeared in the dispatch booth and blasted out too loud over the speaker system, "Now listen up, this is what we got today." He always started out too loud. No touch with the volume control. The buzz kept on as everyone ignored Whitaker while finishing their remarks. He came on again, with the volume lower. "Hold it down. I'm only gonna read this one time."

The crowd stopped talking and bunched in closer.

"Livingston needs two general laborers at Happy Valley, seven tens indefinite. One general laborer for National at Prudhoe, seven tens, two weeks R&R replacement. One general laborer for Jameson-Falcon at Franklin Bluffs, seven tens, two weeks, maintenance. Spencer-Halwell needs two drillers at Delta, seven tens indefinite. That's air track and I don't want any chuck tender heroes trying to fake the air track."

A mixed chorus of boos and cheers stopped him. He let it settle down and continued on in a hoarse voice.

"And we got to have one stud for the pipe yard, for BCI, seven tens, maybe twelves, ten days. He's gonna be a pipe cleaner and they want someone healthy. At least you gotta start out that way. How you come out the other end of those pipes is your own business. And Chena Building Block needs one general laborer, six nines. That's it. One to one hundred on the A List."

A groan surged through the room and the crowd ebbed back from the dispatch window. Some hurried out the door, but most eased along with the crush, muttering and complaining all the way to the sidewalk. A few elbowed forward against the tide with all the moral fervor of a low number on the A List. I went with them.

The Hall was emptying quickly. Those who stuck around broke up into small groups to bitch about the skinny call. Two dozen Labes jammed into the space in front of the dispatch window. I waited at the back of that snarl as the really low numbers picked out the best jobs. The four calls for an indefinite period went first. The last of those was nailed by an old timer with number seventy-one. Most of the elite low number crowd were holding off for an ultimo perfecto job to spend that low number on.

Whitaker picked up the mike again and said, "One hundred to two hundred on the A List." I pushed forward, but I couldn't get all the way up to the counter before the window. The jobs left likely weren't worth a number that low, but five guys occupied the counter anyway.

"What you got left for line jobs?" one of them asked Whitaker.

"There's only that Franklin Bluffs call for Jameson-Falcon, two weeks," the dispatcher told him.

"I'll take it," said a man at the counter. I'm one-seventy-four."

Whitaker reached for the book and started to look up the guy's number.

"Hey," I let out in my heavy voice, "I'm one sixty-nine. I want that job."

I pushed a hand through to the counter and wedged the rest of me into the front rank. One-seventy-four glared at me and made the least possible room. Maybe he knew something dirty about that call, being so taken with it. I was sideways to the window. I turned in and pushed all of them over. Just your basic Social Darwinism.

Whitaker was looking up my number. When he got to my name, he looked up and said, "Hello Rezkel, I thought you were in jail."

"That was temporary. They musta thought vigilantes would work cheaper than the state executioner."

"Somebody might do it for free," a guy muttered behind me.

"You thinking the Teamsters can't find you at Franklin?" Whitaker laughed.

"Well Sam, I figure a fugitive should be well paid."

I signed the dispatch slip and left. Cash For Your Stash was right up Barnette. I made a quick stop and got my .357 out of their care. They hit me for $35, ten of that being two months interest. The gun was a Ruger 6-1/2 inch barrel six round cheapie that I picked up for $75 before the pipeline. That's a crappy gun, surely too small for bear, but I liked having it in the glove compartment. I broke open the loading gate and slipped in six rounds. I gave the cylinder a spin for luck and put it away. It may have been a dishrag as guns went, but I took care of it and it had come through for me both times I'd had to pull the trigger.

Bureaucrats took me prisoner after that. At the Jameson-Falcon Construction office on Dale Road I submitted to torture by paperwork. Eventually, they issued me a travel voucher and sent me off to obtain a badge from pipeline headquarters at Fort Wainwright on the other side of town. That place used to be a full time fort before the oil companies used their stroke to take it over. Back in prehistoric time I had myself been a defender of the Republic stationed there.

In the basement of Haines Hall they were running a small group through the orientation session required before your first pipeline job. That was good duty. The first day on the job was spent listening to speakers who had never been there tell you all about it. They showed movies and topped it off with a lecture on cold weather survival by some guy from Daytona Beach who only went outside to get in his car. Eight hours pay for four hours listening. Got them used to the cost-plus approach.

I'd already been oriented and only needed to get badged. A sleepy clerk typed up my vital stats, took a quick Polaroid and handed me a Trans Alaska Pipeline System badge, still hot from the plasticizer machine and that qualified me for work. I drove out to the airport, freezing because I had to keep the window down as usual, and put the Toyota in the parking lot.

The airport play was two hours of hiding out in a crowd. I walked part way down to the Wien Air Alaska counter and saw that a managerial type was indeed casing the passengers checking in for the next Prudhoe Bay flight.

The pipeline had swamped Wien. Their flights to the camps were being handled away from the main counter at temporary quarters in the middle of the terminal. Twenty or thirty workers built up a mound of suitcases, duffel bags and Arctic gear in front of the line camps counter. The seats were all taken. I lay down on the floor among all the gear, put a stocking cap over my face and got in a low profile nap until flight time.

They hardly looked at my papers and accepted my tale that I had no luggage because I was returning from R&R. I did have all the winter clothing required to board the plane. The Wien manager was doing as he promised Forzano, checking the Prudhoe flights, only he didn't think about me making an end run. I got on the 727 no problem.

We flew north over the birch and spruce forest. The land was flat with occasional hills. The flight was a local that served several pipeline camps. First stop was just north of the frozen Yukon River at Five Mile Camp. Several men and a woman bundled up in parkas and bunny boots trooped down the aisle and off the plane. We took off again and flew on north. First the birch and then the spruce trees thinned out as we approached the Brooks Range. And then even the spruce were gone as treeless rugged mountains stretched to the horizon east and west.

We landed again in the northern fringe of the Brooks, at Galbraith Lake, and another group deplaned. The bald mountains descended into the rolling tundra-covered hills of the North Slope. The plane flew on further over snow-fields and increasing ice fog. We landed for the last time at Happy Valley Camp, a hundred miles south of Prudhoe, and the half dozen of us left got off there.

A bus and a crew cab were parked by a small tower. The others were all going to be working at Happy. They got on the bus. I walked over to the crew cab. The Teamster behind the wheel looked pissed. He was slouched down in the seat talking to himself and stabbing the air with his index finger. I went around to the passenger side and got in. He went still.

"Nick Rezkel, for Jameson-Falcon. You came down from Franklin to pick me up, right?"

He nodded. I wondered if he spoke with others or only himself.

"Let's go."

"What about your gear? They haven't unloaded the plane yet."

"Wien screwed up. They said they'd get it in tomorrow. That means Monday, but I'm OK till then."

He shoved it in gear and took off, but he was unhappy and felt inconvenienced. Even with a slow motion drive to Franklin, we'd get there at four-thirty. Quitting time wouldn't be until five-thirty and his foreman might think up something else for him to do. He'd probably been counting on a lingering coffee break at Happy and later giving his foreman a riff about how the plane was late, maybe getting to Franklin after five-thirty and promoting some overtime out of the deal.

A steady north wind tossed around the ground snow and fuzzed everything out at a hundred yards. Small shrubs grew here and there, most only a few inches high. In sheltered draws some monsters got up to two feet tall. The pipeline ran beside the road in places, sitting up on supports all bright and shiny. I saw a solitary caribou pawing at the frozen ground. Very skinny. Most migrated south. This one was crippled and never would have kept up with the herd. Scratching through snow for grass was better than running the gauntlet of wolves.

The driver was quiet the whole way, but his left hand kept slipping off the wheel to make points that never quite coalesced into words. I asked him how long he'd been on the Slope. He muttered an indistinct sound that I took to indicate that he'd already been there forever and wasn't planning on leaving.

The sun was down and the lights were on when we pulled into Franklin Bluffs. Two beautiful white Arctic foxes were trotting across the enormous parking lot. The camp was laid out like Parsons, only bigger. A central hallway ran on for several hundred yards, with fifty-two man trailers projecting out both sides. Assorted shops were placed behind the main complex.

Franklin had housed fifteen-hundred workers a few months earlier, but the northern section of the pipeline had been built as far south as Happy Valley and now Franklin was shuttered, except for a skeleton crew.

My driver stopped beside the main entrance and sat behind the wheel with heroic patience as I got out. I waved to him and said, "Have a nice chat."

I went inside and considered the situation. It was another forty-five miles to Prudhoe. There were two ways to get there. I could rip off one of the trucks idling outside or I could hitchhike. If the place had been full, I would have grabbed the best truck and figured they never would have known who took it. With only thirty maintenance hands in camp, however, they'd be onto to me from the start. They wouldn't have a chance to stop me, but they would surely get enough noise into the system to hang me up someplace. I also didn't want to burn down my prospects with Jameson-Falcon Construction unless I had to, so I decided to give my thumb a chance. I reported in at the Jameson-Falcon office to cover myself.

There were rooms of desks, filing cabinets and enough office paraphernalia to fake running a large camp, but only one person was in the office complex. The timekeeper. He was waiting to get me checked in so he could slink off for the day. He was six-three and slender with an odd beer belly that started its bulge very low, down by his belt, and then mounded out at a terrific slope. He had a thin face with thin features, light blond hair, tiny blue eyes and pale skin that made me think he lived in a root cellar. He came away from the window and walked with his nose in the air over to a desk. I remained mystified where timekeepers got their notion of personal superiority.

"You're the new Laborer. You're late, but I suppose that's not entirely your fault. Fill this out," he said in a flat, dull voice with sufficient space between each word for a teaspoon of condescension.

I took the W4 form and sat down at the next desk. He hummed and curled his lower lip under his front teeth as he flicked through a notebook. He was sitting there with his pencil poised like a puff adder, ready to strike in one forty-seventh of a second. He stopped on a worn page, noted my job classification, and said half-aloud, "They're bringing in so many unskilled workers it's a wonder anything ever gets built."

I was trying to get along and do the quiet thing, so I could be off to Prudhoe, but I didn't like the guy, even before that crack. I wasn't fond of timekeepers as a genre to start with and this one looked like he hadn't been outdoors for months. He probably thought his double-knit slacks and short sleeve Banlon were the only clothes anyone needed to work the line. All my complaints against timekeepers began running through my head. I was about to write down on the W4 that I had seventy-eight dependents, just to bug him and get an argument started. I held back the urge and prevented any loosure of cool. I simply handed him the form.

A copy of *Oui* in his inbox, open to the centerfold which had such a discrete photo of a petulant and very young harem girl, with a gold nugget in her navel, chained to a bed by gold bracelets. She had a slim figure with small breasts radiating an aura of "touch me and I'll grow." I suddenly thought of a former Alaskan with that taste in women, a guy named Axel Larston, which led me back to a remembrance of the way Floyd Arthur opened his wallet so secretively in the Gold Room at Thalman's on the night he died. A wave of pained realization washed over me. For all I'd learned about what Floyd did that night, all I'd checked out and tracked down, I'd never considered what he hadn't done. I knew I had to check out Axel again. He was an old friend of Floyd's. Seeing that harem girl clicked it for me. Axel had left Fairbanks for good that night. He was in the air flying to LA when Floyd caught it, so he was clear himself. That much I'd verified six different ways, but what now hit me was that I could not place him together with Floyd at any time that night. They had known each other too well, I suddenly appreciated, not to have said good-bye on Axel's last night in town.

I'd stopped looking at Axel once I knew he couldn't have been involved. I knew who gunned Floyd. That was Lou Devery, but I never should have ignored Axel just because he was far away. There was a time that night I couldn't account for. I knew that if I could only learn about what happened then, I'd know who put Devery to up to it.

The timekeeper handed me a room key and told me to report for work at seven in the morning. I took a right at the main hallway and went down to my room. The long corridor was wide enough for two fights at a time, but it was very empty. Loitering in public places the last hour of the workday was bad form. All hands had retired to their rooms for private meditation with their favorite sins.

My new roommate wasn't around. I mussed the bed and wrote a note that I had gotten sick and taken a ride back to Happy Valley to get the next plane to town. It didn't look real convincing, but I hoped it might scrape by if I ever needed work with Jameson-Falcon again.

The phone booth was off the mess hall. A felt tip message on the wall read, "Circus Today, Suitcase Parade Tomorrow," commemorating a famous riot by the 798ers over whether they'd get steak for both breakfast and lunch, as well as dinner, and other constitutional issues. I tried LA information for Axel Larston, but got shutout. I didn't want to get hung up trying to find Axel by phone so I called a pro, Billy Osborne. He was a PI operating out of a nice office in Manhattan Beach, and he was the best solo investigator in LA, whether you wanted a high post offense or a quick fast break game.

Billy had the judgment to be a Celtic fan, but his character was debased by an attachment to the fortunes of the UCLA Bruins. He put up an aggressive defense against accepting the charges, but the operator wore him down.

"Nick, why do Alaskans always call collect?"

"Charm, Billy, and a bush league phone system."

"Well? You trying to get something down on the playoffs?"

"Actually, I'm calling about a trivial murder. Nothing apocalyptic like basketball. I want you to find a guy for me."

"Great. I remember the last one I found for you. A real unfriendly hick. I especially remember his two friends with axes in their hands."

"Come off it. You owe me one."

"Sure, I owe you one. I owe you three, but you owe me five."

"Billy, this is too easy. Your landlord could do it. I got to talk to an Alaskan expatriate named Axel Larston."

202

"Let me guess. You have no idea where he is?"

"Adversity toughens and the way you work, you could do with some. Now, Axel moved down there two years ago. He's five-ten, roly poly, light brown hair, brown eyes, blando face, dresses loud. He's got acute gold fever and lots of money because of it. He will definitely be thinking gold, talking gold, wearing gold, hustling gold. He'd still be up here bobbing and weaving around gold claims if he wasn't so entranced with teenage hookers. There is nothing Axel likes better than young girls. LA is his paradise. He'll be around."

"OK. I gotta do something. The Celtics have been killing me. How much are you paying me?"

"Your usual rates, in trade."

"In trade? You aren't even in the trade anymore."

"Billy, this is a snap. It can't amount to anything at any rates. All I want is for you to get me and Axel on the phone together. By tomorrow night, at your place."

"What's Axel going to think about this?"

"Tell him it's for Floyd and he'll drop anything, absolutely anything."

"Even if she's already taken off her pants?"

"That's right."

"How about some advance green? I might have to try out a lot of young strumpets before I come up with the right one."

"No time for play. This has to happen by tomorrow night."

"Christ, Raz, I suppose you also want me to play it very light, keep things according to British Open protocol?"

"Do it your own way, Billy. West Coast improvisational."

I tried Callahan, but he wasn't at a phone yet.

On the way down the empty Arctic hallway, I saw the factor chalked on the weatherboard—minus seventy-four off a straight minus thirty-nine degrees with a fifteen mile per hour wind. I changed socks and shoved the old pair into my coat pocket. Had to keep the feet dry for that factor. I zipped up, pulled down the stocking cap over my face and went out the doors. The cold hit like the concussion from an incoming 155 round. I cocked my head away from the wind and trudged out to the road. The camp lights disappeared into the ice fog.

I couldn't see the bluffs, but I could feel their effect. They funneled the wind coming down from Prudhoe so it blew steadily out of the north-northwest. I stood with my back to it looking in the direction of my hypothetical ride. Evidently my karma called for me to live out a certain number of hours standing by the road with my thumb out. I was filling out the total. My breath immediately started freezing my beard to my stocking cap and tried to attach an icicle to the front of my coat. I broke it free. No headlights were coming out of the dark and it kept getting colder.

Standing straight with my hands at my sides I focused on kata. I stepped out into Sochin stance, made the first double block and continued through the sequence. I was clumsy in Arctic gear, but it felt good to be alone with an imaginary opponent with just the fighting. Much as I could keep it up, that is. Several times when I made turns into the wind my concentration broke and I fell back into merely making movements. Occasionally I was distracted into noticing that my sleeves had pulled up and freezing air was leaking in. Once I saw a hand with a bloody knife slashing at me. With a surge I moved out of its course and locked down a block, the best karate moment of the entire session.

Headlights appeared after the fourth run through Sochin. I was convinced the rig would stop, but I held up my thumb anyway, like the good hitchhiker. The pickup churned along at thirty-five and went right on past with a blast from the horn. My arm jerked up and I gave them the finger through my mittens. Lousy roadflex. Worse karate. It was illegal in Alaska to pass up a hitchhiker at thirty below or colder. Happened all the time. The only law that works right is the law of gravity.

I returned to kata. After twelve Sochin a line driver with a load of Cat parts hauled his White Freightliner down for me. I ran up to where he got it stopped and climbed aboard. The hot cab was a rush. The driver was a good old boy with a Kentucky fried mind. As he worked up through the gears, he asked me what I was doing out there. I told him I was going to Prudhoe to get laid. That explained enough for his satisfaction. Afterwards, we didn't talk much, so he cranked up the volume on a Jerry Jeff Walker tape and rolled it.

A few miles down the road he offered me a hit of speed out of a bottle of brains he kept in his coat pocket. I passed. I never had liked those tableted highs. They only got you buzzy, a thin and pointless imitation of the cocaine high. I remembered some of my excessive paeans to the thrill of toot, which had been delivered complete with counterpart denunciations of the mere retrograde speed experience. Sitting in the cab of that eighteen wheeler, I felt an embarrassed clench contemplating the silliness of certain easy ecstasies in the past. Cocaine and speed finally felt too much alike, just two dragged out drugs that wired your head and got in your way.

None of that afflicted the line driver. He washed down two white pills with a Schlitz and chuckled to himself all the way to Pudhole Bay.

Prudhoe Bay

Chapter Sixteen

I got out at Crazyhorse. Atco trailers were crammed into the least possible space, basically pipeline frenetic, but as a somewhat obscure camp, a minor chord of placidity lingered about. I went into the mess hall for dinner. The usual sign-up sheet for visitors was on a small pedestal. Those things you could walk past and ignore. With all the turnover in the camps they couldn't keep track of unauthorized strangers. I stopped and signed in anyway. H. Scanlon, Randolph-Lightner Construction. Most of the contractors were on cost-plus and a meal was that much more free money. Randolph-Lightner had a hard dollar contract so they wouldn't like it. I figured they owed me an expense account.

An under-assistant cook with eyes like radishes and blurry tattoos on his arms was going down the steam counter hitting everything with bacon bits left over from breakfast. He tossed a handful each into the boiled potatoes, the peas, the lima beans, the corn bread, the pork chops, the steaks and both green salads. He froze over an American flag desert, red and blue jello stripes with white whipping cream stars. His hand hovered, loaded with bacon bits. At the last second he spared the flag and moved on, sprinkling the apple pie, the pumpkin pie, the cherry pie.

I saw two guys I knew from other jobs, but I sat away from them and was not noticed. After dinner, I went to the phone booths and called Sharon at home. She answered in a sexy voice that made me want to tear the phone off the wall.

"Hello beautiful, greetings from Prudhoe."

"Well, a compliment from the man who ducked out on our first date. What are you doing, chasing Jeanne Dalira?" she teased me.

"Partly, but not for the same reason I started out doing that. You know I didn't want to leave last night."

We shared a silence. I felt myself starting to nod my head, agreeing to some secret promise with her.

"There's something I've been wondering about," she said. "Remember at Tommy's, when Stephen spread his cocaine on the table. Well, did you really feel like snorting up? That first time?"

Pause.

"Not really. I've been getting sour on that stuff. I was trying to decipher if you wanted to. Finally, I was unsure, so I went ahead and did it."

"That's exactly what I was doing, trying to figure you out. I thought I was better at it."

"You do it very well."

"Maybe. Later, when you came back from that phone call and," she paused, "that encounter, I thought you were absolutely decided you weren't interested in tooting up, period. That's true isn't it?"

"A bingo."

"Just checking, Nick. I like to know when I'm right about someone. Anyway. I have sordid news for you. That D9 Cat and every other piece of equipment on that list you gave me was stolen from Barner Oil last April. Randolph-Lightner was using all of it at the time, on a cost-plus contract at Fort Wainwright."

"Excellent."

"You like thievery?"

"I can appreciate that your bosses are conducting a clinic on revolutionary finance with their development. And the names?"

"They all work for Randolph-Lightner, at Livingood, supposedly."

"You see, I'm not a complete washout. You've got some splendid gossip to lay on Hilda."

"Maybe that's all you're good for."

"Let's find out as soon as I get back."

A plumber stepped into the next booth as I hung up. I knew his trade by his soft polka dot cap, worn backwards, and the polka dot bandana down around his neck like Jesse James between holdups. He got through to the operator right off, while I collected a series of busy signals. I listened in as he bragged to his wife that he'd beaten Barner out of ninety-six easy dollars by shutting down a room furnace when he came in from work. After the rooms on either side had chilled off enough for the occupants to complain to the front desk, he was called out to deal with the situation. It only took him seconds to get the furnace running again, but under the contract an after-hours callout was an automatic four hours pay. Meanwhile, after twenty tries I got my call placed, only Callahan still wasn't around.

I went outside to select my wheels. Before the pipeline I'd never once stolen a motor vehicle, except for a trivial episode which doesn't count. The pipeline gave me a new perspective on transportation. Take what you need.

I worked my way along a row of powder-blue Livingston Construction International pickups and crew cabs, but each one was locked up and plugged in. Temptation appeared in the form of a yellow Spencer-Halwell pickup parked there idling and unlocked, but I knew that they had no workers at Crazyhorse. That truck represented a personal pleasure excursion. I wasn't going to interfere. The guy could get stranded at Crazy, not get the foreman's truck back and lose his job. I passed and went around to the shops behind camp.

A newish Livingston pickup idled beside the auto shop. I thought it had a certain élan and was rather a nicer powder-blue than the ordinary LCI rig. I got in and quietly eased it away from the building. The clutch was sickly, but everything vaguely worked and it had a full tank of gas.

I drove the mile up to where Randolph-Lightner had insulation stored on a gravel pad. A hundred crates were neatly stacked two high. There was also a collection of smashed crates that had not thrived on the barge run into

Prudhoe. A snarl of loose pieces was piled up in front of them. I drove down the rows and played the headlights on the crate numbers. It was going to get messy and I wanted as much evidence that Scanlon and Barriss had been cheating as I could get my hands on. I hoped to find some crates that were listed as defective and therefore destroyed. No such luck, so I drove over to Parsons.

I parked behind trailer twelve and walked the few steps to Spacey Acey's room. He was in. When he opened the door and saw me, his face shriveled into an ingratiating quasi-smile. He transformed himself into a completely inoffensive being. He even looked embarrassed that his wing tip shoes were so shiny.

"Hi, Nick," he choked out, retreating back as I came through the door and shut it behind me. No roommate. He gave me another nervous grin and said, "Good to see you. Hope they didn't hassle you too bad."

I looked silently at him.

"Hey, Nick, you know I didn't ever think you killed Phil. I got scared, you see. I had to call security," he squeaked, his voice thinning out.

"Don't worry about it, Spacey. I know that what you think is out of your control. Just relax."

He didn't relax. He shrank back.

"There's a couple things you didn't tell the cops, Spacey. That's good. Now when you tell me, I'll be the only one who knows. Right?"

"Right, Nick. Right."

"How much coke was Phil buying from you?"

"Oh, nothing special," he said, "a gram every week or so."

I stepped over very close to him and stood almost on top of his wing tips. He edged back against the desk.

"Tilt."

"Uh, he bought more than that, Nick."

"How much?"

"Don't get the wrong idea here. I sold him an ounce every now and then."

"Now and then?"

"Pretty steady, actually."

I gave him the least shove and he half sat down on the desk. I was too close for him to be able to sit all the way down on it. He was suspended half on and half off the desk, with more strain on his back and stomach than he was used to.

"How steady?"

"Every week, plus another four ounces whenever his sister was ready."

"You sold to his sister?"

"No. He wouldn't let me. He wanted that action for himself. She was always on him to get me to turn her on to someone in town. I didn't like that idea any better than Phil did. She didn't have anything else set up, so she had to fly up here to score."

"So you knew she'd get here sometime Tuesday night?"

"Yeah, she was picking up a load, only Phil was dead by the time she got here. I saw her in the crowd outside in the hallway and she told me. After things quieted down I sold her four ounces for seven thousand. She liked my price better than Phil's."

"I'm not surprised. How much are you out over Phil getting it?"

"Nothing. I already sold it to him, so his stash got ripped, not mine."

"Did you know Barriss?" I asked and he went ashen.

"I knew him. Phil was always telling me about how he had the hammer on his super. He didn't say why, but he told me Barriss couldn't touch him. He bragged about what a great gram-dealing setup he had going. Hey, Nick," he grunted, trying to ease off the desk, "how about letting me up. I'm telling you all I know."

I stood where I was.

"Did you see Barriss here Tuesday night?"

"Yeah, in the Rec Room before you, uh, before Phil got killed."

"You tell the troopers?"

"They never asked me."

"Why was Barriss here?"

"Come on, man. I don't know why. Let me up. I don't know. Phil only said he was coming over," Spacey said very rapidly.

I stepped back. He was ready to talk to me.

"That's why I went to the movie with Lori."

"What do you mean with Lori?"

"Well, she came over with Phil. He wanted to talk to Barriss alone, so we went to the Rec Room to watch a John Wayne movie."

"Was she there the whole time?"

215

"Yeah. Next seat. I checked her out. You know what she looks like."

"Why didn't Phil talk to Barriss on the job?"

"I don't know any of that stuff. Nothing. He only laughed about how he had Barriss doing anything he wanted. Said he was too busy to stay at CC2. He had to pick up his ounce and the four for Jeanne, see. Something had just come up, he said, and starting right then Barriss was going to be his trained seal."

"Was Phil expecting anyone else?"

"No. Jeanne was only coming because she was dry. Phil dealt a little off here at Parsons, but he didn't let them know where he scored. Like he didn't turn Jeanne on to me, until he had to one day when there wasn't enough time to connect from me and keep her in the dark before her flight. Nobody else knew he was here, except my roommate and he don't know nothing except he likes to toot up."

I went over it again with Spacey and concluded he was telling me a workable version of the truth. He was definite that there had been no knife capable of doing Phil in that room and he told me that Phil didn't have one on him. Altogether, Lori was out, but Barriss, Jeanne, and perhaps even Tyson were still in.

Spacey got very solicitous about my relations with the cops, especially since he didn't want to get mentioned any more. I didn't give him any promises. On the other hand, I didn't bother making him tell me he got his coke from Thalman. The only other thing of interest that he mentioned was that they shipped it up to him in dummy fire extinguishers. I made a mental note to use that when I write *The Illustrated History of Smuggling.*

I drove over to the far side of Prudhoe and checked the other places where Randolph-Lightner had insulation crates stored, but both B and N Pads were clean. I pulled into the back entrance to CC2 about nine-thirty. No outlets were free, so I parked the LCI truck behind D Wing and left it running.

I didn't run into anyone going up the stairs or along the second-floor C Wing corridor. I knocked on Allen's door.

"Cheers, Allen, how's the pleasure level?"

"Nick, come in. Fleeing the state? Across the ice to Norway?"

"No, I came up to catch the rays. Do some foundation work on my tan."

"Kick back. I'll pour something wet."

I got out of my coveralls and coat, then pulled the felt out of my Sorels and put them on a wall locker to dry. The front half of the room was vacant.

"What happened to your roommate?"

"That bumpkin was considerate enough to drag up. May this private suite stay private a while longer."

Allen handed me a glass of white wine, moving with a gangly ease somewhere between graceful and awkward. He flopped down on the bed and leaned against a huge pile of pillows. I rocked back in the chair and put my feet up on the desk. Vivaldi was playing on the tape deck. The strain of travel in a steep chill factor faded away. I savored the warmth, the wine, the pleasure of his company and marveled over the contrast between his relaxed mood and his frenzy as he licked the rug two mornings before.

Allen was not convinced that he should be doing anything so secular as laborizing on the pipeline. He was in continual emotional flux over a lady back in Philadelphia, wondering if gathering vast petrodollar riches was blowing his relationship with her, wondering if his budding real estate empire was worth it. He did the telephone lines like he did cocaine lines. The man was no stranger to thousand dollar phone bills as he tortured himself trying to make up his mind to leave.

His foreman was setting him up as Public Enemy Number One on the crew and Allen was in partial collaboration with the effort. His cush indoor job was in peril, but he constantly told me that it could be for the best if they made his decision for him.

"The man figure out how to fire you yet?"

"Praise the local, brother. The Black Knight will have to take the long way round to can me. I might have helped him out today, though. He came down on my broomsmanship. Told me my sweeping wasn't up to code. I said, 'Sue me for malpractice, muthafucker.' That was the best moment of the day. He ran right off to report me to the General Foreman."

"You no longer care?"

"I don't know. Let'em do me a favor and run me off. Meanwhile, I'll take their money and insult the Black Knight for the hell of it."

"How's Jack doing?"

"He got his rug wet again. Claims we missed a lot of toot the other day."

I laughed, but I felt a twinge of embarrassment over that eye-dropper shot.

"The yellows and purples around your eye are blossoming rather nicely," Allen remarked in his musical voice. "Are lurid colors coming out in your reputation as well?"

"The press has seen to that. The real problem is that I'm running behind events in this tangle. I have to get this end sorted out and hope that a shortcut develops. It's complicated because I get recognized."

"You're famous around here, even with all the talk about the Denali and who's going to connect with the bucks. You were cooling off some, but then Barriss ate it and now you're back to the top of the charts."

"Wonderful. What time does the Denali happen?"

"Six-thirty, tomorrow night. They're holding the formalities in the break room. Luke has been signing them up like crazy. There's over ninety-five thou already. Luke digs it. Lori goes around with him. She flashes those great tits and guys start waving hundred dollar bills in the air."

"No wonder. With five thousand deranged workers up here, the right guy could sell used rubbers."

"Speaking of the persuasive, Daniel Callahan called and dictated a message for you. It's on the desk."

I let the message wait an interval, luxuriating in the opportunity to go slow and attend to the comforts of the flesh. My chair was tipped back on two legs. Holding onto the desk with my right hand I rocked onto one leg only and was just able to reach the wine bottle. I filled our glasses and returned to the stability of a two leg position. Then I read the note.

All your debts are cancelled. This Nancy is a supernova bonus. She says Jeanne and Phil were lovers. Very much past tense. They remained cocaine partners, though with mutual suspicion. Nancy thought it a charming case of applied incest until tonight at the Howling Dog. The God of Drunks smiled upon us and we met one of her old friends who said she knew Jeanne when Jeanne first hit Alaska. She was not Phil Dalira's sister then. Another name—unremembered. Maybe on the run from something. Nancy and I are fleeing to Tahiti tonight, unless we score another gram.

"Good news for Callahan," Allen said slowly, looking for a reaction, "but how about you?"

"It helps and it hurts. I was with Jeanne Tuesday evening. We got close too fast and we didn't get close enough. I went a long way to keep her out of this, only she's not out and neither am I. Maybe it had to be fast or not at all. I was probably thinking outside my brain the whole time. Anyway, I guess I got over her yesterday."

"Did she kill Phil?"

"Maybe she's capable of it. She had the chance. I can't see any reason why and she does things for a reason, as far as I've seen. She didn't have a knife and I don't see how she could have come up with one so fast, unless she was intending to kill him. But that doesn't fit. I was with her just before. She was distracted, but not in any sort of rage, hot or cold.

"Then, there's Barriss. I can get it to fit ninety percent that he took out Phil. I'd like it to fit, but I'm not going to fudge that other ten percent. There's still a chance it could have been Scanlon, but that hardly fits at all. No one else makes any sense, except to those cops who have me holding the knife."

"Callahan told me on the phone about your ice cold alibi for Barriss. Doesn't that tend to clear you for Phil also?"

"With the troopers it does, as far as it goes, but there are city bulls who want to break my fingers to make sure I don't pick my nose."

"What do they care about it? Neither one happened in their jurisdiction."

"Who killed Phil Dalira is off the point. The real problem is that too many things trace back to the night a guy named Floyd Arthur got tapped out."

Allen looked at me, knowing that was one of my least favorite topics. I paused a moment, roving my eyes over the Caribbean posters on the walls while the old anger flared up and then faded. Allen sipped his wine, waiting for me, and then he seemed to know that I finally did want to talk it all out. He asked me what happened that night and out it all came.

"I'm working on it. What I know is that someone showed a cheap hood named Lou Devery how to set up Floyd. Devery did and then he erased him with a .45. You know Thalman's card joint on Fourth?"

"Between Cushman and Lacey?"

I nodded.

221

"I've been there for the local color, but I didn't trust the games enough to partake, not that I know anything about poker."

The tape ended. Allen flipped it over and turned down the volume. He scrunched back on the pillows and I continued.

"It was a slow Thursday night two years ago. I was playing in the big game—five-hundred dollar change in, dealer's choice, table stakes, mostly lo-ball. I had it beat for a couple hundred, but it was no berry patch and had a dismal future.

"A houseman named Vero was running the game for Thalman. He used to be a top card thief. He hustled joints all over the West Coast. The bottle broke him down a hundred times. He finally kicked it and Thalman gave him a job. Anyway, he doesn't move with a deck anymore. He's become a good player, now that he no longer relies on his fingers to help him out. Even worse, he's careful with the house money. And Roland J. Kirby was in the game, with the biggest stack of chips at the table. You know him?"

"The one with all the stroke and the famous dog team?" Allen asked.

I nodded.

"Yet another Man of the People," Allen mocked.

"Definitely. He hired one of the people to put together his team and handle the dogs, while Roland J. takes the credit. I guess he thinks it helps with the outdoor vote. As a poker player, Kirby is damn good. He's extra dangerous

222

because he plays stack poker. He's not just trying to win, he's after your whole stack of chips. He wants them all.

"Hal Scanlon was at the table. He was a shit player, but he wasn't especially drinking in those days and he certainly wasn't tossing away money to see which way the wind was blowing.

"This guy Shakin' John had a seat. He was tight and he played a sound game. And a bartender at the Mecca was in the game. Guy named Joey, dense, but very careful. The seventh player was a furniture salesman from Nerlands. He thought coming up with the ante was a daring play. A miserable game. Lonesome me with three hard rocks, two buzz saws and only Scanlon to work on.

"Then around ten o'clock in walked Floyd Arthur. He was the best news any lo-ball game in Fairbanks could get. He played two ways and they were both terrible. He'd start fast and if he got a few chips ahead of the game, it was going to be a dreary night. Floyd would clamp down and become Mr. Adamant, hardest rock at the table. He'd only draw to maybe a smooth seven, break down his nines and never raise on a pat eight.

"His other style was the bloodbath. Get him stuck and he'd speed up his action beyond recall. He'd lose more, get pissed and forget what little he knew about the game. His face would go red. He'd slump down in his chair with steam coming out his ears. That was the time to raise him. Floyd preferred lo-ball, so that was what everyone would play when he was in the game because they knew he could throw a big party any night.

"He was a dumpy fat guy with puffy cheeks, glasses that slid down his nose and hair that ran with sweat when he was losing. I liked the guy, even though I was always trying to scoop in his chips. Considering the prices he charged at his steak house, that was fair. Besides, he ran a good restaurant and you know how badly Fairbanks needs any one of those it can get. When he was away from the table he was a quiet person with a sense of humor. Yeah, I liked him.

"Floyd's specialty was going busted by hitting the deck trying to outdraw pat hands. When he lost touch he didn't care at all if he had to take two cards. On the gorier nights, I saw him shove in his case chips to suck three cards off the deck trying to beat a pat seven-four. Absurd.

"Anyway, Floyd sat down and the floor boss, big fella named Pinky, sent someone over to sell him chips. The table got tense because that was an important moment. Floyd might come in with only the five bills he needed to get in the big game in the Gold Room, and when he did he held his wallet in the open where you could see nothing else was in it. Or he might have three, four, five grand on him and those nights he was very secretive about his wallet. He'd hold it down below the table as he opened it, where you couldn't see what was in it. How much Floyd brought to play depended on how his restaurant was doing. The worse the food biz, the better the chance he'd dump a full load. The table got excited that night because he held his wallet down out of sight when he got out the five bills for starters. We all sensed that the big water buffalo might be going down.

"About then Joey cashed in his chips. I told you he was dense. I got a mild surprise. Lou Devery sat down next to me and stacked up five yards of chips. I had been busy on a hand and didn't see exactly when Devery had come into the joint. I'd drawn to a straight seven-five and caught a trey making it jam up. Shakin' John had drawn one and come out with a hundred, which was a fair bet at a sixty dollar pot. Shakin' John played solid, but he'd step a bluff out there and he'd make a long call too. You get a lot of yo-yos going to the cloth with any seven-five. That's a strong calling hand after the draw and sometimes worth a raise. I looked for the tell. Shakin' John's lips and fingers trembled most of the time. He looked like a huge rabbit. That time his lips weren't moving. His fingers weren't trembling.

"Shakin' John could be completely still only when he had the Holy City. I dumped the hand. Scanlon was behind me with a two card draw. His nostrils were flaring out as he called the hundred with a smooth eight-six, thinking he had something more than a bluff-catcher. Scanlon even spread his hand quickly, but Shakin' John laid down a six-four and raked in the chips.

"Devery made the game more interesting. He was a greasy, rat face little guy, short and slim, dark hair and eyes, a two-bit hustler who was out of his class in that game. He dealt off grams of coke and I'd heard a couple stories about him waving a .45 around on guys who were slow on the vig to Thalman. Devery was around the cardroom most nights. He was a corrupt angle shooter who played a miserable game of poker, but he won small and steady because he was so widely detested, players were always going out on a limb to try and bust him. He had a deep, croaky frog voice and absolutely no charm.

"He needled the other players with sniveling, obnoxious insults and he laughed at anyone he beat in a big pot. His game was obtuse, but he knew why he won and kept his play tight enough to stay out of trouble. He was cheap and sleazy—peeking at cards, laying string bets, betting out of turn to intimidate weak players, lying about betting in the dark. He didn't move with a deck, but that was only because he didn't know how. That night I thought I liked having him in the game because I usually never had a chance to beat him for anything but maybe fifty bucks. I looked over his five-hundred dollar stack and brightened up."

Allen leaned quietly against the pillows and let me run on. I wanted to let go of it all and was pleased to have him there for an audience. I even began to enjoy describing the poker situation. I always did understand it better than I played it, just like I would have done better as a basketball coach than a point guard.

"The swing pot came up right away. Floyd opened under the gun on Shakin' John's deal with a blue chip, the usual twenty dollar opening bet. Devery raised him eighty from two seats back. No one hopped that fence and it came back to Floyd. He tranced. He pulled a jack out of his hand, held it up, and tranced again. That would be a hundred-twenty to win for an eighty dollar bet, less than a two to one payoff, neglecting what else he might win after the draw, which from Devery would be little. Figuring Devery for better than a smooth eight in those waters and quite possibly a pat seven against Floyd's one card draw, the odds worked out to six or eight to one against Floyd. That's a rotten bet, but Floyd threw in four blue chips, saying 'Give me an ace for this face,' and flicked the jack into the discards.

"Devery arched back in his seat to recheck his hand. He couldn't even hold his cards in the one-handed poker grip, but had to lean away from the table to keep anyone from peeking. I liked it that far. Floyd was going to lose a chunk early, go crazy and scatter chips around the table all night long. Then things moved off-center. Devery got a tinny look of surprise on his face. I was used to his expressions and didn't believe it. He was a simple one-step liar. If he had a good hand, he gave you the sad look, and vice versa. He banged his left hand down on the table and muttered, 'Gimme one.' Then he looked up like he was cursing fate and tossed two cards away."

"Two cards?" Allen asked, leaning forward.

"Yeah, it jolted me. And Vero was right onto it. It looked like Devery had overlooked a pair in the first place, then being angry with himself had mistakenly thrown away an extra card. Only maybe he was holding out or even holding out two cards. I had heard talk that the dealer, Shakin' John, used to move with a deck, but I dismissed the possibility that he was working with Devery. I stared straight at Devery. Vero watched them both.

"Either way this would cost Devery. Four cards is a dead hand and you forfeit all chips you put in the pot. He was last to act and could still change his call and ask for two cards, if anyone spoke up to warn him. That wasn't going to be me. One man to a hand. The other way around, if Devery was sitting on a card or had an ace in his fly, Vero and I were going to catch it and Devery would be eighty-sixed out of Thalman's for good. I liked it. Either he'd lose the pot or I wouldn't have to put up with the creep anymore.

"Shakin' John burned the top card and dealt one to Floyd. Floyd picked it right up and looked carefully at his hand. Devery laid his three cards face down on the table and put a chip on them. Shakin' John flicked his draw card across the table. It slid to a stop beside his other cards. Shakin' John pitched the rest of the deck in the discards. Devery's hand dipped below the table. My heart was pounding in my ears. It looked too easy. He brought his hand up with a lighter and fumbled a pack of cigarettes out of his shirt pocket.

"Then Floyd saw it. He stared at Devery's cards, counting them over and over with his eyes. Devery was distracted getting his cigarette going. Floyd leaned over closer and looked along the edges for a hidden card. Clearly, there were only three of them under the chip. Floyd looked at him and saw that he wasn't holding any other cards. Floyd stopped doubting. His neck corded and he flipped three black chips into the pot, three-hundred dollars.

"Devery had his cigarette lit. He leaned forward and picked up his draw card, leaving the rest of his hand on the table. He looked at it a minute, then pushed in fifteen blue chips. This was the last chance he had to make a move. Vero leaned in a little closer. I was half-turned in my chair ready

228

to grab Devery. Floyd spread his hand and said, 'I have five cards. How many do you have?' Devery's mouth sagged. His left hand went to his cards and spread them face down. There were only four.

"Vero did his part fast. He spread the cards again, called it a dead hand and shoved the pot to Floyd. Devery stood up, bumping his chair over onto the floor. He picked up his remaining chips and left without saying anything. Floyd stacked his chips and started smiling. I caught Vero's eye. He brought in a new deck and slid it over to Floyd to deal the next hand.

"'Stack your chips on your own time and deal. I'm stuck.' Scanlon bitched at him.

"Vero gathered up the old deck and managed to show me that Devery's draw card had been a king. I watched him count down the old deck. Fifty-three cards. Just right, with the joker.

"I was puzzled by Devery's debacle. He hadn't held out. He hadn't moved at all. He'd just been dumb. That wasn't unprecedented, but he'd also been giving out false expressions. Then I was dealt a pat nine-seven. That's a tough hand to play anytime, but Vero called and Scanlon raised. I watched Devery walk out the door, then stopped wondering about it and went back to playing cards. But the game was dying. Floyd had a running start. He clamped down and soon nobody was giving out any action. When Shakin' John and the furniture salesman left early, Pinky closed the joint down. Just as well, as all the chips were nailed to the table anyway."

"Floyd was still way ahead?" Allen asked.

"Right, he walked out with a chunk. I knew that from his wallet play, plus he beat the game for three hundred. Right after Floyd cashed in, the next guy in line at the cashier's cage dropped his chips. A handful of red one dollar and green five dollar chips squirted out of his hand and scattered across the floor. The whole room broke up, laughing at him—a stumpy, bald cardroom bum named Julius, who hung out on the fringes, always on short money. One of the chips was black. A middle-aged lady in the crowd leered at Julius and offered to help him pick up his chips. Everyone waited while he scurried around and ducked under the crap table picking them up. Julius endured the insults in silence. When he got them together, he stood in front of the cage and watched as Fat Georgie cashed him in for a hundred and a half, which was a lot of chips for him. Julius didn't leave when he got his money. He walked over to the bar and ordered up a last one.

"I cashed in next, a stray twenty over seven hundred, a good night, but the thought did cross my mind that it could have been of playoff caliber if Floyd hadn't gotten an early present. I walked out and nodded to the ox at the door on the way past. He pointed to the elevator floor indicator flashing a steady one and thumbed me toward the stairway door instead, telling me that the elevator had just gotten stuck.

"Bells started ringing quietly in my head. That was one too many off things. Stairs are for running. I went down them fast and then very slow and quiet through the downstairs door into the lobby. Nobody there, except for a leg sticking out of the elevator. Floyd was lying on the floor. The door kept trying to shut. It closed a foot, then hit Floyd's leg and popped itself back open again. Floyd was dead, dead in that special way a big gun does. One huge hole seemed to have taken out his entire chest. I patted him down. No wallet. The street outside was empty. I left Floyd there with the door rebounding off his leg and went back up the stairs.

"Scanlon was just coming out the cardroom door. I told him and the doorman what had happened. They agreed not to let anyone leave. I went back inside looking for Julius. He had split down the back stairs and was gone. I got the cops called and then we settled down to the long-term drama that the homicide squad runs whenever they get another body to consider.

"Thalman was flaming mad about everything. He didn't like having a dead guy turning up on his doorstep, especially a good customer. He didn't want anyone to leave either and he had his people enforce that. Thalman went a certain distance to get along with the cops. I did also, particularly when they're playing Rezkels Wild. In that game, if you don't have a suspect, any Rezkel will do.

"By something more than mere chance, we got Thalman's friendliest policeman, a homicide dick named McGarrity. There must have been somebody around town McGarrity hated more than me. There must have been, only none of them had found a body right in the most embarrassing possible place. He had to take care of Thalman and he had to run some kind of murder investigation. He didn't like being all alone in the middle, so he kept me around for company. Or that's what he said he was going to do. I told him everything I knew and nothing I guessed. My citizen's duties done, I retired quietly down the back stairs."

"McGarrity told you to stay and you left. I like that," Allen said. He caressed the air with his hand. "It has a lovely arrogance."

"And stupidity," I continued, "only it got worse. I went and solved his case for him. Devery's move at the table made sense as soon as I saw that stuck elevator light. Anyone who'd played with Floyd knew that if he gets ahead, he won't put any chips in the pot unless he's got his cards in escrow first. The question was, how did Devery know that Floyd had a bundle that night? Devery got to the table after Floyd did his secret wallet routine, so Devery knew before he came to the table. I went to wrap him up, but I was mainly thinking about who might have tipped him.

"But that's what keeps this from quite making sense. I can see Devery blowing Floyd away for a few thousand, but how could that be enough for some sharp guy who was setting up the play in the first place? It doesn't fit.

"I went over to Two Street and had the first cab I saw call Red for me. He was an old time cabbie and I was sure he knew where Devery lived. Devery rode cabs everywhere and Red passed a lot of time at Thalman's. Red knew alright. He drove me across the river to a house on Dawson in Graehl.

"Lights were on inside and I could see Devery moving around. I knocked on the door. Got that? I knocked and he opened it."

"I got it," Allen answered, "only didn't that part come out different in the papers?"

"Real different. Anyway, I was standing on the porch watching his eyes. They were like slate, and they slowly crossed. He started for his gun and then I went for him. I stepped in, grabbed his gun arm, swept his feet and slammed him against the wall. He had a .45 in a pancake holster on his right hip. I jerked his belt open and slipped off the holster without disturbing any prints on the gun. Then I checked him for more weapons, but he had none. He didn't have any particular money either, about a hundred.

"I held him against the wall and phoned McGarrity at Thalman's. I told him that while acting in self-defense I'd found Floyd's likely killer and gave him the address. Then we waited. Devery tried to get me to forget about it for a grand. I laughed and he doubled it. I asked him many times who set it up, but he wouldn't say. And despite what you may have heard, I didn't hit him, though I wanted to.

"McGarrity showed up real quick with two tame cops. He put them together with me, Devery and the .45, and then he searched the place himself. He did a twenty minute number and came back to the front room to announce that the money wasn't there. That fit. Since he only took such a short while, he must have found it. I didn't care. We had Devery and the gun that ballistics later said was the murder weapon. McGarrity told me to take off and watch my step, so I left.

"The next day I was arrested for breaking and entering, plus assault. The DA, guy named Elkin, called me in and gave me his best outrage for an hour, about how I'd ruined his case by smashing into Devery's place. I was a private citizen, but I had destroyed the case by violating Devery's constitutional rights about eighteen different ways, none of which was explained with a crisp clarity. He even took me over to Graehl and showed me where I'd kicked in Devery's front door. He ran down the entire illegal search litany and sent me back to a cell, suggesting that Devery was likely going to sue me for damages.

"Devery never came to trial. He wasn't even indicted. A surprisingly good Seattle lawyer appeared to represent him. Elkin rolled over and shrugged his way through media interviews about how his hands were tied by my extralegal actions. He remained immaculate in regard to me. Never once did he lower his guard and believe a single word I said."

"You were the one who got indicted," Allen laughed. "I remember hearing about that. Callahan told me you appeared very two-fisted and dumb in the *Tribune*."

"Right. That was another form of Rezkels Wild. Any Rezkel makes a good fall guy. Well, Thalman wanted it all to pass as soon as possible and it did. The official take was that a friendly little card game got out of hand. It got so low key and soft around the edges that they dropped charges against me. Only I didn't listen when they told me to forget Floyd. In the end, they tossed away my PI ticket. I took that through six hearings and it's currently being ignored in District Court."

"That's when you made the quantum leap from private eye to loyal 942 Labe?"

"Yes, 942 took me in and truly I'm making as much as before, but the work isn't so suited to my talents."

"Carrying a shovel isn't as aesthetic as carrying a gun?"

I shrugged and uncorked the bottle for another round.

"How much money did Floyd have on him?"

"I don't know. The night manager at his restaurant was definite that he only had a thousand, maybe a bit over, when he left there at five. That wouldn't have been enough for Floyd to do his secret wallet act. Devery was half smart and he knew enough, barely, to run the play at Thalman's by himself. But for just a thou, McGarrity wouldn't have chanced move. There had to be a lot more. Devery was not a likely guy to have found out Floyd was carrying a wad, especially since Floyd only flashed money when he didn't have much.

"I went over every minute of that night, tracking from five o'clock when he left his restaurant to when he walked into Thalman's at ten. I mean, Allen, it took me two weeks of doing nothing else, but I charted every place he went and every person he talked to. Mainly, he was around the bars. He didn't come up with money at any time. I stumbled against a kicker, though. I never could account for where he was from nine-thirty to ten when he walked into Thalman's. I went at that from every angle I could and I never did find out.

"Julius dropped his chips on cue and disappeared that same night. I don't think he meant to. He might have gone skydiving without a parachute. Devery left town also. He paid attention when Thalman told him to stay gone.

"I took a real fine look at all the players at Thalman's that night, especially those in the Gold Room game. Came up empty. Shakin' John and that furniture salesman were clean. Kirby was home most of the day and got to Thalman's at six-thirty. Scanlon had some air in what he said he'd been doing, but mostly he'd been around Thalman's.

"Thalman let Pinky tell me which of the players there had left early or even ducked out for a moment or done any phone work. He didn't like Floyd turning up dead where it would bring heat on him. He helped me, until I leaned on prize pigeon Scanlon too heavily, trying to find out what that tricky bastard had been doing.

"I got nothing but aggravation from the cops. Parading without a permit, you know. Eventually, I took a 942 dispatch and tried to put it aside. But then, yesterday, Lou Devery showed up in Fairbanks again. It got me thinking in another direction. I realized that I'd put too much effort into figuring what Floyd did that night. A divine moment came out of no place and I remembered something Floyd didn't do. He didn't say good-bye over a drink to an old friend of his named Axel Larston who was splitting Alaska for good that same night."

"And you suspect this Axel guy?" Allen asked.

"Not a bit. They were old buddies and Axel never would have set Floyd up. He'd just had enough Alaska, finally. He had too much money and too little love, so he went south on the ten-thirty bird.

"I'd checked him out at the time. He was carousing through the bars before his flight out. I had him ordering a

Daiquiri from the bartender at the Midnight Mine a little after nine-fifteen and then getting a Margarita from the waitress a few minutes before ten. I'd been assuming he stayed there the whole time until it hit me today that I couldn't place him and Floyd together at any time and Floyd definitely hadn't been at the Midnight Mine."

"So maybe Floyd did get more money and the wrong person knew about it," Allen concluded for me.

I nodded.

"When are you going to talk to this Axel?"

"Soon."

We fell silent. The tape ended. Allen had to get up early and go to his imitation job. He went softly into end-of-the-evening behavior by not putting on more music.

"Am I compounding a felony by giving you a place to crash?" he asked, gesturing at the empty front half of the room.

Chapter Seventeen

I slept in until eight, then got up and did a hard workout in the room. The space was too limited for my kata, so I worked on kicks instead and ran through some combinations. After a shower I went downstairs. The night shift was off duty, but there weren't many of them and they tended to be hermits anyway, so the halls were fairly empty. I was able to move around easily without being recognized. The mess hall was closed, which was a loss since breakfast was the only decent meal they served. I put three peanut butter sandwiches together in the break room. As I washed them down with several cups of tea, I refreshed myself on the local geography, since that was the room where the Denali was going to disburse a hundred thou to somebody.

The key point was that there were three doors to the break room. The main door opened into the hallway across from the mess hall. That would be where they'd take tickets. A door in the back wall opened outside to the area behind B Wing. It would be watched. A third door was beyond a coffee urn and fruit juice island in the far left corner. It had a smooth aluminum knob with no keyhole or lock button. I tried it. The door opened into the bakery. Two bakers in white hats looked up at me as I leaned through the door and reached my hand around to the lock button on the bakery-side knob. I pushed in the button as I apologized for taking the wrong door. I shut it again, locked on the bakery side. Any security check they did on that door would seem good from the break room.

My personal stolen truck was still idling where I had left it the night before, a quarter tank of gas lighter. I drove over behind Gathering Center Three where Theo's crew was working along E Line. A green Randolph-Lightner pickup was parked behind Theo's truck. Scanlon. I pulled over to the side of the road a hundred yards back. The ice fog wasn't bad and I could see the line crew putting on a section. Scanlon was outside walking around the work area. That wasn't going to last long. The weather board at CC2 had the factor at minus sixty-eight.

My pickup had no picnic accessories of any kind. No AM radio. No cassette player. Just a CB that was putting out a mix of static and banal air traffic. I was about to turn it off when the LCI dispatcher came on with an announcement regarding LCI vehicle number one-fourteen, the very truck I had taken under my protection. He politely called it missing and asked the rest of the LCI fleet to look for it. What he got in return was a loud, slurpy raspberry and a flurry of bird calls in assorted voices. I took up the mike and chimed in with my rendition of the Tasmanian Devil mating cry. The dispatcher tried to restore order with a recitation of FCC regulations regarding proper CB etiquette. He was laughed out of the air.

Scanlon finished his quickie tour with a few words to Theo and drove away. I pulled my truck up to the rear of the spread as Theo was going into the warm-up shack on the back of the skid. I went in after him. Out of the wind it was a pleasant minus thirty-one. Theo was fiddling with the compressor and looked up surprised when I said hello.

"Rezkel, what are you doing here?"

Theo was from Seattle. I knew how to talk to him.

"What are the Sonics doing in the playoffs?" I shrugged, "Maybe they belong there, huh?"

"They won't always be underdogs, but I don't know about you," he laughed, then pulled off a glove and held out a hand for me to shake. "Scanlon said some hotshit lawyer got you out of jail in time to kill Barriss," he said, growing serious again.

"He was wrong twice. I didn't have a lawyer. I had to make do on innocence. And I was having a drink at the Mecca Bar when Barriss got it."

"I didn't ever think you killed Phil. It didn't feel right to me, or to the guys. Uh, who do you think did?"

"I'm not sure. I have to do the cops' work for them. It's getting so hot all they're doing is waiting for the press to come up with a conviction so they can make an arrest. You can help me out on this, Theo. The thing I've got to know is where all the Randolph-Lightner pickups were Tuesday night. I know you weren't out of camp that night from all I heard about that party you guys got going down in Jack's room."

"We did get high-centered. Jack passed out right there on the floor. We had to pour him into his bed. Funny you mentioned that, though. Barriss borrowed my truck. His was in the shop for a valve job."

"When did he take it?"

"Right after we knocked off. He gave me the keys back the next morning."

"Any troopers ask you about this?"

"No. You think Barriss killed Phil?"

"That's a maybe," I told him, running the numbers again, trying to make them point at Barriss.

"I wondered about that because of the way they argued lately."

"You still working that heavy foam?"

"No, thank God we finished up the last of it yesterday. They hauled off the empties and I hope that's the last I ever see of that shit. We couldn't get any footage. That junk was hard on the guys. Maybe now that damn Tyson won't be underfoot all the time."

"They hauled off the empties right away?"

"Not as quick as when Phil was here, but our Arctic Wrap leader got all excited and gave us so much hassle over cleaning up as we went that we gave them away. North Camp Builders came by wanting empties for work shacks. We gave them the last three."

"Where'd they take them?"

"I dunno."

"One other thing, Theo, that you might know something about. Did you ever hear Huey run down that riff about how he remembers every piece of equipment he ever ran, knows them all by sound?"

"Yeah, goes on about that all the time. I half believe him too. He knows all the equipment on this job blindfolded. He was bragging he made a hundred bucks last fall because he was able to show this biz type he could recognize a D9 he used to operate on another job."

"Did he say who that was?"

"No. He wasn't very clear. You know Huey. He was more hinting than telling, and he was trying to talk up his big connections at the same time. With Huey you can't be sure."

"Theo, I have to check some things out. Would you not tell anyone you saw me here? It could get in my way and I need time."

"Sure, Rezkel. I understand. I'll keep quiet."

We went outside. Theo nodded toward my truck and smiled.

"You gonna take the fifth when the judge asks you where you got that LCI rig?"

I gave him a playful punch and got in my powder-blue pickup. As I drove off Theo gave the break sign to the line crew. Air tools hit the snow and the men hurried toward the warm-up shack.

Had to be time to find North Camp Builders. I drove along the network of roads that connected the various drill pads until I found their show being set up on Q Pad. They had three empty insulation crates lined up side by side with assorted pallets of tools and materials around them. Two of

242

their crew cabs were idling there, but there wasn't anyone outside. One crate was Arctic Wrap number seventy-seven, right off the list of supposedly destroyed crates.

I took a look in the crew cabs. There were usually Polaroid cameras around construction sites. All bosses wanted to be able to cover their own act in case there were questions later about who cut which corner rather than truncate the profit pyramid. I found one in a glove compartment. It took four rounds, but I got a passable shot of the crate, its number and the crew cab parked in front of it. That made it time to see Wayne Tyson.

Another hot truck alert came over the CB on the way to CC1. I decided that I really owed myself a new vehicle. I parked on the far side of CC1. Waste may have been the spirit of the pipeline, but I turned the truck off and plugged it in.

Tyson had a single in D Wing, a room for honchos only. I walked in without knocking. He was in bed reading a gun magazine. He jerked upright when he saw me.

"Hey, what are you doing barging in," he began.

I cut him off. "Here's where you blew it, Wayne," I told him and tossed the photo on the bed beside him.

Tyson swung his feet over onto the floor and sat on the edge of the bed in his shorts. He picked up the picture and glanced at it.

"What's this?"

I sat down on the desk.

"Look at the crate number, Wayne. It's the wrong crate for a Northern Builder's carpentry shack on Q Pad."

He ran his fingers through his lank blonde hair and looked at it again.

"Number seventy-seven. So what?"

I handed him a copy of the letter I'd lifted from the Randolph-Lightner files.

"Forget about lying to me on this, Wayne. How much did Arctic Wrap pay Barriss to install this shit?"

Tyson was red in the face and sweating. I enjoyed the way he curled in his eyebrows and looked like he was being barbecued. Then he got a cute idea and sat back with a grin.

"Are you saying Randolph-Lightner lied to me?"

"I don't care which is the latest company to cheat on the pipeline and I don't care about you. What I do care about is being the bulls-eye in a murder investigation. I don't like that. You come through and I won't pass this on. You mess me up and I'll give it to the newspapers. Then I'll call Arctic Wrap and tell them I called the press because a scared little shit named Wayne Tyson didn't have enough sense to talk to me. What did you do with Dalira's cocaine after you killed him?"

He squealed, "What?"

I stood up, crossed my arms and leaned against the wall. I gave him my nasty smile.

"The troopers are going to come over here to ask you why your Randolph-Lightner pickup was seen driving away from Parsons right after Dalira was killed. They're going to do that as soon as I tell them who saw your truck."

"That's impossible. My truck wasn't there. I didn't take it. I rode over with a friend. We went in his truck."

"I didn't see anybody with you at Parsons. You were alone."

"That was only when you ran into me. Hey, what is this with the troopers?"

"How much did Arctic Wrap pay Barriss?"

"Barriss, that goddamn Barriss. They must have seen his truck. It's just like mine."

"His truck was in the shop, Wayne, for a valve job, like the troopers are going to give you. They don't know yet that I saw you at Parsons Tuesday night. I haven't told them yet. How much?"

He slumped back resignedly and told me in a reedy voice, "Eight thousand, and three more for Dalira."

"You were the bagman?"

"Well, no. I handed the envelope to Barriss, but I wasn't a bagman. And that insulation won't hurt the pipeline. It'll be as good as the rest of it."

"Who else? Scanlon?"

"No. Nobody," he was glancing up at me and then staring at the floor. "Scanlon thinks they buried it at the dump."

"So, why the hurry to do it now?"

"It's because of this guy who oversees the insulation contract for Barner Oil. He's the only one there who really knows what we do. He would have caught on for sure and stopped it, but he's on R&R now. The idiot they have covering for him doesn't know a thing about insulation and believes whatever you tell him. We had to get it done fast, since the real guy is due back Monday."

I didn't say a word. I just looked at him. He met my gaze briefly and looked away. I came slowly off the wall and took the photo out of his hand.

"I leveled with you. You're not going to tell them now, are you?"

"Tell them what, Wayne?"

"You know, about the defective insulation."

"Did you toss in any little lies, Wayne?"

He looked at me and shook his head.

"What's the matter? Don't trust the old voice?"

I stopped at the door and looked back at him.

"You don't want me to find out, Wayne, that you told anyone I was here. You don't want that, do you?"

He shook his head again.

The parking lot didn't afford an innocent such as myself any genuine choice. My former LCI pickup was gone. I don't know if someone else stole it or if LCI did a repo. The day shift had most everything else running. There wasn't even a truck idling by the front door. My field was restricted to one ridiculous, previously vermilion pickup. That's supposed to be a brilliant red-orange, but this example was both formerly red and formerly orange, with a genuinely red "Do Not Operate" tag was hanging on the driver's side door handle. Something about the transmission and brakes. The driver's door was smashed in and wouldn't open. It did have a certain virtue. That was the key in the ashtray. As I didn't know how to get anything else started, it became my ride. Someday I'm going to have to learn how to hotwire those damn things. I considered going back inside and leaning on

Tyson until he lent me his truck, but then I decided to at least determine whether the wreck would run.

It started right up. I got back out the passenger door and unplugged it. From then on I was teased along by marginal performance into driving that dog. It got out of the parking lot without bursting into flames, but I saw immediately what they meant about the brakes. They only existed on the right front wheel and I had to steer against them to keep it on the road. The transmission was perfectly functional, though, as long as I kept it in first. I fought the lever against horrible grinding sounds into second and it popped right back out with an impressive kerwhump. It wouldn't go into third or fourth at all. A constant rattling sound came from underneath, but that was OK. I rolled along at ten miles per hour and did fine except that I had to drive leaning way over to the right to see around the cracks in the windshield.

I went over to the old Mukluk Camp for lunch. They were serving processed cheese on Wonder Bread white, grilled into submission. The place was a trashy trailer slum with raw sewage leaking out. The buildings were painted with a lifeless, near-yellow paint that must have been left over from the Crimean War. It had a single blessing. Being a backwater, I didn't run into a single person who thought I should be in jail.

The only phone booth had a built-in ashtray that was ruining the air. I covered it over with a newspaper, though that hardly made a difference. I put my tea on the shelf and slouched down in the chair for a prolonged dialing session. Busy signals so aggravated my ear that I shut them out and kept dialing on automatic pilot, floating away into luxurious thoughts about Sharon. She had me so distracted that when I finally I did get through to the operator I almost hung up and redialed. In a few minutes Billy came on the line.

"Collect, from Deadhorse, Alaska? Yeah, I'll accept, Operator, but I'm protesting to the league office."

"You should watch that whining, Billy. It makes you sound like a Laker fan."

"I would hardly abandon the Celtics for Jabbar's skyhook. I don't pretend to understand why fate and Jack Kent Cooke should want to offend me with that kind of basketball, though it is effective."

"Did you find him?"

"Listen, Raz, this matter has been highly unprofessional on your part. You had me mingle with the hottest young hookers in the States, and you wouldn't come through with the bucks for me to do it properly."

"Love is free, Billy."

"Who's talking about love? I'm talking about getting my rocks off. It's an outrage."

I knew he had good news so I asked, "How'd you find him?"

"Had to hit the streets. It took most of the night to find a youngie who wanted to do it for gold again. And she was spaced to where I didn't get Axel zeroed in until late this morning. Here he is."

"Nick, thanks for looking me up. That Billy, he blew it for me with my number-one lady," Axel laughed, banging the phone on the table. "She thought I was going to lick her navel and stick the biggest nugget I had right into it." He laughed again and boomed into the phone, "That guy, he'll tell them anything. Where'd you meet him?"

"That's theoretical, Axel. You paying them in gold now?"

"Yeah, mainly dust. They like it and it's a little cheaper for me, though I don't know about that after I make it up with number-one. Hey man," he said, lowering his voice and turning serious, "I heard about all you did to nail that punk who killed my partner and I want to thank you for it. You did right by Floyd."

"Not right enough, yet. Do you know how much Floyd had on him the night he got it?"

"Nope, but knowing Floyd I bet had to be three, four grand. He liked to have too much money. He didn't feel right if he didn't have a roll in case something came up."

"But you aren't sure?"

"No. I was down here and didn't hear about it for weeks. I don't write much. I called my sister in Anchorage one night and she told me."

"Axel, he was killed the night you bonzoed through the bars on your way out of Fairbanks for the last time."

"What? You're shitting me?"

"No, that night. That very night."

"I never knew. I thought… " he paused and then shouted, "Damn, that night Floyd didn't have no three, four grand. He had $37,000 in nuggets on him. That was the last thing keeping me in Fairbanks, selling this claim me and Floyd were in on together."

"You sold it for gold that night?"

"Yeah, we were going to do it that afternoon before the banks closed, but there were all these last-minute hang-ups with the lawyer and we didn't close the deal until nine or ten. I almost missed my flight. We had to wrap it up in the middle of my last tour of the bars. Couldn't pass up the bars my last night in Fairbanks."

"Who'd you sell to?"

"Crazy Harry Menitzer, at his lawyer's office. Dahlquist his name was, an office off Wendell. Just the four of us. Me and Floyd didn't need no lawyer."

"What were the hang-ups?"

"Nothing really, but this Dahlquist was particular about everything. He wasn't satisfied about the work we done on the claim, you know, to keep it active. Something about whether it was in the calendar year or in the fiscal year or in the lawyer crap year. He didn't think the clerk in the Juneau office knew much. But, tell me, what date isn't in both a fiscal year and a calendar year? Crazy Harry was nuts, but cautious. He had the right lawyer for his personality. Me and Floyd got tired of waiting around while Dahlquist phoned around to all the experts he could think of to get it straight. We left. Floyd had things to do and so did I. I kept calling Dahlquist back and eventually he said to come over. Floyd got there a little after. Then Crazy Harry opened his poke and dumped out one of the finest stashes of nuggets I ever saw."

"So Floyd walked out of there with $37,000 in nuggets."

"Yup, and so did I. It felt great on the plane. You know

how us miners love to carry gold around. Floyd weren't no miner, but he loved gold anyhow."

After the call I nursed my disgusting pickup back to CC2. A red baseball cap was lying on the floor. I took it along and went up to Allen's room. His shaving gear was sitting out. I took it down to the washroom and, despite all my vows never to shave again, I took off two years' worth of beard. Actually, it felt good to scrape that razor along my skin. I came through uncut, but I put a Band-Aid on my left cheek to attract the eye away from recognition. Then I went back to Allen's room, sat down in the chair, got my feet up on the desk, and thought through the position.

Chapter Eighteen

"Not even shaving could help you with the ladies," Allen assured me first thing when he came in from work.

"Tonight I'm holding my power over women in reserve and concentrating on invisibility."

"You have a chance there. All they're talking about is the Denali."

We chatted for a while, then Allen opened a small bottle and dumped a load of toot on his snorting mirror. I felt a flare of anger as I watched him blade the powder back and forth. He assumed I wanted to toot up. I didn't like having things assumed about me and I didn't want any cocaine.

Allen offered me a straw. I didn't want to talk about it, I just didn't want any. He saw my reaction and didn't know what to say. We sat there without speaking for what felt like a long while.

Then he said quietly, "You did go for that ridiculous rug hit at the time, remember? We all got to be a bit nuts to keep it together up here." The way he said it, was so gentle and friendly, I was suddenly past my anger and couldn't help laughing with him at how silly it had been. He smiled at me, bent over and whiffed up all the lines he'd laid out for both of us. He leaned back, carried off by his rush. Allen was enjoying it so much that I was happy for him, though I had no taste left whatsoever for that powder. From Jeanne to Sharon, from toot to not.

At quarter past six I put on the baseball cap. Allen wished me luck and I took off. Going out the back door of C Wing, a sharp blast of cold wind iced through my jeans and flannel shirt as I hurried the thirty yards across to the warehouse behind the mess hall. At the door, I pulled out the tail of my shirt and held it over the knob to open the door.

The warehouse was partly illuminated by dull neon lights. I walked past the humming electrical panels and down row after row of supplies. Nobody was there, not even in the short hall leading to the culinary staff's quarters. I looked carefully around the corner into the main hallway, which led past the break room and mess hall down to the camp office and front doors. A hundred feet down the hall a crowd was gathered around the break room door. Security was solid at that point. No one was getting in without a thousand dollar receipt for the Denali that cross-checked with the master list.

Several cooks were out of the kitchen, standing on my side of the crowd. They started cheering on one of their own in a white outfit who was presenting his credentials at the door. I took it as my cue. I walked down the hall without being noticed and turned into the bakery. Nobody there. I pulled the door shut behind me and went over to the door in the back corner.

No sound was coming through the door into the break room, so I had no way to judge when to make the move. I took a deep breath, let the air trickle out and went through the door leisurely. An older man in drab twill work clothes was filling a Styrofoam cup from the coffee spigot. He turned and looked at me over his shoulder, a question beginning to cloud his face. I closed the door and gave it three elaborate twists on the handle, saying, "This one's safe. Locked tighter than our money box now." He nodded and turned back to the coffee urn. I moved away from the door and mingled with the crowd on the other side of the coffee island.

They were coming in fast. The room wasn't crowded, but an intense electricity charged the air. Small groups stood around talking and watching the ping-pong tables being cleared out of the way. A few were holding their paychecks, but most had them tucked away. Downer Dave was in a corner working on a Heineken. He looked extra alert, virtually half-awake behind his hooded eyelids. Paddy was wandering around puffing on a cigarette.

There were three women in the room. A lady Laborer and her hippie boyfriend were telling those around them that they both entered to double their chances for a big score. A tough woman named Rita was helping move the ping pong tables. She drove a twenty yard end-dump and spoke like she had a built-in CB. And then there was Lori, standing off by herself next to a pool table. She was vivid in a slinky, low-cut orange dress with long, loose sleeves, keeping off the hordes with a severe look.

Paddy walked by and glanced at me. He stopped and looked back at my face. I stepped over to him, put an arm around his shoulders and led him off to the side, saying in a low voice, "Yeah, it's me, Paddy, but don't tell anyone. There's something not real right going on and I have to stay cool a while. OK?"

He nodded to me and said in his playful brogue, "Sure, Nick, whatever you say. I know you didn't kill Phil." He opened his coat and showed me a shiny silver flask.

"Want a jolt?"

"Thanks, but I'll pass."

He shrugged and moved off.

The door crew called out that they were only waiting on two more. A big guy with a soft face and dreamy eyes was leaning against the wall next to me. He caught my eye as he pulled a small glass bottle out of his jeans. He unscrewed the lid, tapped some white powder onto the back of his hand, into that little depression at the base of the thumb and whiffed it. It seemed funny.

"Have one before the show, partner?"

I shook my head.

Two stragglers came through the door and were checked out. The door was closed behind them. Luke got up on a chair next to a table and blackboard set up in the middle of the room and called for attention. The crowd peeled off the walls and moved toward the table. Lori didn't move. I stayed in the back.

"Let's go over it again," Luke spoke out loudly, "so everyone knows how we're going to do this."

War whoops and a loud "Alright" answered him. A welder in cowboy boots farted and the crowd cheered the feat.

"OK. OK. We got an assembly line here. You shuffle and let the person, behind you cut the cards. Then you deal out five cards for the person in front of you. The people in front of him verify the numbers on his paycheck. That's gotta be this week's check. Only this week. The checkers write down on the blackboard the last three numbers of the check serial number and the cents off your paycheck, like any checkpool. Five numbers. Then they add the five cards coming off the deck, one at a time, to the check numbers and that's the hand. Face cards don't count. Ones are aces and aces are high. Zeroes are tens, not Teamsters."

The crowd laughed at that. Several guys took the moment to tip up their bottles.

"Best five card hand wins," Luke continued. "Straights play, if you think a straight is gonna be worth a rusty fuck, but we never heard of flushes or straight flushes. Nothing wild. It takes the top cards. Now, you move one spot through the line with each paycheck. After the last spot where you write a hand up on the board, if you can goddamn write, then you can go over in the corner and cry."

More laughs. The crowd tightened up a little. Lori moved off the pool table. I stepped closer to her.

"Here's the money. One hundred-thousand dollars," Luke said, holding up a purple velvet sack. "There was about ten of us counted it and it hasn't been out of our sight since. Ain't that right?"

A knot of men around him nodded and shouted, attesting to it.

Paddy called out, "Get started, you slow fuck."

"Right. Form a line here in front of the table. The guys who start as checkers go to the end of the line after they're done."

Luke held up a new deck of cards and broke the seal. The line shaped up. I got into it two places behind Lori. She was behind a mild, quiet man in a red and green checked flannel shirt. I had a feeling I'd seen him around a Fairbanks card game.

Lori suddenly came alive. She was throwing off burning smiles at the men walking past to get in line behind us and she was dancing in place, swaying around that great body of hers. With that going on in front of me, I gave up worrying that anyone was going to look at me long enough to recognize my disreputable self.

Up front they started dealing out the cards and posting the results. Luke called out each name and each hand as it was written up. The second hand was three sevens with an ace-five kicker. That was an outside shot against a long run of salty cards. The hands tailed off after that, and we worked our way slowly through the line.

A guy in line behind me held up his check and showed those in line around him that he had a natural four sixes.

"And now we gotta do all this with the cards. I woulda won if we went on straight paychecks," he complained.

"Don't fall for that," another guy called out. "He won enough in the other checkpools today to make expenses for the Denali. He's getting a free ride."

The little guy in the red and green flannel shirt handed his paycheck to the checker in front of him. Those who had already been through the line were standing around the table. The guy with the three sevens stood in close and stared down at his feet.

A deck of red Bicycles was lying on a gray wool blanket folded double across the table to make it easier to handle the cards. Lori picked up the deck and started shuffling. She tossed her long, dark hair around and made a lascivious smile through her make-up. Each time she broke down the deck and riffled the cards, she swayed. Her big, firm breasts slid half out of her dress with each move. Ninety-nine percent of the total attention around the table was focused on her cleavage at that moment. I thought how right Barney and Liz had been.

I was standing very close to her, a step back and to her right. My eyes wanted to stray down to her hands, but I didn't have an angle on them. I kept looking right at her elbows. She slid the deck over the blanket to the man in line between us. He cut the cards. She reached over and made the deck up again, giving another flaunting bounce to her body. It was about to happen. I kept my shoulders loose and didn't let them rise up.

Just then the guy in the red and green flannel shirt gave out the loudest belch I'd ever heard, sounding as though it would go on forever. The crowd looked over at him and started laughing. That was it. Lori's right elbow bobbed out from her side and her hands dipped down. I grabbed both her arms, jamming them together and forcing them over her head. I stepped right behind her and shook her. She screamed and stamped at my feet. I felt hands grabbing at me from behind. I twisted out of their grasp and jerked her arms hard. Cards came flying out everywhere. Her right hand was stuck in her left sleeve.

"Hey, what are you doing to her?" a voice yelled.

Others in the crowd were losing their inertia and reaching toward me, but then they all seemed to understand at once as a man behind the table called out in a piercing voice, "Her sleeves. Look at her sleeves."

Red cards were tumbling out of them and sailing through the air. Lori stopped resisting. The crowd went sullen and froze up. I jerked her around and sat her down on the table. She glared at me and hissed, "I know you. You're Rezkel. You killed Phil Dalira."

That brought them back to life. Hands from everywhere tightened on me and I was suddenly in the grip of four men. I didn't fight it. The little guy in the red and green shirt was easing away, but I had no time for him. He slipped into the crowd.

"Count the cards and look at the card holder on her left wrist," I said clearly, raising the volume over the murmur against me that started up as I spoke. "She was bringing in a stacked deck so that guy in front of her would win."

Lori tried to get away from the table, but she had no chance. Three men held her there. One of them jerked up her left sleeve. Just so beautiful. A leather pouch was strapped to her arm, with a few cards still in it.

Cards were gathered up off the floor with great speed and tossed onto the blanket. The checkers looked at their backs. They were all red Bicycles. Doyle was the first to notice a duplicate. He reached over and picked up two cards.

"Look, two aces of diamonds," he announced, displaying them.

That was the final proof. They let go of me at once.

Luke was standing quietly behind the table, waiting to see how it would go. He looked over at the back door, but he didn't make a move. He was going to brazen it out. Someone in the back started to say, "You were going around with her an awful…" but before he could finish, Luke drowned him out.

"Where's that asshole she was dealing for?" Luke bellowed. "Look," he snapped, pointing at the back door closing.

Two men started for the door, but they turned back when one of the checkers said, "Let's call it off and give the money back to ourselves."

"Hey, fuck that, I want to see my hand," one of the men heading for the door shouted. They got on the checker from all sides.

"Just because you got a bum hand, that don't mean you get your money back."

The majority hadn't been through the line. They roared in angry voices at the rest. Lori stood up in the middle of it and walked slowly to the door, expecting any instant to be stopped. They let her pass. Stray insults splashed at her, but she walked through it with her head down. As she got to the doorway a pair of hands came out of the crowd, clamped onto her ass and shoved her through the door.

"How about Rezkel? What's he doing here?" said a man standing beside me and looking around for guidance from the others. My formative years included time spent in the middle of a few Berkeley riots. I had paid attention then to what was successful crowd behavior. I stepped up to my accuser before he got any support and stuck a finger toward his chest, snarling at him, "So what if I'm Captain Kidd? I busted her, right?" I didn't do anything foolish like stick my finger into his chest, because contact triggers a crowd. I only threatened contact. Crowds love intimidation and suspense. He retreated, mumbling something indistinct. That established my rights. I went with it and called for a new deck.

They picked it up and voices were crying "New deck, new deck," all around. Luke produced a deck of blue Bicycles, still in their cellophane wrapper. He was unsure how far to play it. I took the deck out of his hand and did a slow, thorough ceremony of getting out the cards. I tore up both jokers and tossed the pieces on the floor. Then I counted down the deck aloud.

The blackboard had been knocked aside in the confusion. They straightened it and did an inspection. The entries were as before. The guy with trip sevens resumed his vigil beside the table. The line reformed and shortly hands were being dealt again. I stood behind the table as an honorary checker. I didn't care at all who won, just so it wasn't Scanlon's proxy.

A lousy set of trip nines displaced the sevens. They were unimpressive enough that all the remaining players had hope, until the cards stripped it away. Luke hit the table and a wave of resentment and suspicion welled up. His cards were nothing and he was relieved not to hit a big hand. When the couple who said they were doubling their chances got to the table, they were separated so they didn't handle each other's cards.

The champ didn't show until the next-to-last hand. He was fairly slow getting to the line to start with and had to stand aside a few turns while he searched his pockets for his paycheck. It looked to be lost for the longest time, but finally he found it folded into quarters and stuck inside a lid of Hawaiian Senseless he was carrying around for emergencies. Treys full over tens. Not an immortal hand, but it came up on the right night. Downer Dave never did expend excess karma.

Downer dropped his Heineken when they called out his hand. A cheer went up and they started to hand him the purple velvet money bag, but then realized another player was behind him and took the bag back. Downer hadn't noticed. He had reached for the bag, then changed his mind mid-stream to stoop over and retrieve his beer. He kicked it once before he got hold of it and straightened up. The last man's hand was being dealt. No pair showed in the first three cards, but they dealt it all anyway. Downer was looking around for the money without being aware of the last player. When they offered him the bag again, he took it with his free hand and started jumping up and down, whooping, shouting and splashing beer on everyone around him.

The crowd was benign, but not excited. Downer stopped bouncing and opened the bag. He reached in, came out with a handful of hundreds and tossed them into the air. He screamed, "Smutherfucker." and tossed another wad. That got the crowd hyped again. Some bills were caught in the air. Guys hit the floor diving after the rest. Downer walked to the door, sublimely oblivious to it all.

The door opened to a hallway of checkpool fans waiting to see who would come out with the bucks. Downer waded into the crowd yelling "Smutherfucker" over and over. He reached into the velvet bag and showered the masses with hundreds. The way he scattered bills, it had to cost him five grand to get to the long hallway.

At the corner by the commissary I saw Scanlon glowering at Downer. Standing next to Scanlon was a very hard man with a face like a wrench and as much size as Huey. Scanlon saw me in the crowd and pointed me out to the giant with a nod and a brief comment I couldn't hear. They pushed off the wall and walked out the front doors ahead of the crowd surging along with Downer.

"Fuck this sumbitch Pudhole Bay, I'm goin' to town," Downer yelled, throwing away more money.

I waded through the crowd and caught up to him. He was too tranced out to hear anything under a scream, so I shouted in his ear.

"There's some deep shit here, Downer. You lay over tonight and go to town in the morning."

He didn't understand. He reached in the purple bag and pushed bills at me.

"Rez, have some C."

I shoved his hand away and tried again, saying, "Downer, there're men with guns waiting outside to rip you off."

It didn't penetrate.

"Downer, they're waiting on you."

He kept steaming for the door. A cavalcade to the airport was forming. He was pulled away from me into a surge of people. Then he stopped, turned back toward me and said, "Can't stay, Rez. I'd throw it all away by morning." He whooped again and went outside.

I cut away from him and ran down the long hallway, up the stairs to Allen's room and grabbed my down coat. I didn't bother with the coveralls as they'd take too much time. I ran back for the front doors, pulling on the coat as I went. Coming around the corner into the main hallway, I saw Huey stepping out of the telephone alcove with a quizzical expression on his thick face. I went past him without a word, but I did note that the weather board had the factor at minus eighty-nine.

A cluster of men was standing under the floodlight outside, cheering Downer on as he made his way awkwardly over the ice toward a fleet of trucks that was going to escort him to his flight. He slipped and fell heavily, but he didn't let go of the velvet money sack. He had no coat over his cowboy shirt. In the glare of the headlights he looked very cold as he climbed into a packed crew cab.

I got out of the pool of light and wove through the trucks parked in the lot, looking for Scanlon and his heavy. Several dark figures were moving in the shadows. I couldn't make any of them out, so I headed for the trucks that were convoying Downer. Going between two pickups I started to step past a man standing in front of me. In the narrow space I was suddenly close enough to see his face. Scanlon. Alarms rang. He was no threat. I could get my hands on him and take him out, but he was not alone. I didn't know where his muscle was and that scared me. Then, I felt a blast of anger coming at me from behind. I snapped a back fist to Scanlon's face with my right hand as I turned, throwing up my left arm, only not enough time was left for me to block. I couldn't get out of the way. I did the only thing left and turned my head to go with the tire iron as it hit me. Lightning crashed in my head. Red lights flashed before my eyes. I fell to the ground, then I fell much further down into a deep black space.

Chapter Nineteen

I came to lying on the edge of a cliff, hanging over a void with my left arm trapped under me. A loud roaring tore at my ears. The ground felt oddly springy. It bounced and something hard banged into the side of my head, jolting a blinding red flash through my body. I flickered back and forth between the terrible pain and darkness. A deep, rough voice scraped suddenly on my ears and I was awake.

"You didn't tell me there'd be killing."

"There wouldn't have been if not for this asshole. And what's the difference now? It's already kidnapping."

My mind worked like petroleum jelly in the Arctic. It didn't think, it congealed thoughts, but I recognized Scanlon's voice and slowly came to understand that I was on the back seat of a crew cab.

"We kill him, I get double."

"Alright, alright. You got it. Just get his coat and hat off."

"Should I rap him again? Make sure?"

"No. Let him come to out there. He won't get anywhere. I want it nice and slow. I only wish I had time to watch."

Large hands ran over me. They shoved me around the seat, taking off my coat. My head was rammed against the door handle and another lightning bolt roared through me. With each bump as we went, the door handle bit into my skull. I wanted to shift back off of it, but I couldn't move. My muscles felt like they would work, but I couldn't tell them to do anything. I could only lie there in a still pool of pain. Then Scanlon made a sharp turn and I was pitched off the seat. I thudded down onto the floor and went out.

Freezing wind whipping into my face brought me around again. I was being dragged out of the truck. My feet bumped over the floor. I was thrown head first over a bank. I hit and slid down, plowing the snow with my face. I came to rest with snow jammed into my collar. I heard laughter, doors slamming, an engine revving and then all the sounds were swallowed by the wind.

I tried to stand, but I was too weak to do it all at once. I pulled my arms in tight and pushed up on my elbows and knees. With a shove I rocked back onto my haunches and almost went over backwards. I bumped into something and caught my balance against it. A pipe support. I got my arms around it without touching the metal with my hands and rose to my feet.

Six inch pipes ran overhead. Eight of them, without insulation. I knew I was off the edge of a drill pad, close to the control house. I had to get to the control house. I refused to even consider that it might be locked.

The wind was pumping very hard gusts, stripping snow off the ground, swirling it away through the air. Ice fog was thick around me and the pipes disappeared into whiteness ahead of me. I didn't know which way to follow them. I let go of the support and stumbled off with the wind to my back. I almost fell the first few steps, but soon I was stronger and could keep my balance without flailing my arms. One of the pipes overhead turned at right angles and ran off from the others. It had to be going to a well. I was walking in the wrong direction. I turned and went back into the wind.

My head was extremely cold. My face was stinging from the wind. I kept my head ducked down and went as fast as I could without falling. A dark shape was looming above a steep bank on my right. I tried to run up the bank, but I crashed down to my hands and knees and slipped back. The dojo flashed before me. Kiai. I forced out air with my stomach and shouting as loud as I could clawed up the bank on all fours. I struggled to my feet again and climbed stairs up to the control house, A Pad, according to the sign. No lock. I worked the handle holding it with my shirt and jerked with my numb fingers. It didn't give. I kicked the door, then jerked again. It opened grudgingly and I went inside the control house.

The door banged shut behind me and I was in complete darkness. Out of the wind the thirty-odd below temperature felt only cold. I pulled my shirt out of my pants and shook the snow out. I brushed it out of my hair. Each movement sent a spike through my head. I didn't have a beard to ice up any more, or give me its small protection against the cold. My hands hurt as I brushed the snow, but I had to do it or become a Popsicle.

Getting the snow out of my shirt pocket, I discovered a book of matches. Genuine matches. I kissed them. My fingers were so stiff I smeared the first three on the striking surface. The fourth one caught and I felt the glow of a faint heat.

The control house was about ten by twelve, with corrugated metal walls. Wiring drooled out of conduit everywhere. A stand of valves and dials was against one wall. A half-constructed console was in the center of the room. No one had left any mittens or stocking caps around. There was only cold metal and wiring, except that on top of the console was a skin magazine. The cover had an excessively decadent redhead with a lopsided face and mismatched tits. She was sucking a candy cane. It might have been a Christmas edition. The match burned out.

I was out of the wind, but could not stay in the control house. No particular work appeared to be happening on A Pad. It could be days before anyone drove the three miles out here. I didn't like what even a couple hours of minus thirty without winter gear would do to me. I was going to have to walk to the main road, but I had to get something around my head or I simply wouldn't get there. Scanlon had picked the right place to dump a load. He was driving to the airport and A Pad wasn't far out of his way. On foot, without coat, cap or mittens, those three miles might be forever. I guessed that I could handle an hour out in the blizzard. Then I made myself stop thinking about how far I had to go.

I lit another match and looked around again. There still wasn't any clothing in the place. In the flickering light my eyes kept being drawn to the redhead on the cover. Then it hit me that the magazine was going to be my windshield.

I unlaced my Sorels, took off both pairs of socks and laced them back up. If my feet couldn't handle a three mile walk by themselves inside the felt liner, nothing else was going to make any difference anyhow. I tied the thin pair of socks I wore on the inside into a loop. The knots took up a lot of sock, but it worked. I dropped my pants, and starting with the centerfold, pulled pages out of the magazine and shoved them down between my jeans and my cotton long johns. That was the only time in my life I wished for wool long johns. I got my legs wrapped and put pages around my hips, chest and arms. I put a quadruple layer over my head and slipped the sock loop over it. I crinkled as I moved, but everything stayed in place.

I torched off the rest of the matches for their heat and looked around for a way to burn down the control house. A bonfire would have warmed me up for the hike, maybe even bring help, but found nothing to catch on fire. I flattened the staples down and shoved the remaining pages into my collar on the right side of my head, where the wind would be coming from at first. I got the thick socks on my hands and held the magazine in front of my face with both hands.

Going out the door, the first blast of wind all but ripped the pages out of my grasp. I scrunched them further down into my collar and crab-walked sideways down the stairs, keeping my shield into the wind. Cold air washed around the edges and splashed over my face. I was intensely cold instantly.

I walked off the pad onto the A Line road. The eight pipes on my left came together into two bundles of four pipes each. They were insulated from that point on. I turned my face toward them to keep out of the wind as much as I could. The shiny metal skin of the insulation floated in the faint white light and a few feet ahead disappeared into the whiteness of the ice fog.

The road turned and I faced directly into the wind. My legs were a bit stronger. I didn't mind that my knees were stiffening, as long as they worked. My feet were cooling off rapidly. I felt cold air trickling over my long johns, chilling my ankles.

The road was firm and had not been iced by traffic. Occasional drifts cut across. I tried walking through them in Scanlon's tire tracks, but the tracks were too narrow to stay in. I walked out of them, tripped over a drift and almost fell. I looked ahead for the tracks. That opened my collar. Cold air whistled over my chest, sneaking down behind the slick pages covering me. It didn't feel good. I went back to walking hunched over and stopped looking ahead. I stumbled a lot and had to wander around to find the tracks through the drifts, but I didn't open up for any excess cold.

I tightened and loosened my fists. My hands ached too badly for it to help much. My head was worse. The coldest part of my body, that spot in the middle of my forehead, was screaming. It hurt even more than that place behind my left ear where the tire iron had crashed into my head.

The magazine pages over my head helped. Actually they were essential. But what I mainly felt was where the cold

271

eddied around them. I was glad I could still feel. The greatest danger of the Big Cold comes when it's worked its way inside and numbed your mind. Your brain turns cold, then stupid. Once your thinking gets idiotic, you will make a bad mistake.

I trudged on and tried not to think about how far I had to go, only about putting down the feet one in front of the other. My face was stinging, except for my nose. It felt alright and that was not a good sign. I switched to inhaling through my mouth and exhaling the warmed air through my nose. Left foot, right foot, in mouth, out nose. The wind slashed at me like razor blades. I leaned into it and kept going.

Many steps along, the wind came to feel less cold. It became more a heavy thing pounding into me than exactly something cold. My knees had passed the line from cold to numb. They felt dark. My head felt dark. The wind had become dark. Cold was no longer whiteness, but thick and murky. Then I tripped and fell on my face. The magazine fell out and lay on the snow with its remaining pages flapping. And I was sharply cold again. No more numb. I grabbed the magazine and stuffed it back in place, holding my arms tighter around my head than before.

The cold was white again. I could see white ground and white air for twenty feet and a solid impenetrable whiteness beyond that in all directions. No road. No pipeline. Just whiteness. I stood there trying to figure which way to go, but all my brain wanted to consider was how much better it had felt walking with my eyes closed.

"Think," I ordered myself. Finally, I got enough neurons firing at once to arrive at the concept of following my footprints back to the road. Only there weren't any footprints to be seen on the hard ground with the wind constantly shifting the top layer of snow. I felt very dumb.

Then it hit me to go with the wind. I had been walking into it. I hadn't crossed the pipeline, which had been on the left of the road. Therefore, I concluded in slow motion, I should walk with the wind to my right and I would be going back toward the road.

I shifted the magazine to cover me and trudged in that direction. I thought about how the pages were keeping off the direct wind and found myself wishing the pictures on the pages were of Sharon. I walked on, dreamily, thinking about her but keeping my eyes open.

When I got back to the road, I saw that A Line had jogged left. I'd missed the turn and blundered out onto the snowfields a hundred yards before a ridge in the snow had tripped me up. Falling down did tend to wake up the mind. It was a message from the body that things were not right.

I resumed walking on automatic pilot. The new heading of the road made it somewhat easier. The wind was hitting me obliquely from the right instead of head on. Less air leaked down my collar and up my sleeves. My head didn't hurt so much anymore, but my stomach was cold for the first time. I started shivering, but then I held my arms tighter about me and it stopped. I tried to remember how far the turn in the A Line road was from the spine road. I knew the Prudhoe roads fairly well, but I hadn't been on A Line

273

since the year before and I hadn't been walking then. I just couldn't remember.

Gradually I found my mind turning to another winter, a time when Callahan and I set the world's record for consecutive behind-the-back Frisbee catches at twenty below zero. Eighty-two straight. That was done with the throwing hand bare. You can catch well enough with gloves, but you can't throw very well wearing them. After each toss we'd stick the bare hand into a parka pocket and then make the return throw, behind the back, with a gloved hand. Musing on that as I walked along, it occurred to me to take the sock off my right hand. In a vague way, that seemed like a good idea.

I held the magazine with my arm a second as I slipped off the sock and dropped it on the ground. I kept walking. I considered that my hand was open to the air, freezing as I gripped the magazine. More steps thinking about the cold of my hand. Everything felt spacey and slow motion.

I woke out of that with a snap, turned around and ran back. The sock had blown off the road. I was lucky to see it on the bank. I climbed down, picked it up and shook the snow out of it. The pages rattled in the wind as I held the magazine one-handed. I got the sock back on and started walking again, faster. The pages I had wrapped around my chest and around my left leg had slipped down. The wind cut through my clothes there and I felt a painful, biting cold. It frightened me that the factor was getting to my head. I concentrated on stepping and breathing. My mind tried to wander off again. I slowly bent it back to the rhythm of left foot, right foot, in mouth, out nose.

I was shivering again. My whole body was shaking and I could not stop it. I walked for a very long time into the cold.

Someplace down the road a strong gust blew the ice fog apart, showing the red lights on a communications tower. The lights were off to my left. I wanted to walk straight for them even though the road I was on was the shortest route to the main road and a truck. I wrestled with the choice. Then the ice fog thickened and the red lights disappeared back into the whiteness.

I was shaking harder and harder. I sped up, but I was afraid to run because breathing too much cold air could frostbite the inside of my throat. I pressed on and wondered what the factor might be doing to me. I shivered uncontrollably and a burst of anger rose up in me that I could not stop. I clenched my arms tighter about my head and walked on. And then I stopped thinking about anything and only paid attention to breathing and walking. And I saw an image of a man with a greenish hue in a high cave. Wondered if he was cold.

I walked a long time.

I didn't recognize the main road when I got to it. I walked all the way across and just caught myself before I went down the bank on the other side. At first I thought I'd blundered off track again, but then I saw where I was and a tremendous rush came over me, snatching away the feeling of cold for an instant, as I wondered if I could get to the Deadhorse airport in time for the last flight to Fairbanks.

Headlights suddenly glared right on top of me. I stepped in front of them and waved the magazine. Aggressive roadflex. No passing up the hitchhiker that time. I didn't step back until a powder-blue LCI pickup came to a complete stop.

The cab was wonderfully warm, even before I slammed the door shut. I felt dizzy from the heat, pulled off the socks and unbuttoned my shirt. The driver gave me an odd look as I pulled the cold pages out of my clothes.

"Hey, man, you OK? What happened?"

"I got separated from my truck. I'm fine."

I didn't believe it until I got the rearview mirror turned around for a look at my face. The driver snapped on the dome light and I saw that the flare of my left nostril was white, and I mean dead white. There were gray spots on both cheekbones, but they were no problem.

"You got coffee or something hot?" I asked.

He produced a Thermos and I poured a cup. I threw down a fast swallow. Then I scooped snow off my clothes and dumped it into the cup. I cooled it down too far and had to pour in more from the Thermos to bring the temperature back up to a touch over lukewarm. I bent over and stuck my nose into the cup. It stung as it warmed, though not badly. I liked that. Maybe it hadn't been frozen. Maybe it wasn't going to turn black in a week and fall off my face. Nothing more I could do about that, except keep it in the coffee.

I talked with the driver with my nose burbling in the coffee. It sounded so funny I had to laugh and then I couldn't stop laughing. Cold wasn't funny, but heat flowing into me was a delight. My head started aching again where

I'd gotten rapped and that was pretty funny also. I laughed louder and snorted waves in the coffee.

My savior turned out to be a nightshift electrician foreman from Gathering Center One, just out floating around. He was unsettled by my laughter and wanted to humor me. He agreed to drive me to the airport. In fact, he claimed that if I thought Prudhoe Bay was that funny, it was a very good idea for me to catch the next plane out.

I warmed up the coffee once and dipped my nose in it the rest of the way over to Deadhorse. I downed it in a gulp when we pulled into the parking lot and took another look in the mirror. I had flesh color back in my nose. The stinging was gone. The gray spots had turned pink. I had no way to know if my nostril was damaged, but I felt good about it because the stinging had been so low key. And, I had lucky skin. I'd had lucky skin all my life. I thanked the driver and went inside the terminal feeling good, though my knees were still too cold and stiff to concede the possibility of ever being warm again.

I stood at the coffee urn and downed two cups. The heat flowed though me.

Fifteen passengers for the nine o'clock to Fairbanks and Anchorage were already in the boarding area. I didn't see any hundred dollar bills lying around, so they must have gotten the place cleaned up after Downer went through. I paid the sixty bucks and walked through the electronic searcher. It chirped and the attendant started her riff about taking everything out of my pockets. I backed up, composed my mind, and walked through again producing no sounds.

Lori and the shill in the red and green flannel shirt were sitting together, trying to fade into the wall. They saw me alright, but they weren't letting on. She had on the same highly eroto dress, but she was using the parka to cover up. I went over to them and sat down in the chair next to her. She turned away and tried to ignore me. It didn't work.

She finally turned around and faced me, asking "What do you want? Get away from me."

"Sssssh," I said, holding a finger to my lips and nodding to the others in the boarding area, "you don't want them to hear."

"Hear what? You got nothing on us," she snapped.

"That's only because I stopped you in time."

The shill leaned over and said quietly, "The cops have no beef with us. Let us alone."

"How about this jury of your peers around here," I said, motioning around the room. "They've heard about the Denali. You want I should point you two out for a round of cheers?"

Lori wanted to slap me in the worst way, but he held her back, telling her, "He's right. Just cool it."

"Or, maybe you'd like to tell the troopers about how you rode over to Parsons Tuesday night with Phil?"

"I was watching a movie the whole time. Sitting right next to Spacey Acey. You can ask him." She leaned back in her chair and looked at me defiantly.

"But you'd still rather not discuss it with the troopers, right? They're still wondering how Phil's truck got back to CC2."

"What do you want, Rezkel?"

"That's better. I'm going to ask you some questions nice and quiet, and you'll answer them because you like the way I'm helping you duck out of here. Now, first, did Scanlon ever pull this stunt before?"

They both looked at me and couldn't decide at first who was going to answer. Then the shill opened up.

"Last fall, in Valdez, only it wasn't for so much. Just thirty thousand in the pot. It only took five hundred to get in. Scanlon didn't know how easy it is to get guys to put up a grand. Worked the same way, though. And real smooth, even."

"What was your cut this time?"

"Two thou for me and five for Lori. Right, Lori?"

She paused and then made herself speak. It came out strained.

"Yeah. Luke was getting five, same as me. Phil would have gotten more, but... We got these jobs, too. Scanlon gave us two weeks on the payroll. But now, I don't know if we'll even see that." She went quiet, feeling very sorry for herself.

"How did Scanlon take it when Phil was killed?"

"He went right for the Chivas Regal," Lori said, "and I thought the deal was all off."

"How good a hand were you putting out of the cold deck?"

Lori looked back up at me and said, "Five eights. It was going to be five eights."

"Yeah," the shill seconded. "We thought five aces might be going a little strong so we backed off a bit."

"What if you got edged by a natural five nines?"

"That's the breaks," he said with a minute smile.

"Come off it. Scanlon's not that good a loser, is he?"

"No," he said, shaking his head. "He's not."

Fairbanks

Chapter Twenty

The Aurora Borealis was spectacular over Fairbanks. Shimmery red wands slid along the horizon, wavered, dissolved and then reappeared as a purple wave washing back across the sky, obscuring the constellations as it went. There were other lights, bright blue flashing lights, at the edge of the airport parking lot where several police cars had a Checker Cab surrounded.

I got a sweater, coat and cap out of my car and joined the crowd standing around watching a photographer work the scene. Downer was sitting in the back of a trooper car with a dumpy guy who was wearing a Checker Cab hat. Scanlon was in the back of another stater car. A body was lying on the ground next to the cab, covered by an official sheet. The area was thick with troopers, scurrying around trying to find things they'd look good doing and keeping away from the gaze of Forzano, who was standing in the midst of them, arms folded over his chest, glaring at everything.

"Tucker," sneered Forzano, drawing out the name, "do we have this situation under control?"

Tucker stopped scurrying and looked up, unsure what to answer. He tried a crisp, "Yes, Sir."

"Then turn off the goddamn flashers," he said, lashing out a hand and pointing at the blue lights on a patrol car. "They're giving me a headache."

Tucker hopped to it.

Forzano saw me walking up to him and crossed his arms again. His upper lip curled as he said, "I told you to stay put, Rezkel."

"I was only helping out, Lieutenant, like a good citizen."

"You think this borough needs a freelance card game cop?"

"Oh, you heard about that."

"Yeah, I heard about it."

I stepped over to the corpse and drew back the sheet. Scanlon's guy, with bullets in him. Must have thrown him off balance. Scratch one from the list of people I had business with.

"You know him?"

"A little. I was hoping to know him better. He and Scanlon made me unhappy with a tire iron. I got over it."

"That why you didn't come in on the same flight?"

I nodded.

"Any charges you want filed?"

"How about you fill me in on this scene first?"

"Com'ere," he ordered and led me over to the car with Downer in the back. Forzano got in behind the wheel and I took the other side. I leaned over the front seat and smiled at Downer. He was very nervous. He didn't like cops.

"What happened, Downer?"

"I got ripped twice, man. That guy over there," he said pointing at Scanlon in the other car, "and the one that got shot, they were standing at this stop sign here with their backs turned. We didn't think nothing of it. When the cab stopped they turned around and had guns on us. They had stocking caps down over their faces. We couldn't do nothing. They were right here, man. That one in the car, he opened the back door where I was and pointed his gun at my face. He didn't say nothing. He took the sack with the money from the Denali, what was left," Downer said, laughing uneasily.

"What do you mean, what was left?" Forzano asked with a mean look.

Downer looked at his feet, shrugged and squeaked out, "I gave a lot away. I guess I got excited."

"You said that before and I didn't believe you then either," Forzano sneered.

"I was there, Lieutenant. He went batshit and tossed it away by the handful, but he left camp with eighty or ninety thousand and that's enough for a grand larceny rap."

Forzano eased off with a grunt and went back to listening. I turned over my hand as a cue for Downer to resume. He wiped sweat off his forehead and went on.

"These first two guys, they didn't get nowhere. Two more guys appeared out of nowhere, right behind them with guns drawn. There was a big guy and a little guy with a funny, deep voice. They had stocking caps pulled down, too. The big one smacked that guy over there with his gun," pointing at Scanlon again. "The other one of the first two, he tried to turn and get his gun around on the little one and that guy, the little guy, shot him just like that, two times. He got knocked back and fell down. I'm pretty sure he's dead. The little one, he came around the cab and took the money sack. The back door was still open. This little prick leaned in and told us to lie down on the seat. Rez, I thought that was it. He was pointing his gun at me and I thought he was going to empty it. Didn't you?" he asked, turned to the cabby sitting next to him.

The cab driver sat there, quite disdainfully. "No, I knew he wasn't gonna. Them punks is all talk."

"Shut up asshole," Forzano barked at him. "When the officer got here you two were still lying down on the seat." He turned to Downer and said, "Go on."

"With what? We laid there. They left. I heard something drive off, but I didn't stick my head up to look. He wanted to shoot. He wanted to. This guy," he said, jerking his thumb at the cab driver, "he called it in on his radio and we waited."

"You two are coming downtown," Forzano announced.

"Hey, what do I know," the cab driver complained. "This is gonna blow my whole shift."

Forzano looked at him with his usual disgust and got out of the cab. As I was getting out, Downer motioned to me. I came around to the back door on his side. He got out handing me a small bottle.

"Nick, you gotta take this. I never been in jail and I'm not going back."

I looked at it and then back up at him. I didn't want to touch it, not in any way, but I didn't want to see him run into a dumb bust.

"Just dump it, Downer, and don't worry about it. They don't want to pop you. It'd screw up their case."

He pulled the bottle back.

"Yeah, yeah. That's right," he agreed, shakily. Then he got a burst of confidence and chuckled. "Hey, I could use a hit," he said and started unscrewing the cap.

"Christ, Downer, wait till you get out of sight, at least," I told him and walked away.

Forzano was standing with his arms crossed again, watching his crew at work. He motioned me over with a jerk of his sharp chin and nodded at Scanlon, who looked completely dispirited, pathetic and even somehow drunk. Scanlon had a bandage on his forehead. I hoped that came from the back fist I gave him before I got clipped by his dead friend.

"Lamest hold-up I've seen in twenty years. I made the arrest. Gave him his rights myself. You know," Forzano said, nudging me with his elbow, "he's the most prominent citizen I've busted since I got the ex-mayor for shooting at his wife. That was discharging a firearm in a dangerous manner and it didn't stick anyway. This one's perfect. It's not just attempted armed robbery either, because Scanlon got away with it, even if for only ten seconds. And later I'm going to arrest him again for gunning Barriss."

Forzano laughed and I chuckled along with him. I rarely saw him in a loquacious mood. I was afraid it might go on for a very long time.

"Why? Why'd he do it?" Forzano asked me.

"Scanlon arranged the whole checkpool scam. Phil Dalira hustled the tickets. Scanlon set up his shill and a card mechanic with phony jobs to get them in position. But you know about the mix-up. Seems the wrong guy won. Scanlon tagged along with a rod man and took the first chance he came across, without covering his own back."

"Dumb, not to figure a pro might be after a cupcake like that Downer."

"Yeah, all of that, and desperate. This goes back to Scanlon's development out on Old Nenana, S&B Enterprises. There's money trouble landing on him out there. His sandcastle was only half built and the tide was coming in next Wednesday. He needed fifty thousand to keep his end alive. And that could also be the reason Barriss killed Dalira."

"Barriss, huh? That's cute, their way out, you're still on that. Why is it always so much easier to pin a murder on a dead man?"

"Come on over to my car, Forzano. I've got some stuff I brought back from the Slope. Evidence they call it."

"Right, Rezkel, evidence, lots of evidence. Remember, evidence is different than proof."

On the way over I ran down the defective foam scam Barriss and Dalira had going and explained how the water on the Randolph-Lightner payroll tied right in. At the Toyota, I handed him a collection of papers to punctuate my explanation.

I was not fully convinced about what had happened to Phil Dalira. Barriss still didn't fit better than ninety percent, but I pushed him on Forzano anyway. I didn't actually care about Dalira at that moment. I wanted to do something for Floyd Arthur. Floyd had waited two years. Now Dalira could wait a while.

"That's all context. Here's the one-eyed Jack, Dalira's notebook. I found it in the bottom drawer of his wall locker at camp. It's all in his handwriting."

"I don't know his handwriting."

"But you'll check it out, won't you? Anyway, look at this number 66A6139. That is the serial number of the D9 Cat Scanlon and Barriss were using at their development. It's ripped off from Randolph-Lightner, along with most of their other equipment. Dalira came up with this number, put it together, and he hit Barriss up for a bigger cut of the action."

"Keep it up, Rezkel. You might talk yourself into it. I'm still looking at your girlfriend Jeanne."

"Listen, at least, Forzano," I said, wanting to get it all out as fast as I could. I knew he had to think he had it all before I'd ever be able to clear out of there. I believed enough of it, except for one part.

"Dalira had too much figured out. Barriss had already turned the corner on his share of S&B and he was no longer interested in padding the payroll with phony workers. Too risky. Remember how fast he cut that off the day after Dalira ate it. He was playing in the big time with his development and he didn't want any cheap hustler like Phil Dalira messing with it.

"At the same time Scanlon was blowing his end of S&B. That was getting the whole development into bad shape.

They barely had enough cash to do it in the first place and had to steal the equipment to make it work. But Barriss was going to win big if Scanlon could be knocked out of the partnership. And, just exactly then, Dalira was trying to squeeze Barriss while helping Scanlon put on the Denali Checkpool."

"So, you telling me that made it knife time for Barriss? That's why he chopped Dalira to pieces and poured cocaine all over him?" Forzano queried, rubbing his chin.

"Barriss had a bad temper. The cocaine stunt was clumsy. He knew nothing about cocaine. It fits."

"I like some of it, Rezkel, but I'm not going to take Barriss' body and throw it in a cell. This is just fluff. What you got to back it up?"

It took another twenty minutes to tell him everything about the Randolph-Lightner truck Barriss had borrowed and how both Jeanne and Spacey had seen him at Parsons. In the end, Forzano was still unpersuaded, but leaning. He didn't like hearing news from me that his investigators had missed and I could see him throwing a penalty flag in his mind. Finally, he just got tired of listening.

"Rezkel, I'm not going to forget that you went up there after I told you not to jerk me around with the oil companies. I'm not forgetting, but I am condoning it this time."

I made my pitch.

"Thanks. How about I come by in the morning and make a statement? It's been a hard day and now that this is over, I just want to get some rest."

He made me wait while he thought it over, then answered, "Make it early in the morning."

The Toyota wouldn't start, naturally. I got out the jumper cables and promoted a jump start from Tucker. He wanted to scope out what I'd told Forzano, so for a tidbit of information he turned helpful and got me started. No headlights bloomed in the rearview mirror. By the time I took the left at University Avenue I felt clear of the troopers.

I wanted to drive straight to Sharon's place, but I couldn't. I knew where I had to go. I had to finish it off for Floyd.

The bank's temperature sign at College Road showed an encouraging minus eight. Nearly sun stroke conditions after Prudhoe. I didn't want to press my luck with frostbite, so I drove with the window rolled up and scraped the windshield as I went. Out Farmers' Loop. Left on McGrath. Near the top of the hill I made another left and pulled over just beyond a driveway that led to a very expensive house.

Before I got out I flicked on the dome light and did a quick inventory of the body parts. Rosy flesh tones. My nose was acceptable, or if it wasn't I wouldn't find out about it for days. My knees were cold and stiff. Any sensation felt a big improvement. My formerly black eye, now purple and lemon, was among my more functional parts. The ache in the back of my head was getting worse, which proved that my mind had continued to thaw, possibly enough to be capable of thought again. And my feet. Even without socks, they were perfect. My Sorels had performed out on A Line, only Sorels weren't going to cut it any longer. There would be three men inside with guns. I might have to move and Sorels were entirely too clumsy for that. I took them off, got socks back on my feet and slipped into the tennis shoes I had stashed behind the seat.

I got the Ruger out of the glove compartment and flipped open the chamber. Six rounds. I gave the cylinder an extra hard spin for luck and snapped it shut. My Wham-O Frisbee was sitting on the passenger seat. I touched it for luck also. I like luck. Then I pulled my stocking cap down over my nose and got out.

Up toward the crest of the hill the temperature was warmer than the minus eight down in the valley. Maybe zero. The Lights were splashing across the sky, but I didn't watch them. I turned into Kirby's driveway and walked softly over the snow.

Halfway to the house one of the huskies started howling. I knew the rest of them would take it up, so I stepped into the birch trees flanking the driveway and stood still in the shadows. An aspen near me rustled faintly in a light breeze. After a moment all the dogs were howling. Maybe wolf scent was coming up the valley. Maybe they had heard me. Maybe they smelled me. It didn't matter. Someone would be out to shut them up.

A crack of light appeared in the doorway of the small cabin below the house. An old man with a white beard and silvery hair came out in his long johns and slippers. Kirby's dog trainer. He shouted at the huskies. They gradually cut it out and settled down again. The old man went back inside. I didn't like extra variables floating free, but I decided that I could ignore him.

Two pickups were parked in a turnaround lit by a flood-light on a pole. I left the cover of the trees and ran lightly toward the porch. I stayed in the tire tracks to keep the snow from crunching under my feet and stirring up the huskies again. The only light on inside the house was in the room just beyond the porch. For a few seconds, anyone looking out could have seen me, but no figure appeared in the windows. I eased open the porch door and stepped inside. I closed the door and stood in the darkness.

Light was coming through a small window in the door. It took a moment for my eyes to adjust, but then I could make things out clearly enough. On the left split birch was stacked to the ceiling. On the right a table against the end wall had small tools scattered over it. A crate with two five gallon kerosene tins was on the floor by the door. Cross country skis and snowshoes leaned against the wall. I shook out the muscles in my legs to get loosened. Then I stepped past a chopping block with a double-bitted axe sunk in it and moved quietly to the window in the door.

Through the glass I saw a slice of cedar-paneled living room. A full bar with four stools and lots of bottles was in the left rear corner. Kerosene lamps burned on either end of the bar. A door in the back wall led to darkened rooms beyond. In the center of the room stood an island of cedar cabinets. Stained wood dowels ran up from it. Philodendrons twined up them to the ceiling. Sitting on top of the cabinets was a purple velvet sack.

I knew right then the smart thing to do was back off and get to a phone at one of the neighbors. I did consider letting

Forzano take care of it. Then I got closer to the window and saw Lou Devery and Huey sitting in black leather armchairs in the near left corner, just inside the door, looking sullen. That changed it. It wasn't anything I didn't know. I expected them to be there, but the instant I saw Devery I didn't care anymore about doing the smart thing. I felt a burn in my guts and knew I had to take care of it personally. It made me feel reckless. With a gun in my hand I didn't mind the sensation.

It didn't make me completely dumb, however. I stepped left to look at the other side of the room. In the far right corner was a wood stove. More black leather furniture was along the right hand wall as far as I could see. And Kirby stood there, elegant in a pearl-gray suit. He was in the middle of the room with one hand behind his back and the index finger of his hand laid beside his mouth as he looked down thoughtfully at the rug. I'd seen him get like that at the card table when a pigeon had made a rash bet and Kirby was checking his cards again before raising. It looked like a decent chance to conduct some personal business. I didn't care how it might sort out in court.

No hinges were showing on the door. It opened the wrong way, inwards, like a politician's heart. I bumped it with my shoulder and stepped in, bringing the Ruger around on Devery. I was expecting him to reach for his .45 and then I was expecting him to stop his move when I had him lined up. If he didn't stop, I was going to shoot him. But he didn't move and neither did Huey. Just as I was understanding that, I heard her say, "Drop it."

I stopped and looked over my shoulder at Jeanne. She was standing in the corner behind me, with a blue steel .32 automatic in her hand. A small gun, hardly able to maim. It was only big enough to kill and she was too close to miss. The blue steel didn't go with her burning green eyes at all, or with the slinky yellow-on-green dress she was wearing. It did go real well with the rage and triumph in her face, however.

"Let me help you, lover," I said quietly, keeping my gun on Devery.

"Drop it, Rezkel," she yelled, her voice vibrating with anger. She jabbed the automatic at me. "Now, or I'll drop you."

She was ready to. She was very close to squeezing the trigger. I heard it in her voice. I wondered if Phil had seen her like this. About Jeanne, just a single unknown remained.

A slight smile played over Kirby's face. I let go and the pistol fell to the carpet with a dull thud.

"What are you doing here?" she demanded. "Why are you interfering with me?"

"Hardly that. I just now got Forzano pointed away from you in Phil's murder."

"Did you confess to stabbing my brother yourself?" she asked with a sneer.

"No. I pitched Barriss at him. He bought it, mostly, but isn't that bit about Phil being your brother getting a little dated?"

Her gun hand clenched as another burst of rage ran across her face. She steadied the automatic on me, but a

295

question was shining in her eyes. She motioned me over to Devery and Huey. I thought I might get help from Kirby and the others if I went for her, but I was the one closest to her gun. I answered her unspoken question instead of making a move, because I thought it useful to involve Kirby as much as possible.

"What I meant, lover, was that Phil only became your brother a little while ago, in Anchorage, when you needed cover. I don't see what he got out of that except dead."

"Bullshit. That's a stupid rumor."

"Too late now. Kirby's got the idea and he'll look into it."

A bitter look hardened her face. I could see quite clearly what she might be like with a knife in her hand. I could finally see that. I just didn't quite believe it before because I didn't think that she could have come up with one so fast on Tuesday night.

Kirby tensed like he wanted to try something or rather, like he wanted Devery and Huey to try something. I was exactly in line between Devery and Jeanne. I took an easy step away from her toward the center of the room so he couldn't use me for cover. Kirby looked around. I thought he must have another cannon around somewhere and tried to find it from where he looked. Then Jeanne stopped that.

"Stay right there, Kirby. No, wait. I don't like Rezkel loose. Tie him up. We have to talk."

Devery started to get out of his chair. She swung on him and he stopped dead halfway to his feet.

"I said for you to tie him up, Kirby."

Devery receded back into his chair.

"These do?" Kirby asked, stretching his left hand slowly toward the cabinet island. Jeanne tracked him with the automatic. Kirby picked a pair of handcuffs off the counter, dangling them in front of him to repeat the question. Jeanne nodded me over to him. I stepped over and presented my arms in front of me. I had to try.

"Stuff it, Rezkel. Turn around," he said.

I turned and looked over my shoulder. They were Peerless cuffs. Toughies. Kirby laid the key on the cabinet top and slapped the cuffs on my wrists. He cupped his hands around them and gave an extra crank to make the steel bite into my skin. He put his soft, smooth left hand on my chest and marched me backwards. I went with it.

Another black leather couch stood against the wall behind me. Jeanne was standing between it and the armchairs in the corner behind her. Kirby kept pushing me and then gave me a last shove onto the couch. I sat down opening my hands behind me to take up the impact. As I landed Kirby was delightfully open for a front snap kick to the nuts. I almost fired it off, but I couldn't see how it would help. Maybe I should have anyway, because Kirby turned his last shove into a step toward Jeanne. She wasn't ready for it. He reached and immediately had her gun hand tied up.

Devery got there quickly and they took the automatic out of her hand. Huey lumbered up too late, uncertain what to do, so he grabbed Jeanne from behind and held her. Devery walked away toward the cabinet and Huey was left holding Jeanne. She twisted around, elbowed him and spat in his face. He half let go of her and tried to grab her arms.

She stepped back before he could catch her. Devery laughed. Huey shot a dark look at him and stood there trying to figure what to do next.

Kirby changed focus right off. He slipped the gun into his coat pocket, walked over to a table in the corner and picked up a manila envelope. He turned on a standing lamp and, carefully pulling up his pants leg, sat down in an armchair. Jeanne walked slowly toward him. Huey was right behind her. He didn't grab at her again, but he stayed in reach and leered. She stopped and he stopped.

Huey's big gut stuck out through the black and white striped work shirt he was wearing. He had a .38 stuck in his belt. It looked ridiculous indenting into his belly. He couldn't have pulled it out without sucking his gut in first.

"You didn't have to do that, Kirby, to read that material," Jeanne said. "That's why I brought it, for you to read."

"Why'd you pull the gun as soon as you came in the door?"

"I thought you'd be here alone. When I saw you weren't it scared me. I didn't trust them. I don't trust them. Especially that oaf," she said, dismissing Huey with a glance.

"Go over there, Huey, and keep an eye on Rezkel," Kirby said, smoothly waving Huey away.

Huey peeled his eyes off Jeanne with an effort and walked toward me. He got an oak chair from the wall next to the wood stove, put it a few feet to my right and sat down. The pistol poked into his belly and made him uncomfortable. He pulled a chunk of birch out of the wood pile by the stove, stuck his left foot on it and rocked the chair back on two legs.

Devery paid marginal attention to me and didn't worry about Jeanne at all. He took out a two gram coke bottle with a silver spoon attached to the cap by a chain. He tooted up and then kept on snorting spoons of cocaine at a steady pace. He threw back his head with each hit and breathed in a full load of air, shaking his head and making a sharky smile. He seemed to think he'd grown two feet and didn't need a .45 anymore. He swung around and offered a hit to Huey, who got uptight and turned him down with a grunt. Devery thought that was funny. He lit a cigarette and laughed dully as he blew out a lungful of stale smoke.

"You're too straight, Huey. You're a joke," Devery croaked in his frog voice, firing off another toot.

Huey glared at him, then turned away and glared at me.

Jeanne walked around our half of the room in agitated circles. She was very strained. I thought she was missing a lot of what was happening.

"I've got copies of those documents, you know," she announced in an overly loud, jerky voice.

Kirby muttered "Hmmmmm" and continued reading. His face didn't look as smooth and shiny as usual. His cheeks were drawn in and he wasn't controlling his expression the way he always could at the card table or politicking around Fairbanks. Anger was leaking out all over his features. That was good news. I saw an opening, a small one, and Kirby being angry was just what I needed.

Chapter Twenty-one

Kirby finished the last sheet and put down the papers.

"It's all there, isn't it, Kirby? Enough to send you to jail," Jeanne hissed at him.

"So you say. Frankly, I don't think this material has much connection to anything I might have done or not done."

"Come off it. Look at the file numbers. They came right from the Department of Mines files and they've got your signature all over them."

"Who did you get these from?"

"Does it matter? They're genuine and you know it."

"The weather has changed since last time, Miss Dalira or whatever your name is, from sunshine to thunderstorms, but it's still the same shake down," he told her, hitting the last words with bitter emphasis.

"You don't really want to talk money," she said, looking around the room, "with all of them here, do you?"

"Why not?" he asked in a level voice, crossing his arms and pulling his face into neutral.

"Your track record as deputy commissioner would look sorry even in Chicago."

"Pardon me, but I have an excellent record as a public official. You might call it distinguished."

Kirby said it automatically. He was giving himself time to think and he was controlling himself while he did it. That wasn't healthy for me. Jeanne didn't pick up that he had already decided what he was going to do and was working out the implementation. She'd been quick about my reactions, but I hadn't minded displaying them. She wasn't reading Kirby at all. She still thought she held aces.

Jeanne moved about the room as she talked. Kirby stayed in the armchair. He was at his best sitting down, whether you were on the other side of the card table or the other side of the checkbook.

"Your record is distinguished by a lot of help you gave certain partners. Expensive help. Like the way you moved in on S&B Enterprises. There were four tries to patent the land S&B is building on. The same shady application kept getting turned down each time, until you approved it two years ago. Then like magic you appeared as a partner in Associated Interior Investors, which happens to own Arctic Diversified, which happens to own S&B Enterprises."

"Is this where you demand twenty thousand dollars again?" Kirby asked in a hard voice, counterpointed by a mocking chortle from Devery.

301

Jeanne's eyes were wild. She still wasn't getting it. She thought she could make some deal with Kirby. I knew there wasn't any deal they could make that I would survive, or Jeanne either. But I saw that if they stayed close enough together, close enough for me to reach them before they could fire, I saw half a shot at getting out of there alive. Only it was going nowhere without Jeanne and it had to be soon because the Peerless cuffs were shutting down my hands. They hurt and I was going numb quickly.

When Kirby cuffed me, he laid the key down on the counter top, ten feet away, with no one paying any attention to it. Devery was standing against the counter a few feet from the key, but he was snorting up and not watching anything carefully except his spoon. I wanted Jeanne to get desperate, very desperate, enough to see she needed me. So I got obnoxious and provoked Kirby.

"Shoot higher, Jeanne. Try eighty grand. They've got it right here."

All their heads swiveled toward me. After that teaser I changed the subject. I spoke to him, but I was trying to get something through to Jeanne.

"You did more than muscle in on S&B Enterprises, Kirby. Your partners were on the edge of a cliff from the start. You helped them push each other over. That's why you gave Phil Dalira the serial number to that stolen D9. You knew Dalira couldn't pass that up. He was too much of an angle junky not to put the bite on Barriss. Huey had to give you the idea about the D9, but how'd you know Phil so well?"

"Dalira was around," he answered cautiously.

"I think you figured he'd hit up Barriss for a cut. That would crank up the pressure, help Barriss make mistakes. Only then Dalira wound up dead and that was even better for you. It almost blew Scanlon's checkpool fundraising. Scanlon was in bad money trouble. You knew all about that, didn't you? You beat him out of enough at Thalman's to help him get that way in the first place."

"That's widely known. Anyway, why should I make his money trouble worse, since that hurts my interest in Associated?"

I caught Jeanne's eye. She gave me a neutral look, no burning hatred any longer. She stopped pacing around and leaned against the counter, taking in what I was saying.

"Because it didn't hurt your interest," I answered Kirby. "It could help you in a big way. That's how you always were at the card table. You didn't want some of Scanlon's chips. You wanted them all. When Barriss was taken out, his interest passed to his wife. Anyone looking at the charter will find that Mrs. Barriss owns a share that now has no vote. Isn't that right, Jeanne?"

"Yes," she confirmed guardedly.

"And now you're even luckier, Kirby, because Scanlon is blown out of the water," I said and paused as a quick look passed between Kirby and Devery. "What's next? Are you going to up the ante? Maybe declare an assessment on Associated's partners, high enough so Mrs. Barriss and Mrs. Scanlon can't cover? Do you wind up with the whole works?"

"Neat, Rezkel. Were you ever in business?" Kirby asked.

"No, I just naturally think dirty," I answered, becoming more of an embarrassment all the time.

As soon as I paused, Huey spoke up.

"I didn't tell nobody but Phil about that Cat."

"Shut up," Kirby snapped. "You told someone or he wouldn't have found out."

Jeanne looked over at Kirby when he barked at Huey. She was starting to see what Kirby had on his mind, but she wasn't convinced. I decided on revolutionary tactics because it had to get much worse before it could get better. I had to give Kirby a good reason to kill me.

"You had the perfect partners for your style. They had enough money to get a large-scale development going, but not enough to finish it. Plus they hated each other. You took chances and you got lucky. Scanlon's checkpool was in trouble. I saw his face when he first got the idea that Barriss had killed Dalira. Scanlon brought in a relief pitcher, a Teamster named Luke. Barriss then messed with Luke. Tried to run him off the job. That was all Scanlon needed to figure Barriss was the one trying to knock him out of the game. Scanlon pre-empted Barriss with a .38. That was an easy win for you."

"They're not usually so easy."

"How'd you know your partners were using Phil to water the Randolph-Lightner payroll?"

"That's another thing you'll never know."

"It couldn't have been Huey. He was there, but he's too damn dumb to figure out something like that."

Huey's chair legs slammed down to the floor and he came out of his chair at me. He rocked my head back with a punch before Kirby got him stopped and told him to sit down again. Huey went back to his chair. He didn't tilt it back as before. That was a complication, but I couldn't do anything about it.

As long as I was telling Kirby what I knew about his business, he was going to listen. I knew he had just one question for me.

Jeanne was staying put, leaning against the cabinet. She wasn't ready yet. I figured it was time to get her ready.

"You're good at setting up a play. I've seen you do that at Thalman's, for instance when you set up Floyd Arthur. You showed this asshole over here," nodding at Devery who only laughed, "how to dump a few chips Floyd's way to keep him tightened up until he could be taken out in a certain elevator. You were real helpful then, when I was checking out the murder, weren't you, showing me you'd been home or at Thalman's the whole time. I almost crossed you off the list, only there was one thing you didn't tell me. A certain lawyer called you here late that afternoon. Guy named Dahlquist. He was working the deal where Floyd Arthur sold his mining claim and you had him stall the sale until you could get Devery into position. Tell me, Kirby, did Dahlquist know what he was doing or didn't he think about things like that when you gave him orders? Tell me."

"You tell me, Rezkel, who else knows about all this? Who did you learn that from? Dahlquist?"

"You know me. I get around. I talk to everybody."

He didn't like the ambiguity, but he didn't press it. I could see him file his question, to ask again after I ran dry on him, with some persuasion behind it.

"You really should go for eighty grand, Jeanne. A guy I know took a short ride in a cab and lost all his hundred dollar bills. They're right over there in that purple sack."

She looked at it and then right back at me. I carried on with a rush.

"Scanlon and a hired hand tried to steal that sack. They didn't get two feet before a little man with a big gun and a big man with a big gut ripped them off. Scanlon's helper got dead. Ask Devery about it, Jeanne. He might remember which bullet it was."

The atmosphere went ozone. Devery eased off the counter and looked to Kirby. Kirby started out of his chair, but thought better of it and leaned back without saying a word.

It came to Jeanne completely and at once. She knew she didn't want to be hearing it, but she was fascinated and didn't want me to stop. She looked right at me with her gray-green eyes. The gold flake in them was molten as she stared at me like she had on the tugboat.

I looked her away to the key. She didn't get it. I met her eyes again and then cut my glance sharply to the key on the counter beside her. The third time she followed my eyes, only she looked too far and thought I meant the money bag farther across the counter. She had enough of the idea. To cover her I rattled on, committing suicide with Kirby.

"Scanlon set up the Denali checkpool using Randolph-Lightner troops and a designated winner. Only the play soured and the wrong man won. Some cheating at cards or something. You can appreciate that," I said to Kirby, getting a hard stare in return. He wasn't bothering to control his face anymore. He was flushed red and only waiting for me to finish.

"Scanlon lost it days ago. He's been improvising ever since. He needed the Denali score to cover his end of the development. Between you and Thalman, he was crazy for bucks to keep afloat. He had no way to turn back. He had to win big or lose it all. He tried that amateur holdup, but Devery finished it off for him. Now Forzano is giving him the heat and he probably still thinks you're his pal. But Thalman isn't going to think that. The only thing he can collect from Scanlon now is a share in Associated Interior. How are you going to keep him from running over you?"

"I thought I'd do the honorable thing and pay off my former partner Scanlon's gambling debts with that money over there. After all, that's partly why he tried to steal it," Kirby laughed.

Devery cracked up. Huey rocked back in his chair and started chuckling. I looked at the counter. The key was gone.

"You're right, Scanlon was hopeless, only it happened long ago. He and Barriss were in trouble form the start. If not for me, the development would have long since sunk out of sight. I had to do something to ease Scanlon out of the partnership. Thalman abhors a vacuum, you know."

That got his help laughing again, even if they didn't exactly understand what he meant. Devery loaded up his little spoon and snorted up another round. He was still laughing as the rush hit him. Then he turned his head and stared at me. His laughter lapsed into a stuttering exhalation and his dark eyes slowly crossed, becoming flat and dull as his high turned barbed, dank and vicious.

I'd been quiet too long. Kirby looked at me like the sand had finally run out of my hourglass. He was about to say something when Jeanne interrupted, stepping away from the counter.

"I can see it, Kirby. You don't have to spell it out. You were just going to ignore me, weren't you? You were going to let me try and scare you and then you were going to bluff it out. Only not now."

She wheeled toward me and spit out, "Because of you. You couldn't stand the idea of dying alone. You had to go and say all this that Kirby couldn't afford to have me hear, just so you'd have company. You're too much of a coward to die alone."

It was going over. They loved it, all three of them. Kirby sat back in his chair to watch the show. Huey didn't particularly listen, but he leered at Jeanne's every movement. Devery tooted. Jeanne gave a fine performance, especially since she meant most of it. I didn't know the direction she would take it, so I threw in an insult for her to work off of.

"Can't help yourself around me, huh lover? You're getting all excited like the night we made it."

308

"You think you're real hot, Rezkel," she said, turning around and picking Devery's cigarette out of the ashtray with her right hand, "only you'll have to get even hotter to turn me on."

She walked slowly toward me with smoke trailing up her arm. Her left hand was closed. "I'll heat you up," she taunted me, her voice going shrill.

Devery snickered.

"Just because of that one night, you probably thought you owned these, didn't you," she said, thrusting her breasts at me. "You had to be an asshole, didn't you?"

She brought the cigarette up and pointed it toward my right eye.

"Having trouble getting it up, Nickie? Need a little help?"

She sat down in my lap, slipped her left hand behind my back, and held the burning end of the cigarette a foot from my eye. She was facing Kirby. He couldn't see behind my back. Devery and Huey were entranced. They watched the cigarette as she slowly moved it in toward my eye.

"Getting hotter for me, Nicky?"

I felt her reaching around behind me. She was playing it too close. I felt the heat of the cigarette all around my eye, a quarter inch away. The glowing tip was a brilliant red and huge. My eyes unfocussed. I turned my face away and arched my back to give her more room.

"Keep your eye on the ball," Devery croaked.

Jeanne shifted on my lap and brought the cigarette in again. As she moved I felt something hard on the inside of her thigh. A terrible thought roared into my mind as I remembered the moment we had been slipping half out of our clothes on the tugboat. She had been so graceful undressing in an awkward position, until she made that odd abrupt movement. It was as though she had slid something around her thigh and right after that one of her legs made a thunk against the bulkhead. I knew then that it had been a knife in some sort of sheath. The very thing I thought I knew, that she could not have had a knife, I had been completely wrong about. I became afraid that she was going to burn out my eye after all.

My eyelids kept closing on their own, like when a hammer strikes and they slam shut no matter how hard you try to keep them open. I forced them apart again. The glowing tip was closer than ever, so hot that I knew it would ruin my eye even if it only stayed right there for much longer. I could see Jeanne smiling and feeling her power over me.

"Don't you think I should, Kirby? First this eye, then the other," she purred, and as she said it the cuff around my left wrist opened. The sound was huge. I thought they had to hear it and I tensed to move. They did nothing. I eased the steel off my wrist and held it with my other hand. Feeling and pain surged together back into my left wrist.

Jeanne wrenched her face into an anguished expression and pulled the cigarette back away from me. She was trying to look close to tears, but I could see there wasn't any hurt there. Kirby didn't observe that. She jumped up and walked toward him.

"I can't," she said, almost breaking down.

I scrunched forward in the couch and covered it by whistling with relief. For the first time since I'd come in the door, I started feeling I had choices. I finally had a move I could make with some part of me other than my mouth. Images of Floyd and Sharon slid through my mind and then I came fully back to the present.

"I couldn't," she choked out. "I couldn't stick this in his eye," she said, looking back at me. But I knew she could. I looked her hard to Kirby. Once. And she caught it.

"In, in his eye. I couldn't," she whimpered. "Do what you want with him, but don't kill me too. You don't have to. I won't, I won't." she choked out, trying hard for a tear.

Kirby was twenty feet away to my left, in the corner of the room. He was watching with an amused smile. He was getting used to Jeanne's rapid shifts in manner, and he was feeling good as she pleaded and slowly approached him.

I checked back on the other two. Devery was about eight feet in front of me, leaning against the counter that divided the room. He was unscrewing the top of his cocaine bottle and getting ready for another jolt. I noticed that he was wearing an absurdly electric blue sport coat, shiny in the extreme, over an orange shirt His coat was unbuttoned and through the opening I could see the butt of his .45. He was good with that thing, and quick. I had to take him completely out, only Huey had to be first.

Huey's chair was half way to Devery and a little to the right. His left foot was resting on the stick of birch again. He leaned back, staring at Jeanne, twitching his left leg whenever she moved.

311

The first time around, he'd blown his advantage when he surprised me in the Randolph-Lightner office. He should have come right for me in that narrow space. Instead he got a bright idea and reached for a hammer, as if his fists weren't big and hard enough. Now he had a gun in his belt, right where he could reach for it. He was tough, but not with guns. I wanted him to go for the iron instead of me and I planned to give him the chance.

I pulled my right foot in close to the couch and got my weight on it as much as I dared. I slid my left foot out ahead. The cuffs were off my left wrist. I held them in my right hand and wished it was the other way around because Huey was on my right and that hand was numb. I quit worrying about it and looked back at Jeanne, wondering how fast she could get her knife out.

"I'm not going to tell anyone about this. Nobody," she pleaded to Kirby, tears forming, giving him the line he most wanted to disbelieve.

She took another step toward him and stopped five or six feet away. I glanced back at Devery and Huey. No change in position. The coke spoon was getting loaded. Suddenly the room seemed much brighter. My hearing became very acute.

"You have to..." Jeanne began and held out her hands in supplication. It looked like she'd forgotten she was still holding the cigarette and had dropped it, but the motion was a bit off. She bent over as though to pick it up. I almost fired out of the couch right then, but I held back as she immediately got hold of the cigarette again and brushed the rug with her right hand.

"Oh, I'm sorry," she said as she picked it up.

Kirby suddenly didn't like it anymore. The smile evaporated from his face as his lips closed. He snapped a look at me. I almost went again, but Kirby had not quite realized that he was suspicious. It could get just a little better for us. I gave him a blank look. Jeanne was still bent over. Her right hand was partly under her dress. Kirby was catching on, but he didn't know to what. Jeanne looked at me. Devery was raising the coke spoon to his nostrils. I judged Kirby would be in suspension for another second. I waited as the coke spoon got very close to Devery's nose. I relaxed my shoulders. Mind like water. I didn't look at any of them, but kept everything in peripheral view and felt their energies as the timing matured.

Devery snorted, tossing back his head. At the sound I exploded off the couch and kicked Huey's chair out from under him with my right foot. Blur off to the left. Devery's head snapped down. He dropped the spoon and went for his gun. I planted my right foot and made that the start of a round-house kick with my left foot. He got the .45 out of the holster and was raising it as my kick arrived, knocking the gun against his stomach. He was partly stunned, but his arm had absorbed much of the force. It didn't matter. I was driving the snap-back of the kick to the floor and throwing a punch in the same motion. I had his whole head to pick from. First I was going for his chin, but he was turning his face away. As my foot slammed to the floor my fist crashed into the hinge of his jaw. I felt the shudder of impact run through me after the contact, then rebound off the floor

313

through me again back to his jaw, ba-bang, like I'd hit him twice with one punch. His jaw snapped with a dry, brittle sound and Devery crumpled.

An agonized scream came from off to the left.

I jerked my head back to the right. Huey was untangled from the chair and getting to his feet. He might have had my legs if he had been diving, but he wasn't, he was reaching for his gun. That gave me a world of time. I skipped sideways toward him, squeezing up my right leg and firing a side thrust kick to his ribs. I never could kick high, but catching him in the ribs was enough. He went down in a heap.

Another scream shrilled from the corner and then I blew it. Devery was out. I wasn't certain about Huey. He'd taken a lot of hits the last time. I stepped in ready to kick again. It wasn't necessary and I changed my motion into reaching for his gun. He was lying on it moaning. I would have had to roll him over to get at it. Very late, I got my mind unstuck from that idea and spun back to Devery, but it had slowed me a half-count. The .45 was lying on the floor beside him. As I reached for it a shot rang out and a slug buzzed past my face.

"Freeze, Rezkel," Jeanne shouted at me, and I did.

Kirby was lying next to the door with a knife in his ribs. His left hand clutched the knife, but he wasn't moving. Blood spread slowly over his suit coat, turning the lime green into a rusty, orangey red.

Jeanne was standing over him. Her lips curled up slightly, somewhere between a smile and a grimace. She wasn't beautiful anymore. Her face was too hard and her

314

long hair hung lank, without luster. She was pointing her automatic right at my stomach.

I stopped reaching for Devery's gun and straightened up. The handcuffs dangled from my right wrist.

"That was nice, Nickie. You did both of them. Too bad you were so slow getting to the guns," she said, bringing back her mocking tone. "Now I suppose you want to call the cops."

"You haven't committed any crime here. Don't mess with anything and they'll see that it's self-defense."

She took a step toward me and began speaking through a very giggly laugh.

"Don't lie to me, Nickie. That's not what you'll tell Forzano now. You hate me. I can see it. It was in your face when you felt my knife. You figured it out right then and you hated me. I saw it. Don't you think I noticed all those times you didn't ask me if I had a knife Tuesday night? That's something you wanted to know, wasn't it?" she poured out, faster and faster, with her voice losing its smoothness. "You never asked me if I had a knife."

"I thought I knew you didn't have one that night. We were in too much of a hurry on the tugboat or I would have found out then."

"You liked me then, especially when I came," she said with her words turning into strange laughter that went up higher and higher and broke up into a loud bang as she whipped her gun hand around and fired a round into Devery. His body shook and one of his legs twitched.

"Don't you think he shudders like I did on the tugboat? Don't you think you're going to shudder?"

I almost went for her then, thinking she was about to shoot me anyway. Then she seemed a little further from squeezing the trigger and I decided to string it out. I thought she wanted to talk herself up to it, so I gave her a topic.

"You fooled me alright, only I don't know from what point. Were you going to kill Phil all along?"

"No. That just happened. He'd been screwing me on toot. I imagine you harassed that out of Spacey?"

"Yeah," I answered, hoping she would go on talking as I looked around.

"See, Phil wouldn't let Spacey sell direct to me. And he'd only sell me small amounts. An ounce or so. He wouldn't mail it. He wouldn't turn me onto anyone in Fairbanks. So while I was getting set up, I had to fly to Prudhoe every time I needed to score. That was Phil's price, or most of it, and I had to pay because I didn't have another connection."

I mostly looked at her, but I got two quick glances around the room. The most interesting thing I noticed was the pair of kerosene lamps burning on the bar behind me. Another way to play Rezkels Wild is to burn yourself into a corner.

"And then that night the fucker tried to jack up the price on me. I'd seen Barriss leaving his room as I got there. I knew he drove one of those Randolph-Lightner trucks like the one you had. That's why I thought I could get away with pretending that it was you I saw driving away. I had to try that, once you as much as told me at the airport that you saw me there and weren't telling the cops. But I thought that up later. I killed Phil because he got me so mad. He said he wanted more money. And he told me he was going to knick my ounces a gram a piece."

Then I interrupted. She was talking faster and faster and her voice was catching on some of the words.

"And so you dumped all that extra coke on him to make it look like Barriss tried a clumsy misdirection of some sort."

"Yes. I didn't know you were coming along so conveniently or I would have done something else."

She went silent. I didn't like it. I wanted to keep something going, so I slowly, elaborately picked up the Denali Checkpool sack from the counter, as though to give it to her.

I had it by the neck with my left hand and moved it deliberately across my body from right to left, watching her eyes, something from one of the katas, Empi, give them the wrong thing to watch. And she did look at it, expecting me to throw it at her. She kept the gun on me and watched the sack. As it passed from in front of me her eyes followed it. The moment her eyes switched past me to the sack I whirled, ducked and ran for the bar.

A shot slapped behind me. For an instant I had the counter between us, but I could hear her coming after me. I drove off my right leg and rolled over the bar. Another shot sounded as I was in the air. I landed on all fours on the wood floor behind the bar. I spun around. I saw a window in the wall at the end of the bar, but no way to get that far in time.

317

I swung the Denali sack up and smashed the nearest kerosene lamp to the floor. I scuttled down to the other end, straightened just enough to smash over the second lamp. It crashed into the side wall of the house. kerosene splashed everywhere and boomed into flames.

Two shots banged out. Louder than before. She had Devery's .45. Slugs ripped through the veneer bar front and tore holes in the wall behind me. An unlit lamp stood on a shelf under the bar. I threw it against the back wall. It shattered and kerosene splashed over the short end of the bar, bursting into more flames. The whole space from the cabinets to the bar was burning, but Jeanne could still get to me by going around the cabinets. I tore liquor bottles off the shelves, grabbing anything. I used one bottle to smash the necks off the others and threw them over the bar, one after the other. Flames roared up with each one. There wasn't a boom as they ignited, but the fire was instant and the bar was completely surrounded by a leaping belt of flames.

Two more .45 rounds ripped through the bar front. Close. She must have seen where the bottles were coming from. I scrambled to the corner away from the window. The wall above my head was on fire. The cedar cabinets were catching fire. The curtains on the back wall went up with a whoosh. Smoke was filling the room and reflections from the flames played across the ceiling. Another round slammed through the bar.

I pitched the velvet bag over the bar and heard her go for it. Then I grabbed more bottles and threw them through the double-glazed window at the end of the bar runway. Four bottles, one after the next, taking out a lot of the glass. Fresh air excited the flames. Then the front door opened and they surged. Time to pull the pin.

I ran and dove head first out the window. A jagged spike sliced my leg. Jeanne was around the corner of the house and running at me. Just as I hit the snow the .45 crashed again and a bullet whanged past my face, coming close on a tough shot. I was rolling to my feet. I caught a glimpse of her raising her arm. I kept the roll going. She fired. Flatter sound, maybe my Ruger.

All the huskies were on their feet, snarling and jumping around. I kept rolling until I crashed into one of them. We were tangled a moment, then he leapt free. I crawled past him among the other dogs. They ran out to the ends of their chains, barking and howling. They were chained separately, as always, so I had room to move between them. I stayed down and crawled between two more angry huskies before I risked a look back at Jeanne.

She was at the far edge of the dogs, looking for me in the shadows. I crouched lower and went left to where I was mostly obscured by a doghouse. Flames were coming out the broken window and licking up the wall, backlighting her and scaring the huskies. In the moonlight she was going to pick me out any moment. She was fifteen feet away. If I ran, she'd have an easy one. If I crawled, she'd see the movement and be on top of me.

The cabin door opened and the old man stomped out, still in his long johns. He hollered at Jeanne. He was so enraged to see her among his dogs that he didn't notice Kirby's house was on fire.

"Hey, what are you doing? Get away from them dogs."

He stepped off the porch and started toward her. The huskies escalated their howling, straining against their chains. Jeanne swiveled and fired a shot at him. I started toward her, carefully. The old man retreated back onto the porch and ducked inside the cabin. The huskies went completely insane. Then a brilliant floodlight on a light pole came on. Jeanne saw me instantly. I charged.

Two huskies and a doghouse were between us. Both dogs came for me as I moved. The first one nipped an arm as I went through the reach of his chain. I stayed on line with the doghouse and I stayed very low. Jeanne was tracking me with her gun. At the doghouse I was six feet from her. The husky chained there spun and jumped at me. I cut right. Jeanne fired, but the dog was still between us and she hit him. Then I was around the dog and coming up out of a crouch at her.

She was lining up on my face. It seemed forever that I was stretching out my left hand toward the gun and it was almost exactly that. I caught her gun hand and pushed it aside as she fired. The shot blasted past the side of my head. I caught her wrist and twisted the pistol out of her hand. Huskies were leaping against their chains all around us. I tossed the gun, then pulled her arm behind her and walked her away from the dogs. Jeanne went still and didn't resist me.

The old man stormed out the door again with a shotgun leveled at us.

"Don't shoot," I shouted at him. "I got her out of there."

He suddenly saw the flames pouring out the windows of Kirby's house behind us, but he paused to be sure we weren't among his dogs. Then he turned and ran back into the cabin. Through the door I saw him pick up a telephone.

"Nick, I didn't want to shoot you. I meant to miss and I did," Jeanne said quietly, her voice cracking. "It happened so quickly, I didn't know what I was doing. I only wanted to scare you. I...I..." she choked, eyes filling with tears that I didn't believe any more than Kirby had.

"Did you tell that to Phil, too, after you stuck him?"

The Denali money sack was lying on the snow beside the house. I walked her over there and picked it up, glad Downer would get his bucks back. The heat was a searing intensity. Walking her back away from it she started to speak again.

"Nick, you don't have to."

"Shut up," I screamed at her. "I know what I have to do. Just be glad I don't do what I want to do."

She went quiet and didn't say another word to me, except some beauties later, in court.

Two sets of neighbors roared up in pickups. There may have been someone still alive inside, for a while, but there was no possible way to go in and get them out. The old man didn't even go up to the house. He hurried around freeing the huskies. I made sure he called the troopers.

Fire trucks arrived quickly. The firemen reeled out their hoses and started pumping. They gave up on the house fairly soon, but they saved the other buildings. I stood toward the back of the crowd with Jeanne right in front of me. I didn't touch her. I didn't have to and I didn't want to. She stood there completely still and stared into the flames.

When Forzano turned up, I gave him Jeanne, the money, the quick version and held out my right arm for him to take the cuffs off. Instead, he slapped the other one on and arrested both of us.

"Thought you were tired, Rezkel, going home to take a nap or something," he complained.

"Well, I got an idea and checked into it. Worked out pretty well for you."

Forzano looked at the flames and snorted. Then he took me over to his car alone and made me tell it all the way through three different times. Finally he took off the cuffs and forgot he'd arrested me. I didn't want to talk to him all night long down at his office, but I could see it coming.

One of his understudy cops bandaged up my leg, doing a perfectly crude job. When Forzano got out of the car to coordinate something with the firemen, I worked the bandage loose and got the bleeding started again. Then I went and found a Samaritan among the neighbors who were standing around watching the show. He said he'd drive me to the hospital. I took the guy over to Forzano, pointed out the lousy bandage work, showed him a puny trickle of blood and made my pitch. Forzano relented, maybe because he thought I could testify better if I didn't bleed to death. He agreed to let the neighbor drive me to the hospital.

"But after that, you come to my office," he told me. I nodded and he went off to direct his crime scene.

322

We took my car. I made a miracle recovery around the very first bend. I had the guy pull over and give me the wheel. I drove him down to his place, dropped him off, and then headed out to Gilmore Trail. The Aurora was glowing in the sky, pale greens, streaks of red, pulses of white. I looked at the Lights and finally felt right about Floyd Arthur. It was every bit as late as the last drive to Sharon's place, but this time I didn't turn back.

Richard Anderson is a former ditch digger, a former cab driver, a former phone booth cleaner and a former game developer. He also did computer stuff in Indonesia for a couple years and has 100,000 miles on his thumb. These days he's a database developer in a town to the left of Berkeley, with a writerly wife, three cats and a nighttime crime writing habit.

http://DeathBelowZero.com